THE VISITORS

Marion Zetland lives with her domineering older brother, John, in a decaying Georgian townhouse on the edge of a northern seaside resort. A timid spinster in her fifties who still sleeps with teddy bears, Marion does her best to shut out the shocking secret that John keeps in the cellar. Until, suddenly, John has a heart attack, and Marion is forced to go down to the cellar herself and face the gruesome truth that her brother has kept hidden. As questions are asked and secrets unravel, maybe John isn't the only one with a dark side . . .

CATHERINE BURNS

◆

THE VISITORS

Complete and Unabridged

CHARNWOOD
Leicester

First published in Great Britain in 2017 by
Legend Press Ltd
London

First Charnwood Edition
published 2018
by arrangement with
Legend Press
London

A catalogue record for this book is available from the British Library.

ISBN 978–1–4448–3703–2

Published by
F. A. Thorpe (Publishing)
Anstey, Leicestershire

Set by Words & Graphics Ltd.
Anstey, Leicestershire
Printed and bound in Great Britain by
T. J. International Ltd., Padstow, Cornwall

This book is printed on acid-free paper

Dedicated to the memory of my parents, Cath and Bob, for teaching me to love books.

In the Night — 1

Like a white bird, the scream flew up from the depths of the cellar, then became trapped inside Marion's head. As it flapped its wings against the inside of her skull, she wondered how it had got through three floors of the big strong house to her dusty little room in the attic? If the scream managed to reach her, surely it could find a way to someone else: Judith next door or old Mr Weinberg opposite, who liked to walk his little Pomeranian dog along Grange Road in the small hours. Lying on her side made her hip bone ache, so she turned onto her back, but this position strained her knees. The sheets had wriggled to the bottom of the bed, so the woollen blankets scratched her skin, but when she pushed the blankets off, she was freezing cold. She tried to stop herself from wondering what had caused the person to scream and what it might be like down in the cellar in the middle of the night. Don't think about it, she warned herself, or you'll go mad, just like Great Aunt Phyllis. They'll send you to one of those places with bars on the windows, and you'll have to eat your dinner with a plastic spoon.

Then she heard Mother's voice: *John is doing what is best for them; you have to trust him — he is your brother and a very clever person, an Oxford graduate, no less. If you can't trust John, your only living family, then who can you trust?*

1

But what if Judith or Mr. Weinberg did hear the scream? What if someone called the police and they came to the house in the night? Would they bang on the door and wait for someone to answer, or just knock it down and come right in? Would they be dragged from their beds? You heard people say that sometimes: 'They dragged them from their beds in the middle of the night.' But surely the police allowed a person time to get up and get dressed, didn't they?

Perhaps you ought to have something decent ready just in case, suggested Mother. Those baggy black trousers with the jam stain on the knee and that scruffy brown jumper you dropped on the floor before getting into bed would hardly do.

While she and her brother were taken off to the police cells, the home she had lived in all her life would be ripped apart in search of evidence. The thought of strangers running around the house horrified her. What would they think of all the mess? The mould on the bathroom wall, all those broken appliances that John refused to let her throw away, yet never got round to repairing, the tins of food piled in the kitchen, and years and years of newspapers blocking the hall? And that Tupperware container on the top shelf of the fridge, the one full of black slime and greeny-blue fur; she wasn't even sure what it had in it to begin with, and now she was too frightened to open it. *If I weren't already dead, I would die from shame that you let things get into such a state, added Mother.*

She saw herself on the front page of a

newspaper (Marion had never taken a good photo; even in her eighteenth-birthday portrait she looked like a matron of forty), that frizzy brown hair sticking out in all directions like a madwoman's, all the world judging her. What would Judith say? That she had always thought Marion and her brother were odd? And Lydia? The shame of Lydia finding out about all of this would be too much to bear.

'It won't happen, Marion. Nobody heard the scream. Nobody's coming. Who'd be looking for them anyway?' said Neil, holding her in his arms and stroking the hysterical hair.

'But they will, if not tonight, then another night,' replied Marion. 'And no one will understand that John only wants to help them.'

Marion Zetland was eight years old when she first discovered she was plain. If she'd had friends, someone might have pointed this out sooner, but Mother's nerves, delicate as a glass cobweb, couldn't stand the strain of other people's 'snotty-nosed scamps' cavorting around the Grange Road house, dirty feet clattering down the oak stair-cases, squeals bouncing around the large wood-panelled rooms, the possibility of someone breaking or even stealing one of the many 'heirlooms', so aside from her brother, John, Marion rarely saw other children outside of school.

Sarah Moss's mother was young and pretty. She dressed in clothes bright as sweetie wrappers and her shiny blonde hair bounced as she bent over to talk to Marion outside the gates of Saint Winifred's Primary School one Friday after-noon. Marion's own mother's hair was set into a mass of interlocking iron and steel curls at Pierre Micheline's once a week and could withstand Northport's sharpest seafront breeze without shifting.

'Would you like to come over to our house tomorrow?' she asked with her smiling voice.

Marion saw Sarah over her mother's shoulder. She was standing by a yellow car, her new grown-up teeth bared at Marion in a way that said, 'I'd prefer you to drop dead than come to play.'

It was as if Sarah had grabbed her by one arm and the nice lady by the other, and they were trying to split her into two halves.

★   ★   ★

'They probably know my family owned Northport Grand until the war,' Mother said loftily. 'They're using her to get in with us.'

But Dad insisted that Marion should go. 'She spends too much time locked away in her own little world. She needs to get out and about, start making some real friends.'

Dad drove her to Sarah's house on Saturday afternoon, smoking a cigarette with one hand and steering the Bentley with the other. The car was hot and leathery like the inside of a shoe, and with each jolting stop and start of the fifteen-minute journey, Marion felt as though she was about to be sick. They pulled up outside a new, boxlike house with huge stone snails crawling across a hump-shaped lawn.

'I'm popping over to the office now. I'll pick

you up seven-ish,' said Dad, biting on his black moustache. On weekends he often spent long periods of time at his office above the huge warehouse of Zetland's Fine Fabrics.

'But, Dad . . . I don't know if they want me to stay that long.'

'Well, just ask if they can let you wait until then.' He crushed his dying cigarette, alongside the bodies of several others, into a little metal container attached to the car door and clicked it shut.

'It'll be all right, Chuckles, don't you worry,' he said, pinching her cheek with ashy fingers.

The Bentley had already driven away before she reached the end of the gravel path. She rang the bell, and a shape appeared behind the bubbly glass door panels. When the door opened, a suntanned man with a brown side-swept fringe and blue jeans was standing there smiling at her. He crouched down so their heads were the same level.

'Hi, I'm Sarah's dad. You must be Marion.' He let the golden-brown fringe fall forward, and Marion felt the urge to reach out and feel if it really was as soft as a silk tassel.

Marion's dad never wore jeans; he always dressed in a suit even when they went for walks along the promenade. Sarah's mum and dad seemed so young compared to her own parents. Marion's father had been fifty-two when she was born and her mother forty-three. They were the same age as most of her schoolmates' grand-parents, and their lives had the sepia tinge of a bygone era when people rode penny-farthings

5

and had kitchen maids.

Marion followed Sarah's dad into the house, which was remarkable for its lack of antiques, wood-panelling, and curtains with mad swirling patterns. Instead, everything was made from sunlit pine and crayon-box colours. Through the French windows she could see Sarah and her friends standing on the patio. When they saw Marion, they gathered into a group and began to whisper.

Sarah's mum came from the kitchen, wiping hands as small and soft as baby mice against her pale blue jeans. Sarah's mum and dad were like a pair of those fashion dolls you saw in toy shops. The ones that stood side by side in cellophane boxes, dressed in matching outfits with plastic leisure accessories like miniature bikes and BBQ kits.

'Hi, Marion.' She beamed as if they were old friends. 'The girls are out in the garden playing with Robbie. You go and join them while I get lunch ready.'

Marion got a tight cold feeling in her tummy as if she were being sent out to fight in a battle.

'Please don't make me go,' she wanted to say. 'Let me stay inside. We can watch TV, and I can pretend that you are my real mum and dad.'

Sarah's dad let her out through the French windows, and she found herself standing on some paving stones, all different jagged shapes and sizes that had been cleverly fitted together like a puzzle. Sarah and her friends were taking turns stroking the grey fur of a large cuddly toy. The creature's nose twitched as if in annoyance at Marion daring to step out onto its fantastical stone garden.

'How does it move? Is it a magic toy?' asked Marion.

'*He* is a chinchilla called Robbie, and he can move because he's alive,' said Sarah in a tone that implied only an idiot wouldn't know that. 'Don't let her touch him,' she ordered the other girls. 'She'll probably do it wrong and squish him to death.'

Lucy Clements, by far the biggest of the girls, readied her walnutty knuckles to punch, then placed herself between the chinchilla and Marion. The others petted Robbie with exaggerated daintiness, sweeping their fingertips downward and allowing them to alight on his fur for just an instant.

Marion went and stood alone at the far end of the garden. 'White trousers, twill — brushed cotton red trousers with flower on the pocket — rayon pink skirt — black pants, serge — no — canvas — pants — black — no, white pants — towelling — towel — towel,' she said to herself, identifying the fabrics of items on Mrs. Moss's rotating washing line. She knew how from having spent so much time at Dad's warehouse looking through sample books.

When Mrs. Moss called them in for lunch, they ate things that Marion had never seen before: peanut butter and a drink called Lilt that had pictures of palm trees on the can and tasted like sugary sunshine. Sarah and her friends began being overly nice to her, but in a pretend way.

'Judy, would you most kindly pass the peanut butter sandwiches to Marion?' said Sarah with a sharp-edged smile stretching her pretty face. 'She looks like she is almost dead from hunger.'

'Would you like another Jammie Dodger, Marion? You have only had six or seven already,' asked Lucy. The other girls giggled until a frown from Sarah's mum shut them up.

After tea, Marion and the other girls went upstairs to play. Sarah declared that they would pretend to be brides by putting a lace curtain over their heads and parading up and down the space between the frilly pink twin beds that served as a church aisle, holding a vase of plastic lilies of the valley borrowed from the downstairs loo.

'Who's next?' Sarah said, when everyone but Marion had a turn.

'Marion hasn't had a go,' said Hazel Parkinson, who had so many freckles on her small nose that they melted into one big browny splodge.

'But she can't be a bride. She isn't pretty enough. Who would marry that fat potato face?' said Judy Blake. Hearing these words made Marion's insides burn like the time she ate the bad berries from the garden because they looked like candy.

'No, she must, everyone has to do it,' said Sarah ominously.

Reluctantly, Marion put the curtain over her head and took the flowers that had the harsh, headachy smell of cheap air freshener. As she walked, Sarah began to sing:

Here comes the bride
Forty inches wide

They had to knock the church door down
To get her bum inside.

The mattresses of the twin beds shook as the girls that were sitting on them began to giggle.

★   ★   ★

When she went home, she found Mother cleaning the Edwardian silver teapot. Beautifully decorated with exotic animals and birds and standing on four tiger paws, the pot was too valuable to be trusted to the meaty hands of Mrs. Morrison, the housekeeper. Mother listened to Marion's tale while carefully rubbing a soft grey cloth over the gleaming curve of the handle.

Marion wanted to be told that Sarah and her friends were wrong, that they were just saying these things to hurt her feelings, but instead Mother looked at Marion with an expression of vague disappointment, as if she were something that had lost its shape in the wash.

'It's not your fault, Marion; you take after your dad's mother. She was a very plain woman, but she was going to inherit the fabric business. That's the only reason Grandfather Zetland married her.'

'Maybe I'll be pretty when I grow up, like the ugly duckling,' Marion said optimistically.

Her mother said nothing but put down the teapot, lit a menthol cigarette, and exhaled. As the realization she might never be loved enveloped Marion with the cloud of bitter smoke, she wrapped her arms around Mother's angular hips for comfort. Physical affection wasn't encouraged, however, in the Zetland family, and she soon felt herself peeled off with extreme delicacy.

As Mother returned her attention to the teapot, Marion ran upstairs to her attic bedroom. She arranged all her soft toys in a circle on the floor, then got into the middle and curled up into a ball with her head tucked between her knees. She often did this when she was upset. It made her feel as though the toys were protecting her with their magical power. While she was still curled up with her eyes closed, someone came into the room. Marion did not look up, but she knew it must be her older brother, John, because she could smell strawberry shoelaces, and those were his favourite sweets.

'What's up, Mar?'

'I'm not pretty. I'm never going to get married because I'm far too wide.' The sob that came deep from Marion's chest sounded like a saw being dragged across wood. 'I expect I will die alone.'

She heard John snap a shoelace between his teeth.

'Who told you that?'

'Sarah Moss and her friends. And they wouldn't let me touch Robbie in case I squished him.'

'Robbie?'

'He's a chinchilla — that's a cuddly toy brought to life by magic.'

'Where does she live?'

Marion sniffed. 'It's called Copperdale Estate. Near to that place Dad takes us, you know, Frank's Yard. They have giant snails in the front garden. Pretend ones, though.'

When she lifted her head, John was gone, but a slick red strawberry sweet lay next to her inside the protective circle. Marion picked up the strawberry stick and put it in her mouth. As soon as the pink-flavoured sugar fizzed on her tongue, she began to feel a little better.

A few weeks later Mrs Moss was about to drive Sarah and her little brother to school when they found the skin of Robbie the chinchilla spread across the windscreen of the car. No one knew how the skin had got there or what had happened to the inside bits of Robbie. Marion did not go back to Sarah's house again. If ever she was invited to things, she pretended to be poorly. Instead, she preferred to stay in what Dad called her 'own little world' with the door firmly locked against intruders.

@devushka.94
July 6th
Hi today this is Sonya. This is a normal day for me I clean/fed everybody all morning. Sometimes I play with the white rats and they don't eat my fingers now because they know I am friends. Many children come to the store to look at the puppis. The Mrs Boris tells me I am ask them what they want and if they do not buy I must stare at them with angry eyes until they leave. But I am not as good as Mrs Boris at making angry eyes and the children do not leave. They

poke their fingers through cage and scream making the puppis bark, then the parrot make Kaakaaakaa sound and the cats hisssss and my head gets so big with noise I think it might pop.

At night I watched TV show about horses. One day I like I will work with horses. Big animals better they can run free not like the little things in cages. Sorry for not so good English I will try harder please be patience with me!

August 8th
This day is hot very and daddy gecko died. I cry because I am sad it died but also because I am sad about many other things. Boris says it is my fault because not enough water for daddy gecko. Boris says daddy gecko cost a lot of money. The Mrs Boris says the money must come from me.

August 9th
Again very hot and my hand hurts because I was bitten by the bad puppi. Even with bitten hand I have to clean and feed and clean more. Boris says it is my own fault. Everything is Sonya fault. Puppi is growing very big. Someone must buy him soon because if he gets too big he is not cute enough to be loved. We must not tell anyone he bites. Even the fishes look scared when the bad puppi barks.

Sept 9th
Man bought the bad puppis for his little girl birthday. But then the puppi bit girl on leg and the man brought back to store. He threatened to go to politzia if Boris did not give him money.

Boris is angry with me though it is not my fault. I thought he would hit me. He says the puppi must be killed. He took it to the river. I am sad even though it was the bad puppi.

I called one puppis Adrian because he has the curly hair like you. He was the best one. He didn't bite anyone and has gone to nice home. I hope he is happy.

Sept 10th

Clean and feed and clean and feed all day long. I am teaching the parrots English. Then they will know my secrets. I will tell them about you Adrian. I wish I could set them all free. I wish they could set me free. Sometimes I am so hungry I eat their food.

Dec 12th

Now is winter very cold. This morning I find a yellow bird and two of the baby mice not moving. Things die when it is cold things die when it is hot. The cats are in bad mood with me for some reason. The big cat with thick fur coat like rich lady scratched my face I do not know what I have done to upset her.

Feb 23rd

My English is so much better now — I watch many TV programs in English at night but I have to keep the sound very low so no one hears me. It is a program about animals in a big American zoo. I want to study about animals and become maybe a vet or work in a zoo. Do you think that will be possible Adrian to study these things in

13

England? Of course I will need to get a job too and save up very much money I know this and I am prepared to work hard, do you have any animals? We were not allowed to have pets in the State Children's Residence, but I loved to read books about all kinds of animals. This is why the supervisor obtained me the job in the pet store, but really it is the worst because the animals are treated so badly, but even then not as badly as some people!

Feb 25th
I received the money you sent yesterday. I am so excited to come to England! Of course I am a little scared because it is a very long journey, a bus, two trains and then a big boat. Then I wait at the McDonald's for the Mercedes car. I hope I do not get lost on the way. No one will miss me here, except maybe the white rats.

Lunch with Judith

As she waited for the clock to move to half past twelve, the inside of Marion's thin nylon raincoat began to feel as hot as a carnival tent in summer. She had put it on well before going out, because getting the zip up could be a bit of a struggle, and she didn't want it to get stuck at the last minute and end up being late. Of course, she was only going next door to Judith's house for lunch, but it was a drizzly February day and Marion felt safer with the layer of orange nylon between her and the outside world.

She held her handbag clutched in her lap as if afraid someone might snatch it, which was unlikely, of course, since she was alone in her own kitchen. The clock twitched to twelve fifteen. Appointments made her nervous. If only she could have come up with an excuse! But saying she already had plans for the day would have been an obvious lie, as Marion never had any plans.

A pile of mail lay on the table in front of Marion. Mostly it consisted of leaflets and brochures encouraging one to do things like buy a new sofa or stay in a cottage in Cornwall.

YOU CANNOT AFFORD TO MISS THIS OPPORTUNITY
SAVE £££££ SWITCH TO GREEN NET BROADBAND

screamed a bright orange-and-green leaflet on top of the pile. She wasn't exactly sure what broadband was; her brother, John, made all the decisions about that kind of thing, but perhaps she ought to keep it in case the opportunity was one they *really* could not afford to miss. Marion suddenly imagined them falling into poverty, becoming homeless and having to sleep on the streets as a result. Even though part of her knew she was being silly, a superstitious fear that she found hard to explain prevented her from throwing it away.

Beneath it was a blue leaflet with a photograph of a pizza. The red circles of meat between bubbling cheese made her think of pictures of skin diseases in a medical textbook that John had once dared her to look at when they were children.

**Fratelli Pizza Delivered Directly to your Door
50% DISCOUNT with this leaflet**

Neither she nor John ate pizza, but it did seem like a very good offer. The people who owned the restaurant were obviously trying very hard to sell their pizzas; perhaps business wasn't going well, and they needed to reduce prices in order to gain new customers. It seemed cruel to just throw the leaflet in the bin when they had gone to so much effort, so she put that into the save pile too. Then she came across:

**RAY'S RELIABLE ROOFING —
FREE QUOTES GIVEN**

and:

BRIGHTEN UP YOUR WORLD —
MORLEY DOUBLE GLAZING

What if they really needed double glazing or the roof needed fixing? Who would they go to? Should she not keep these for reference or in case of emergency? Just by throwing a leaflet away, might she not be tempting fate to break their windows or damage the roof? Suddenly the thought of sorting through all these leaflets and deciding which ones needed to be kept and which should be thrown away seemed too much for Marion to cope with, especially on the day she had to undergo something as daunting as a lunch appointment with her neighbour, so she gathered them all together and shoved them into a cabinet above the sink.

As she crossed the kitchen, dark fluff and grime filling the gap between the sink and the refrigerator caught her eye, making her think of hairy armpits. She really ought to do some cleaning when she got back, but there was so much that needed doing, where to start? Why pick one place rather than another? The bathroom tiles were all black around the edges, dust balls got fat beneath the beds, and each room was filled with so much junk and clutter that it was hard to cross the floor without tripping.

The six-bedroom house, once so immaculately maintained, had tumbled into a state of domestic chaos in the twenty-odd years since Mother's death. Cobwebs draped the high, corniced ceilings, the Meissen figurines were surrounded by white drifts of dust, Georgian dressers were heaped with piles of old newspapers, and the fine oak flooring was cluttered with broken toasters and TV sets that John said he intended to fix but never got round to it. Before Mother died, the housekeeper, Mrs Morrison, kept everything in order; but no sane person would even think of taking the job on with things in such a state, and even if they did, John would never allow a stranger into their house.

In fairness, Marion tried to keep some areas of the house clean; she had a dustpan and brush that she used to clear biscuit crumbs and bits of fluff from the big leather living room chairs and the sofa where she lay while watching television in the afternoons. The kitchen and bathroom surfaces were wiped down regularly with a cloth soaked in a weak solution of bleach, the smell that lingered on her skin afterwards always bringing back miserable memories of school swimming lessons.

And as usual, whenever she thought about all the mess, she felt as if she herself were just another piece of nameless junk trapped underneath one of the many piles that littered the house. So as not to have to look at her surroundings, she tightened the drawstring of her hood until it covered her eyes, leaving only her mouth and nose framed by a small oval of puckered nylon.

As the bolt behind the cellar door scraped back, a little worm of anxiety crawled around in her stomach. The door swung open, letting a whiff of old-church smell into the kitchen, and Marion held her breath so she wouldn't have to breathe the same air as *them*. Then John appeared panting with effort from climbing the steep cellar steps. It wasn't until her brother had slammed the heavy door behind him and locked it that Marion allowed herself to breathe again.

John used his handkerchief to wipe sweat from cheeks crisscrossed with tiny red veins. Well over six feet tall and with a huge belly that hung over his leather belt, he seemed to fill up the whole kitchen. Marion noticed that his well-polished, black leather shoes had rubbed his ankles raw.

'John, why aren't you wearing any socks, love?' asked Marion.

'Couldn't find them.'

'I left the clean ones on the bed in the spare room.'

'In Mother's room?'

'No, the spare room.'

'The room with the cracked window?'

'No, the spare room with the face wardrobe.'

The face wardrobe was the polished-oak wardrobe where winter coats were kept. In the dark grain of one of the doors you could see a shape that, as children, Marion and John thought resembled the face of a screaming man. Marion had been too afraid to go into the room by herself until she was nearly fourteen.

'Why didn't you leave them on my bed?'

'I always put them in that room. You don't like me going in your bedroom.'

He made a huffing sound, then shook his

19

head, jiggling the heavy jowls around his neck.

As he walked past her, the scent of the cologne she had bought him for his birthday tickled her nose. It was called Apollo, the one with the advert where a man from Greek legend was riding a white horse. She had chosen it because he was so fond of classical mythology. His hair was combed carefully across his scalp in a manner that even Marion knew was considered old-fashioned nowadays; most men shaved off the remaining hair the minute they began to go bald. Around his wrist was the watch with the stainless steel band that had belonged to Dad. The same watch that had been recovered miraculously still working from the river after the accident.

John went over to the sink, took off the watch, and placed it on the ledge before turning on the hot tap. As steam clouded the kitchen window he put his hands under the running water, and then began scrubbing them with a bar of dirt-streaked, coal tar soap. Marion noticed a neat round scar on the inside of his wrist.

After drying his hands on a kitchen towel, her brother switched on the radio, then stomped across the kitchen and began chopping up tomatoes for sandwiches, drumming his knife in time with the music playing. Little piles of seeds slid across the cutting board like frogspawn tinged with blood. These sandwiches would be for the visitors, and even to look at them made Marion uneasy.

'Why are you sitting there with your coat on, Mar?'

'I'm going to Judith's for lunch.'

'Does Judith even eat lunch?' He snorted. 'She

looks like she lives on fresh air and tap water.'

'I suppose she must eat now and then.'

'I'll bet she wants something.'

'Don't be silly. What could she possibly want from me?'

'You're a soft touch, Marion. That's why she uses you.'

Marion didn't mind the idea of being used; surely that was better than being unused, like a forgotten carton of milk going slowly sour in the fridge.

'All that babysitting you did for her and without paying you a penny.'

'But I enjoyed babysitting for Lydia. I would never take money for that,' said Marion, a little shocked by the idea.

'Well, it's a shame Lydia can't be bothered to come and see you now she's all grown up.'

'I'm sure she is too busy with her studies and friends to bother with an old thing like me.'

Despite regularly sending parcels of treats, and sometimes a card with a bit of money stuffed inside, Marion hadn't heard from Lydia since she began her studies at Birmingham Met more than a year ago. It wasn't so much Lydia's behaviour as John's relish in pointing it out that gave Marion a tight feeling in her throat.

'Oh, I forgot to tell you, John, a delivery arrived for you this morning. It's in the hall.'

John left the room, then returned a moment later carrying a package. After placing it carefully down on the table, he stood looking at it for a few seconds as if savouring the moment. The brown wrapping made a papery shriek as he ripped it off with a knife; he then ran the palm of his hand across the box upon which was printed a picture of a dark grey aeroplane.

'What do you think of that then, Marion? The Avro Lancaster.'

'Very nice, I'm sure.'

'Nice?' John chuckled. 'I don't think the people of Hamburg thought this beauty was very nice; the Lancaster was used by the RAF to bomb the city in World War II. One of the air attacks took place after a spell of such warm, dry weather that it created a firestorm nearly a thousand feet high.' John paused to flick his tongue across his bottom lip. 'The roads and even the water in the rivers burst into flames. People were swept up into the blazing tornado like dry leaves.' He removed his gaze from the picture of the plane to fix it on her. 'Can you imagine that?'

Marion gasped. 'How awful!'

'It had to be done, to win the war.' John patted the box affectionately. '*People sleep peaceably in their beds at night only because rough men stand ready to do violence on their behalf.* George Orwell said that, Marion,' he said, wagging a thick, red finger for emphasis.

'It never ceases to amaze me the things you know, John.'

★　★　★

At twelve thirty exactly Marion rang the bell by her neighbour's front door. Judith appeared dressed in leggings and a wraparound cardigan, dyed-black hair pulled into a bun. Her clothes

22

and posture gave her the controlled, impatient look of a ballet mistress. She squinted at Marion as if unsure who she was or what she was doing standing on the step, then her thin red mouth curved into a smile.

'Oh, there you are. Well, come in then, lunch is already on the table.'

Marion followed her into the house, which despite being built in exactly the same style as the one next door, seemed to exist about a thousand years in the future. Everything in the open-plan kitchen/dining room was as sterile as a laboratory, and as she entered, the brightness of a dozen overhead spotlights stung Marion's eyes. The entire rear wall of the house had been replaced by glass, through which you could see a Japanese-style garden and small gazebo over-looking a pond.

'Shall I grab your coat?'

'No — no — it's all right — I'll keep it on, thank you.'

'Isn't it warm enough in here for you?' asked Judith.

In fact the house was much warmer than Marion's; the outdated boiler next door did little to fight the sharp draughts that were forever chasing each other around the edges of windows and doors. But Marion was thinking of the struggle she had getting the zip up in the first place. If she got it stuck again and had to struggle to get out of her coat, Judith would get that annoying amused look on her face as if Marion were a clown brought in especially for her entertainment.

'Maybe I'll take the hood down.'

She must have tied the knot too tightly beneath her chin because it was impossible to get undone. Marion had to stretch the hood back over her crop of dark frizzy hair. She sat down on one of Judith's funny modern chairs made from a piece of curved plastic, then struggled not to slide straight onto the floor, as her nylon-covered bottom offered no grip against the shiny surface. The room was decorated with artworks from the gallery on Northport High Street that Judith owned. A giant abstract picture that looked like it might have been a lady's breast hung on one wall, and several disembodied dolls' heads that had been, for reasons incomprehensible to Marion, roughly crammed into an old medical cabinet stared out at her.

On the opposite wall hung two black-and-white portraits of Lydia. One had been taken when she was about five years old, her round face was framed by a puffy halo of hair, and there was a solemn look in her huge eyes as though the camera had disappointed her gravely. In the second, taken more recently, she was wearing a white linen shirt and sitting on a wicker seat, her fine features framed by long straight hair. Marion felt a surge of warmth as she looked at the pictures.

The table was set out with things like tomatoes, peppers, and artichokes drowned in bright yellow olive oil, all arranged on glossy white plates, so they looked like medical specimens.

'I've got bottled water, Marion, or would you prefer tea?'

'Tea would be nice. Milk and two sugars, please.'

24

'I don't have sugar. Or milk. If I have a drop of dairy, I swell up like a balloon. The human gut isn't really designed to handle it. You know you must have a real *espresso*,' said Judith, forcing the word from between her lips with a hiss. 'Greg bought me this fancy coffee machine back from Milan.'

She went over to a huge metal contraption that sat on the counter and then began messing with tiny cups and pouring jugs of liquid through funnels.

'Go ahead and eat,' said Judith as she began cleaning already spotless surfaces, taking things out of cupboards, wiping them, then putting them away again, moving with a whirr of sharp angles like some kitchen apparatus set to fast motion.

Marion tried to cut off a piece of baguette, but the bread was so stale, it shattered instantly into sharp brown crumbs, leaving with her with a small elbow of crust. There was no butter, and the crust cut into her tender gums as she took a bite. A tiny cup of black coffee appeared in front of her. Marion took a sip. The coffee was so bitter that her tongue shriveled like a slug doused with salt.

'So, Marion, what have you been up to?' Judith, having completed her flurry of activity, positioned herself on a plastic chair, pulling up a bare foot and placing it across her thigh.

'Well, not much really.'

'You know, Marion, you should get out more, take up a hobby or join a club. They have all sorts of classes at Northport Methodist Church.

Someone left a pile of leaflets in the gallery — here, I brought you one.'

Judith pulled a crumpled sheet of paper from her bag and began smoothing it out on the table.

'Monday is adult literacy, then on Tuesday an AA meeting, well, presumably you wouldn't need either of those, Wednesday is computer skills, and basic maths, but look, on Thursdays they do beginners' French — ooh la la — you never know, you might meet someone.'

'Someone?'

'A man. A *romantic interest*, Marion.'

The sound that came out of Marion's mouth was more like a screech of fear than laughter.

'Oh gosh, can you imagine me meeting a man at my age?'

'Well, why not? You know sixty isn't considered old these days.' Marion, at fifty-four, was a year younger than Judith.

'Of course, I should take you clothes shopping sometime. We need to glam you up a bit.' Judith reached out and patted Marion on the arm. 'I hope you don't feel offended, but I am only saying these things because I want to see you bloom. You have to live life to the fullest, my dear, and no one can do that in polyester trousers and an old raincoat.'

'I don't know, Judith, it sounds like a lot of fuss and bother really,' said Marion, ashamedly picking a fuzz-berry from the knee of the offending trousers.

'But you don't want to miss out on everything, do you Marion? And time passes us by so quickly.'

'I suppose it does. But I'm quite all right.'

'Are you really all right, stuck in that big old house with John?' Judith asked.

The house didn't seem that big to Marion; it was so filled with things that sometimes she felt like a little mouse trying to burrow through it all to get where she wanted to go.

'You never seem to go out anywhere or see anyone.'

'I go out all the time,' Marion protested. 'I go to the shops and I walk along the promenade. And I see John, of course, and you now and then.'

'But that's hardly enough, is it?' She took a sip of coffee, and the thin red smile left her mouth and stuck to the edge of her cup. 'Can I ask you a question,' then without waiting for an answer she added, 'have you even been in love?'

'Well, of course — everyone has been in love — haven't they?' Marion replied vaguely.

'Oh, come on, don't be such a tease, tell me all about him — or her, of course.'

'It was a boy — I mean a young man. He worked in my father's warehouse years ago.'

'What was he like?'

'He was very tall with red hair, and his name was Neil.'

'Did you get engaged?'

'Oh goodness no, nothing that serious. I used to talk to him while he was on his break. He liked reading paperbacks. You know the ones, Penguin Classics. The other workmen made fun of him; they called him the Ginger Professor. You see, he was only doing the job to save money for university. And he always brought a packet of cheese and onion crisps to eat with his lunch. Sometimes he gave me one.'

Judith pressed her fingertips against her lips to stop the giggles escaping. Marion felt as if she had shown Judith a treasure that she had carried around with her for years, only to be told it was a piece of trash.

'Did he taste like cheese and onion crisps when you kissed him?'

Marion's raincoat crackled as she shook her head. 'No, I don't know — we didn't kiss — nothing like that happened.'

'You didn't even kiss him? I'm sorry for laughing. That really is a sweet story.'

Marion felt sometimes that Judith was playing a cruel game; pinching her hard, then gently patting the bruise better.

'But don't you ever regret not getting married, having children?' Judith asked.

'Well, no, not really. I've never thought about it much.'

'But you must have. Most women are desperate to have a baby at some point in their lives.' She held both fists to her flat stomach, as if to show the exact spot where the baby-hunger came from. 'Though perhaps if one has a career or pursues some artistic goal, I suppose that might provide a similar sense of fulfilment.'

Wondering if she was expected to apologise for having none of these things, Marion lowered her head, and the drawstring of the raincoat pulled tight around her neck.

'Though in some ways you are probably better

28

off,' Judith added quickly. 'Kids give you no end of worry. You know Lydia is switching courses again? This time to film studies, which probably means I'm paying out thousands for her to end up serving tequila shots in TGI Fridays. That's a restaurant, by the way.'

'Yes, I've heard of it.'

'And she's so careless. She lost her mobile and all her credit cards in some bar last month. I had to phone all round the banks to cancel the cards and lend her money for a new phone. Of course her father doesn't do a thing, though he has Krish to worry about — and she is practically a child herself.'

Judith's ex-husband, a high-flying management consultant, had left her for a twenty-five-year-old silk printer called Krishna. 'And to think I had been getting all these hideous bloody scarves as presents for birthdays and Christmas, and I had no idea why!' Judith had wailed when she found out.

'I've made it quite clear to Lydia she isn't moving back here after graduation. I have my own life now.'

Marion felt a throb of disappointment. Lydia coming back to live on Grange Road had been something she was looking forward to. Suddenly Judith's phone sang a tinny little tune.

'Oh, this is Greg, you don't mind if I take it, do you?'

Judith's boyfriend worked as her assistant in the gallery. From the next room Judith could be heard saying; 'No, I really don't know where the damn scissors are. I suppose you will just have to open them with your teeth.'

Marion pictured Greg, tall, bearded, and nearly twenty years younger than Judith, frantically gnawing at cardboard boxes tied with string.

She began picking at the cold, vinegary food, thinking that it would probably give her terrible indigestion for the rest of the day. She took a barbed salad leaf from her plate and nibbled it warily; if she had gone out into the street and eaten some leaves straight from a privet hedge, they might have tasted more appetizing. Then she attempted spearing an olive with her fork, but it rolled across the table and plopped onto the floor.

'Sorry about that,' said Judith, coming back into the room. She saw the olive and frowned. After picking it up as carefully as if it were a tiny, unexploded bomb, she placed it in the shiny stainless steel bin, washed her hands, then sat down.

'And what about John, what has he been up to?' asked Judith briskly.

'He keeps himself busy.'

'Is he still poking around in that cellar of yours? You know, you really ought to have it renovated. I'm thinking of having a mini-gym and a sauna in mine. How many rooms do you have down there, three, four? You could have them made into a little flat.'

Mention of the cellar made Marion feel as though little spiders were crawling across her skin.

'I don't think John would like that,' she

mumbled. 'He has his workshop down there, you know, for his hobby.'

'What hobby is that, then?'

'Didn't you know? He makes model aeroplanes.'

'Model aeroplanes?' Judith's fine nostrils flared contemptuously.

'They are really quite, I don't know . . . ' — Marion hesitated, trying to find the right word for what essentially were plastic toys a grown man spent hours gluing together and painting and which then hung from his bedroom ceiling — ' . . . *impressive.*'

'Well, get him to make them somewhere else. Just think of the extra money a lodger would bring. You could go on holiday somewhere fabulous. That reminds me: I must show you the picture of the villa.'

Marion made agreeable noises while Judith showed pictures of a resort that she and Greg had visited recently on their holiday to Turkey. Not having her glasses on, all she saw was a blur of swimming-pool blue and scorching sunshine as Judith's phone was waved before her eyes.

The phone rang again. This time the noise was shriller and less frivolous than before.

'That's Greg again, texting about some earthenware cats we're having delivered. They really are quite charming, all one-off pieces. The woman who makes them served five years in prison for prostitution and drug dealing — that's where she learned her craft.'

She paused, perhaps to assess if Marion was shocked.

'Anyway, it's a fascinating story. You should

come in and have a look, Marion, might be your sort of thing.'

Then Judith began picking up things from the table, even though Marion's tiny cup of espresso was still half-full.

'I hate to rush you off. We really should do this more often — oh, before I forget . . . ' Judith's mouth, now the dull maroon of overcooked meat, tightened. ' . . . there was one small thing I needed to ask you. You know that large sycamore at the end of your garden? Well, several of its branches are overhanging my wall, and I think it might be diseased. You really ought to get it cut down. If you like, I could give you the name of a man.'

A weight pressed against Marion's heart. She had played around the sycamore tree as a child, believing fairies lived inside the trunk and the spinning seeds were their discarded wings. At the same time she was afraid of saying no. Judith could get so angry when she didn't get what she wanted. Her words came out in a stuttering confusion.

'I don't really — the sycamore — diseased — but — but are you sure? Perhaps — '

Judith's sharp tone sliced through Marion's mumbling.

'Yes, Marion, it clearly needs to be cut down. That ugly old thing is rotten through and through. Also it blocks all the light from my gazebo.'

Marion pulled the raincoat hood back over her head as if it had suddenly started pouring with rain inside Judith's hallway.

'I suppose you're right, but I don't know. I'll have to ask John about it.'

'Make sure you do as soon as possible and get it dealt with before something awful happens.'

When she reached the refuge of her own hallway, Marion pulled the raincoat off, and then threw it down on top of a pile of old scientific magazines. She went straight into the kitchen and looked out the window. To her, the tree was a kindly old man spreading out his arms in welcome. It was impossible to believe it could be dangerous, yet why would Judith make such a fuss otherwise?

Marion filled the kettle to make a cup of sweet tea that would wash away the bitter taste left by lunch. John was right, the only reason Judith had asked her over was because she wanted the tree cut down. And all that talk about falling in love. Didn't she realise that of course Marion wanted affection and romance just as much as anyone else? While other people went around having things happen to them — getting married, having children, getting divorced, then married again to someone else — it seemed she was fated to just drift through life without being touched or touching anything else.

She realised this was probably down to her looks. Her face wasn't hideous, but it seemed unable to hold anyone's attention longer than, say, a brick or tree stump. Plain women got husbands, but they tended to be the pushy kind. If she had been more forthright, she might have got herself a man, but she hated to *impose* on anyone. That was how she had been brought up:

not to force her needs or opinions on anyone else. Wait for them to come to you, Mother always said, only no one did. She already knew that her life had been a disappointment by most people's standards. For Judith to point this out seemed unnecessarily mean.

Marion knelt down on her hands and knees and then took a battered tin from the cupboard. On the lid was a picture of a ruined castle surrounded by lush green foliage. She put her fingernails under the edge of the lid, and the tin opened with a satisfying metallic pop. Inside was a shiny brown Dundee caké covered with almonds. Picking up the cake with her bare hands, she began to break off big, crumbly lumps and then ram them into her mouth.

That lunch of nasty green things wouldn't have satisfied a flea, thought Marion, revelling in the feeling of solid, sweet cake filling her mouth and stomach.

As she was sitting on the floor chewing mouthfuls of cake, she imagined something bad happening to Judith; perhaps she would be wrongly accused of a crime and forced to go to Marion for help.

'You were the only one I could turn to, Marion,' Judith would say penitently. 'Even Greg has turned his back on me.'

'I will do all I can to help you,' Marion would say with a noble expression on her face.

And then Judith would go down on her knees and weep with gratitude. When Judith was finally proven innocent, they would stand outside the courtroom to be interviewed by TV cameras.

34

Judith would say, 'I'd like to thank my good friend Marion Zetland for standing by me in this time of difficulty. And I just want to say I'm sorry for being such a bitch to her in the past.' Then she would take hold of Marion's hand and raise it into the air.

After eating over a quarter of the cake, Marion began to feel disgusted with herself. She knew she at least ought to cut it into slices and eat from a plate while sitting at the table, but she had no more control than if someone else were shoving food into her mouth, so she kept on eating more and more until it was all gone.

Feeling sour and overstuffed, Marion dragged herself upstairs to the top floor of the house. The walls of the attic bedroom, where she had slept since she was a child, were covered with faded roses, and little grey bunnies raced in and out of the folds of the curtains that hung at the windows. Against one wall stood a glass-fronted cabinet containing her collection of animal figurines; next to that was a small bookshelf that housed her favourite books: *Beatrix Potter: The Complete Tales*, *The Secret Garden*, *Ballet Shoes*, C. S. Lewis and the Harry Potter books that John had bought for her a few years ago.

A dusty landscape of assorted items covered the dressing table by the window. There was a bottle of lavender water that smelled like vinegar and rust, but Marion could never have thrown it out because the picture on the label of a peasant girl picking flowers outside a thatched cottage filled her with sweet, achy nostalgia for summers in the country that existed only in her imagination. This and the other perfume bottles had rested on the same spot for so many years, they had burned circles in the varnish. Behind a box of sun-faded tissues, a bottle of Mum deodorant and several small containers of things like nasal spray and decongestant was a music box. If you opened the lid, a tiny, crook-backed ballerina with ragged skirts would jerkily turn to 'Lara's Theme' from *Doctor Zhivago*. The jewellery inside consisted of mostly costume pieces along with yellowish pearls given to her by her mother when she was eighteen.

Marion sat down on the bed. Looking at the half-open, cherry-wood wardrobe that had several old fleeces and a pair of grey pyjama bottoms spilling out of it, she felt once more the sting of Judith's comments about her clothes. She only wore things made from soft, stretchy material that did not cut into the plump folds of her body. She was, in fact, rather fond of the dark brown trousers that Judith had been snooty about, though it was true the hem on the left leg had come undone, so it trailed on the floor and got a bit dirty sometimes.

She never thought what clothes might make her more attractive or fashionable; in fact, she never considered how she might appear to other people at all because, in general, people did not look at her. Of course, John might, but in the way that people who have known someone for a very long time look at them; that is, without really seeing at all, their minds having built an impression of one's appearance over many years of familiarity that is nearly impossible to alter.

On the single bed, all piled on top of one another, were Marion's friends. She lay down so the soft toys were crammed beneath her body and then hugged them to her breast, pushing her face into their musty fur, feeling the cold hard glass of little eyes pressed against her cheek. There was Ben Blue, a lively little chap, with his cream fur and blue dungarees. Though she loved him, she still felt the hot burn of shame when remembering the time he had fallen out of her satchel in French Conversation and all the other girls had laughed at her for bringing a toy to school at fourteen. Big Woof was a long-legged, doglike creature whose remaining black glass eye was filled with sorrow.

She had found him in the Age Concern shop for fifty pence and always sensed there was some tragedy in his past; perhaps the child who once owned him had died. Freddy Fatpaws, a tough guy who picked fights with the others if she didn't watch him closely, had been found sticking out of Mr. Weinberg's rubbish bin. Marion had had to sew back together the places where his fur was ripped from being chewed by Mr. Weinberg's dog.

Marion tried not to have favourites, but if she could only save one from a fire, she would no doubt pick Bettina, a large, silky grey rabbit. She was very proud of her beautiful sky-blue velvet bow and preferred to keep to herself rather than mix with the other toys. Bettina had been given to Marion by her aunt Agnes for Christmas when she was eleven.

That was the year Agnes had come to eat

Christmas dinner with the family. Aunt Agnes, who wore fashionable trouser suits and had her blonde hair cut in a short fluffy style, was Mother's younger sister. When she was a child, Marion loved her in that swoony, yearning way little girls reserve for fairy princesses and angels.

Normally they went to the Northport Grand for Christmas dinner, but this year Mother wanted to stay at home because they no longer allowed smoking in the banquet suite, and she 'Just couldn't face the thought of sitting amongst all those people in paper hats chewing at once like a herd of cows.' Marion and Aunt Agnes helped Mother to cook the meal, since Mrs Morrison had Christmas off.

While they worked, the three of them joked around, singing along to Christmas songs on the radio, wearing baubles as earrings, and draping tinsel around their necks, even Mother smiled and laughed, though normally she just rubbed her forehead like she had a headache at any kind of horseplay. Mother and Aunt Agnes showed Marion how to jitterbug, a dance they used to do when they were girls, and the three of them practiced in the middle of the kitchen, grasping one another by the hand and spinning around until John came in, with the expression of someone serving a summons, and said Dad wanted to know if they were likely to be eating before New Year's Eve or not.

When Agnes set the turkey down on the table with a triumphant 'taaa-daa' Dad glowered as if it were a roasted rat. During the meal he kept moaning about everything: the carrots were overcooked; the meat was dry; the gravy was full of lumps.

Then Aunt Agnes, who was known for speaking her mind, suddenly shouted out, 'Go and get fish and chips from the end of the pier, Philip, if you don't like it.' Marion still remembered that feeling of cold horror when Dad had got up from the table with his fist clenched as though he was about to hit Agnes. Instead, he had thrown a full jug of gravy on the floor, where it smashed, leaving a pool of brown sludge with shards of white porcelain sticking out like monster's teeth. When Agnes left, Marion had been so devastated that she went out and deliberately ate several of the berries in the garden from the bad bush and ended up having her stomach pumped a second time.

Marion took hold of Bettina and hugged the rabbit tightly to her chest, but soft toys were not enough to comfort her, and she felt bad inside as if the poison berries were again rotting her tummy. Then Neil came into the room and sat on the bed beside her. She felt the weight of his hand as he began to stroke her back, and the bad feeling faded.

'Everything will be all right,' said Neil, because that was what she wanted him to say.

School

When they were small, John and Marion both attended Saint Winifred's Primary School. John was two years ahead of his sister, and though he was far from popular with the other children, no one ever dared to bully him. Even as a boy, he was tall and square with mousy hair that stuck flat to the dome of his large head and then formed a thin fringe over those puddle-grey eyes. Marion was proud of the fact that her brother was by far the cleverest child in the school and that everyone, including the teachers, seemed a little afraid of him.

Each morning they would walk to Saint Winifred's bundled up in thick coats and heavy brogues that had been made to order for their exceptionally wide feet. On their way, they often came across troops of rough kids from Northport's council estate. They would call out names like fatty and snob and sometimes even threw stones. But the stones never hit either of the siblings; they just landed near enough to make them jump, which seemed to satisfy the scally-wags, making them screech like heartless monkeys. John told his sister to ignore them, these kids were worthless trash. When they grew up, they would trade glue sniffing and cat torture for burgling houses and wife beating.

Even at Saint Winifred's, Marion found school-work difficult. Fractions especially troubled her, the number on top wobbling on its little tight-rope with the cruel number underneath waiting to slice it up into pieces. John tried to help her understand them by taking a packet of Mr. Kipling lemon curd tarts from the kitchen and cutting them into pieces.

'See, Marion,' he said, grinding his teeth as he explained it for the umpteenth time. 'I've cut one cake down the middle. Those are two halves. Now, can you cut it into quarters?'

But Marion learned nothing, and they ended up with a pile of sticky yellow crumbs, which they would stuff into their mouths before Mrs Morrison realised they had taken the cakes without permission.

At eleven John started Golding's Grammar School for boys. Two years later when Marion took the entrance exam for Golding's sister school, Ladychapel High, she failed miserably. So she went to Turner House Comprehensive instead until one day she came home with her coat ripped and fatso knifed into her leather briefcase (none of the other kids had briefcases; instead they carried nylon kit bags with *Bowie Rules* or *Bay City Rollers Forever* written in Biro all over them).

Mother refused to let her daughter go back to Turner House, and in return for a substantial donation from Zetland's Fine Fabrics towards Ladychapel's new swimming pool, a place was found for Marion.

Ladychapel girls were high achievers; they excelled at both sports and academic subjects; they were graceful and at ease with themselves in

41

social situations. Marion was none of these things. At the new school, she felt like a zoo animal that had strayed into the wrong enclosure: a bear trying to blend in with flamingos. Every other girl had slim ankles, a tiny waist, long hair, and a delicate neck. There were a few plain girls, but at least they were brilliant at schoolwork. Marion stuck out because she was stupid and plain and had hair that looked like the aftermath of a bushfire. While other girls plotted out their futures as doctors or businesswomen, her only dream was to be allowed to stay at home and eat buttered toast in front of the TV all day long.

The nickname Manatee was given to her by Juliet Greenhalgh. In biology class, they had learned that a manatee was a pale and bloated river-dwelling beast with female breasts. During a swimming lesson one afternoon, in the very same pool Marion's dad helped to pay for, the other girls slipped one by one into the water, while Marion stood with her thick legs stuck to the tiled floor.

Her slim shoulders bobbing in and out of the rippling pool, Juliet shouted out, 'Come on, Marion, why don't you want to swim? Manatees are supposed to love water.' Then the teacher, Miss Oberlin, had said, 'Yes, thank you for your comments, Miss Greenhalgh, we all have better things to do than wait for Manatee — I mean Marion — to dive.' Whether Miss Oberlin had called her the name on purpose or not, Marion would never know, but the slip triggered giggles from the other students that echoed around the tiled room.

Running out of patience, Miss Oberlin gave Marion's lower back a hard shove, sending her headfirst into the pool. Strange shapes swirled before her eyes, and chlorinated water gushed up her nose as she sank with the inevitability of a tombstone pushed into deep water. She had been quite prepared to drown when Miss Oberlin's callused hand grabbed her wrist and pulled her to the surface.

At Ladychapel the teachers seemed to accept that Marion was stupid and therefore any attempt to help her achieve better grades was a waste of precious time and resources. They never asked her questions in class or even bothered to comment if she did badly on test papers or gave in poor homework. They would wordlessly return her work, red ink covering the paper like scratches on skin, while other girls were kept after class for scoring Cs or even B-minuses.

For Marion, trying to follow the logic of mathematics or science was as dizzying as being trapped in the fun house on Northport Pleasure Beach, surrounded by crazy mirrors and twisted hallways. She was so far behind the other students, she sometimes feared being made to join the sleepy-eyed special kids that flapped their hands (in what could have been excitement or panic) as they were herded onto the bus to the Elizabeth Simon Institute each morning.

John was the only person who seemed the least bothered about her education. He tried to help with her homework, but by the time she had got to secondary school, even he grew frustrated with her lumbering brain.

'You see, it is red because that symbolises death, Marion.'

'But in the other poem black meant death. I don't see how I am supposed to know which one it will be every time.'

Perhaps her schoolwork would have improved if she could have studied alone, but just sitting in a classroom surrounded by sharp-minded girls, their expensive fountain pens racing across the page, turned her brains to mush. She spent entire lessons worrying that she might break wind, make gurgly tummy noises, or sneeze in a weird way. The time she had tripped in geography, smacking her nose against the teacher's desk, then trying to pretend she wasn't hurt, only to have the other girls point at her laughing because blood was pouring from her nose, still haunted her. Something so embarrassing would never happen to Juliet Greenhalgh.

Mostly the other pupils at Ladychapel didn't bully or tease Marion; she wasn't important enough to attract their valuable attention. Instead they behaved as if she was invisible as she stumbled down long, airy corridors and beneath classical porticos, from one elegantly high-ceilinged classroom to another.

Juliet Greenhalgh played tennis for the county, and her parents owned a chain of restaurants called Café de Cuckoo. Her mother was a former actress-model and had appeared in a commercial for a popular brand of kitchen roll. Juliet was so pretty and popular, Marion was almost flattered to be mocked by her.

In the canteen queue, Marion had felt a flush

of excitement as Juliet's warm breath tickled her neck. 'Don't eat everything, Manatee, leave some for the rest of us,' she whispered before ramming her tray into Marion's plump behind.

It had been during a trip with Mother to Pennington's department store that Juliet and John crossed paths. Marion was fourteen and John was sixteen. Mother left them in the café eating coffee cake and drinking hot chocolate while she went to search for dust mite-proof pillowcases in the bedding department.

Juliet was sitting at a table across the room with a group of smartly turned out tennis-club girls. They were snapping open compacts and applying makeup they had just bought from the beauty department when Juliet pointed and shouted out:

'Look, it's Marion the Manatee!'

As she got up from her seat and approached their table Marion felt sick with dread. Juliet, in a tweed miniskirt, black tights, and shiny pumps, blond hair held back by a velvet Alice band, stood over them like a queen meeting beggars.

'How simply charming. Mr and Mrs Manatee all dressed up in their smart winter togs,' she said.

Both Marion and John were wearing heavy overcoats that Mother had just chosen for them in the clothes department. It was warm and steamy in the café, but Mother was worried the new coats might get left behind if they took them off. Marion wriggled uncomfortably in her red gabardine, suddenly hating the garment that she had fallen in love with just an hour earlier.

45

'How adorable — are all those Christmas presents for the little manatee children?' said Juliet, looking at the parcels that Mother had left for Marion and her brother to keep watch over.

John kept forking cake into his mouth without even looking up at Juliet, but Marion knew that he was furious. And it was her fault for being fat and stupid while attending a school full of sleek, brilliant princesses. It was one thing to be mocked by scallywags from the council estate, but a beautiful rich girl making fun of them in Pennington's was unbearable.

Three weeks later, a dog walker found Juliet lying unconscious in the frozen mud of Albert Park. She had been struck with a rock while cycling home through a thickly wooded area near the council estate. The mild fracture to her skull healed quickly, but she suffered from severe anxiety afterwards and was forced to take months off school and give up tennis permanently.

A boy from the estate was caught trying to sell her missing bike. When the police questioned him, he said he had found it propped up by his grandmother's garden gate. There wasn't enough evidence to bring charges against the youth, so the crime went unsolved. At Ladychapel they had a special assembly during which the headmistress talked to them about Juliet's attack, and students were warned not to go through the woods alone. Marion made a card for Juliet and took part in prayers for her recovery.

As she lay down in bed one night a few weeks after Juliet's attack, Marion felt a hard lump behind her head. Reaching underneath the pillow she took out the black Alice band that Juliet always wore. With her thumb she rubbed off a few specks of dried blood sticking to the velvet. Just touching it made her heart beat faster, as if it contained some mysterious essence of Juliet's spirit. She got out of bed and went over to the mirror, sliding it onto her own turbulent hair. She felt overcome with a strange power, as if she had tried on a crown belonging to a mythical queen. She hadn't hated Juliet; in fact, she had almost been in love with her and that made what happened all the more significant. How thrilling to have a secret like this! Now she was no longer just a plain fat girl who people felt sorry for. This made her important and interesting, like a dull brown field with a seam of gold hidden deep in the ground beneath it.

Dinner with John

Marion was in the kitchen preparing their evening meal when John next came up from the cellar. Without saying a word to her, he went straight into the dining room and switched on the small TV set that was so old, it didn't even have a remote control.

'The Seven Years War,' he shouted from the next room.

Marion stirred the pan of oxtail soup to stop the gritty lumps from sticking. Mother would have thought it was common to have a TV set in the dining room, but John liked to watch *Brain of Champions* while they ate. Marion sometimes imagined answering one of the questions correctly herself: 'Well done, Mar,' John would say, 'that was a tough one, fancy you knowing that.' But this never happened; the pace of the quiz was so quick that she didn't have time to even think before someone else answered.

And of course most of the subjects were things like science and history that she knew nothing about. Indeed what kind of question might Marion be able to answer? She could never remember the capital cities of countries, or kings and queens of England. If someone asked her to name the prime minister she could manage that, but who, apart from an imbecile, couldn't?

Sometimes she got cross with herself for not being more knowledgeable, or at least attempting

48

to read interesting books and newspaper articles rather than wasting all her time daydreaming or watching what John called that 'American made-for-TV trash' (even watching the same film more than once, if it was one of her favourites, like *The Disappearance of Jodie-Lee* or *A Home for Malcolm*). Perhaps if she were a well-read and less-ignorant person, then her intellectually minded brother might want to spend more time with her, rather than staying down in that cellar practically every minute of the day. And he wouldn't get angry and call her dummy for not knowing so many 'obvious things'.

During the evenings they might sit together on the sofa, drinking tea and discussing 'the history of France' or 'space travel'. After hours and hours had passed Marion would look at the clock and say, 'Goodness, John, is it 2 a.m. already? We've been talking so much, I didn't notice the time, but now we really ought to get off to bed.'

And John would reply, 'Oh, but can't we sit and chat for a little while longer — I was having such a good time. How about you make us some toast, then we can discuss famous explorers of the Amazon rainforest?'

'The Prague uprising,' she heard John shout from the next room. 'And the answer is — the Prague uprising,' echoed the quiz show presenter.

Marion carried the tray of food from the kitchen to the dining room and placed John's bowl of soup on the place mat before him. The place mats belonged to a set that had been used by the family for years, and the picture on it was of a Scottish mountain called Ben Lomond, which had been close to an area they often visited as children with their parents. The name had such a lovely sad sound to it. Marion imagined herself as a young peasant girl climbing that mournful mount, carrying a basket of eggs to a sickly relative. She would have to pull her shawl tightly around her long black hair to keep off the driving rain. How glad the relative would be to see those eggs, and even gladder to have some company while he ate them!

Marion sat down at her own place mat: Loch Lomond, a lake at dawn and an old man fishing at the edge. She always felt sad for the old man. Did he have anyone to look after him, or did he live alone in some stone croft, worrying about the day when he would be too weak to go down to the lake and catch a fish for his supper? In the background you could see a boat sailing across the waters.

'Do you remember that year you ran away on *The Maid of the Mist*?' asked Marion.

'What?'

'We were on holiday in Scotland; I was thirteen; you must have been about fifteen. You had an argument with Dad and then stowed away on the ferry that took tourists on trips around the loch.'

John shook his head dismissively.

'No idea what you are talking about, woman.'

How typical of him, thought Marion, he never remembers things. Memories, however, were everywhere for her, firmly glued to each object in the house. The Royal Crown Derby dinner service they ate from evoked childhood meals when the china, now covered with hairline cracks, was as creamy and unblemished as the skin of a young girl.

She took a mouthful of brown soup, savouring the familiar dark meaty taste. Almost everything they ate was reheated from either a tin or a packet. For breakfast they had toast with margarine and tea.

Lunch was sandwiches or perhaps a pork pie. Evening meal would be something like soup, spaghetti hoops on toast, cheese on toast, or tinned stew with packet mashed potatoes. Sunday dinner was always sliced beef from the supermarket deli with instant gravy. If either of them was hungry between meals, they filled up on biscuits or Mr. Kipling cakes. Marion liked the Bakewell tarts; John preferred the lemon curd pies.

John, of course, prepared food for the visitors himself; she had nothing to do with that, though sometimes he asked her to buy special items from the supermarket, *foreign things* that she presumed were for them; jars of pickled gherkins, goats' cheese, and a funny type of spiced sausage called kolbasa.

'I went over to lunch at Judith's today,' said Marion, trying to remove a little speck of something floating in her glass of orange cordial with her finger.

'I know, you told me already.' He sighed as if weary at having to bear twice the weight of worthless information.

'Lydia has changed from fashion to film studies.'

John dipped his slice of white bread in the soup and bit off a soggy brown chunk.

'Fashion and film studies, what kind of rubbish is that?'

'Well, I don't know. I suppose these things must be important if the university goes to the trouble of teaching them.'

'University should be for proper academic subjects like science and maths. Good luck to her trying to get any kind of job, that's all I can say.'

The speck refused to be caught, so Marion gave up and drank it down instead. As John reached for the salt, the round scar on his wrist caught her eye and she noticed it was made up of several little red lines, were those *teeth* marks? Had one of them *bitten* him? What terrible circumstances might have led to such a thing happening? A picture of John down in the cellar with them flashed into her head, but she refused to let it stay for more than a second. No, I'm being silly, it's just his eczema flaring up again, I must get him some cream, she told herself.

'Judith wants us to cut the tree down. The sycamore.'

'What?'

John's face went dark with anger. Dad used to get exactly the same expression: 'Don't upset him,' Mother would say, 'he's got that look like he's ready to murder someone.'

'She says it's diseased,' said Marion timidly.

'You tell her that tree is on our property and

it's nothing to do with her. You know that I don't like people interfering with our business, Marion.'

'I'm sorry, love — it's just I didn't know what to say to her — so I told her I would ask you about it — '

'Well, the next time she asks, tell her to fuck off.'

Marion flinched as if he had thrown a rock at her. She hated it when John used that kind of language, it didn't seem right coming from an educated person like him. Then he got up from the table and switched off the TV.

'You know that programme you like is on tonight, love — the comedy show,' she said, trying to soften the atmosphere.

John kept his back turned to her.

'The one with the tall skinny woman that makes you laugh.' She felt a sudden need not to spend the evening with only the television for company. Even John in a mood was better than no one at all.

'Why would I want to watch that crap?' said John.

She searched her head for something that would make him stay, but all she could come up with was: 'L-last week you said you thought it was funny — when she did that thing — you know — pretending to be a nun.'

Without answering, he left the room; a minute later she heard the cellar door open, then slam shut. Well, she thought, a lump of resentment swelling inside her, I suppose my company just isn't good enough for him, not compared to what *they* can offer.

Maid of the Mist

Two hours into the drive to Scotland, the Zetland family stopped for lunch. After bolting down his mixed grill, Dad kept looking at his watch and glancing through the restaurant window to check that the car hadn't vanished, while John ripped up a red-and-white Little Chef napkin, letting the shreds fall onto the floor. The two of them had barely spoken all day. For some reason Marion didn't fully understand, a form of low-level warfare had been rumbling on between father and son over the last few months, and the forced proximity of the car journey only served to heighten these tensions.

Marion ate her fish and chips slowly, each forkful feeling heavy under the weight of Mother's gaze.

'A lady never *completely* clears her plate, you know, Marion,' Mother said, having barely touched the ham salad before her except to stub a couple of cigarettes out in the yolk of the boiled egg.

John rolled up a piece of napkin and flicked it at his sister.

'John!' exclaimed Mother tremulously.

'Time to make a move,' said Dad, scraping his seat loudly as he got up from the table.

Mother insisted that Marion accompany her to the restroom, while Dad and John went out to the car. Marion had to check each cubicle to find a suitable one, then hold Mother's coat and bag while she 'went'. Marion waited outside the cubicle until Mother said, 'Marion, I just can't relax. Run the taps, would you.'

When Mother finally came out, she washed her hands, squeezing the soap, scrubbing and rinsing, no less than three times.

'Did you wash, Marion?'

'Of course.'

'And use soap?'

'Yes. Are you ready now? I bet Dad has the engine running.'

'Just give me a minute will you!' she said, snatching her bag from her daughter.

Mother took her pills from the large snakeskin handbag and popped one into her mouth. As she was screwing the lid back on, the bottle slipped out of her hands, and little white discs fell onto the floor, bouncing and rolling in all directions.

'Oh, oh!' she wailed. 'Now, that's your fault for rushing me.'

Then, to Marion's disbelief, Mother got down on her knees and began searching for the pills that had gone just about everywhere one could imagine.

'Don't just stand there like a slab of lard, help me.'

'But they've been on the floor!'

'What else am I supposed to do? We're hundreds of miles from home, it's not as if I can call Dr Dunkerly and have him send over another prescription.'

Mother's need for the medication must be pretty bad, Marion realised, if she could override her extreme fussiness to scramble around on a toilet floor picking them up; so she got down on her knees and began collecting pills in her cupped hand, hoping no one would come in and witness what they were doing.

'Make sure you get every single one,' urged Mother.

'Oughtn't we rinse them under the tap?'

'No, no you can't do that, they'll dissolve just like little lumps of sugar.'

After they had retrieved as many as they possibly could, Marion and Mother returned to the restaurant car park, where John and Dad were waiting in the Bentley. They had been driving half an hour or so when John spoke:

'Can we stop to get something to eat? I'm starving.'

'But, John, you hardly ate a mouthful of your steak pie at the Little Chef,' said Mother.

'I told you, it tasted funny.'

Mother, sitting next to Marion because John got carsick in the back, tapped her husband on the shoulder. 'Should we stop somewhere, Philip? Acid on his stomach could cause an ulcer.'

'Nowhere for miles and miles,' Dad answered resolutely. 'He'll have to wait until we get to the hotel.'

'If you're desperate, I have half a banana sandwich.' Mother took a limp cellophane package from her handbag and reached over from the backseat to hand it to John. He grabbed hold of the snack, ripped off the cellophane, took a sniff, then threw it back so it bounced off

Mother's cameo broach and landed in her lap.

'I'm not eating that shit, you stupid cunt.'

After shooting a furious glare at John, Dad did something violent with the gears of the Bentley that made the engine howl in pain. As they sped forward the car filled with ear-splitting silence as in the aftermath of an explosion. Marion saw Mother reach into her handbag for her medication, then place two white discs on her narrow, slightly furred tongue. Marion's lip curled back when she remembered picking pills up from close to the porcelain base of a public toilet, blowing on them to remove fluff and grit.

The rest of the journey went by in deepwater slowness. Mother gazing blankly out at the heather, the sandwich growing stale in her lap; Marion chewing Bettina's ears for comfort and staring so hard at a single spot on the back of the car's passenger seat, she wondered how it didn't singe the upholstery.

It wasn't until almost 8 p.m. that they rolled up along the gravel driveway of the Brigadoon Hotel: a daunting stone building with a single turret overlooking Loch Lomond. The interior of the hotel was filled with tartan and taxidermy; a stuffed stag's head with great twisted antlers stared out from above the reception, while the sweetly startled faces of deer lined the wood-panelled hall and sweeping oak staircase.

Mr Galloway, the owner of the hotel, greeted them. He was dressed in kilt and blazer, his jolly smile propping up jaded, bloodshot eyes. Mother and Dad were shown to their usual room, the Balmoral Suite. Tam O'Shanter had been reserved for John and Marion.

As soon as they got to their room, John threw his case next to the bed and then went into the bathroom and slammed the door. After unpacking her suitcase, Marion wandered around examining the various stuffed birds and animals that decorated the room. A dusty mongoose was sprawled on the window ledge, a small white hare glanced nervously over its shoulder beneath a glass dome on the mantelpiece, and several stuffed birds stared down at her from the walls.

'Don't you think now I'm almost thirteen and John is fifteen we should have our own rooms?' Marion had asked Mother a few weeks before the trip.

Mother seemed surprised by the suggestion. 'But the two of you have always shared. I don't see why this year should be any different.'

'But wouldn't some people consider it weird?'

'What could possibly be weird about a brother and sister sharing a hotel room?' Mother inquired innocently.

Marion thought of the funky, spicy smell her brother had recently acquired and the habit he had of staring at her as if she'd just sprouted a second head, but she knew that if she tried to explain these things to Mother, she would be told she was being silly.

* * *

At 9 p.m. they were the last guests eating dinner in the Walter Scott Room: brown soup, beef in gravy, ice cream in small metal dishes. Their

58

parents chain-smoked from their own individual packets of cigarettes, Mother's green and gold and elegantly feminine, Dad's red like the uniform of a royal guardsman. No one mentioned the incident in the car. It had become a feature of family life that such moments of brutal drama often slipped from everyone's mind a few hours later, so that Marion was left wondering if she had imagined them altogether.

After the dinner they went to the bar. Marion had a little bottle of Britvic orange. Mother had a small sweet sherry and Dad drank whiskey. John insisted he wanted beer.

'Why not?' said Mr Galloway, pouring himself a whiskey from the same glowing amber bottle he had served Dad. 'The lad needs a few hairs putting on his chest.'

So John was given a half glass of milk stout. After the first sip he licked away the foam mustache and gave a little sigh as if he were a working man unwinding at the end of a long day.

Relaxed by the sherry, Mother got into conversation with Mrs Galloway. Having presumably forgotten, if not forgiven, John's earlier outburst, she began to brag about her son's academic achievements. 'John — John what was the name of that thingummy — you know what I mean — the prize they gave you?' she asked, her voice slurring a little.

John gave an impatient huff.

'The Wilkinson Award for promise in scientific achievement.'

'Yes — the Wilson Award — '

'Wilkinson!' he snapped.

'Oops — silly old me. *Wilkinson*,' said Mother, shielding a guilty smile with one hand.

When Mrs Galloway asked about Marion, she gave a shrug and said, 'Marion is Marion,' as if that required no further explanation.

★ ★ ★

The next morning they went down to the pier to take a trip around the loch. The boat they took was called *The Maid of the Mist*. When Marion was a small child, she had believed it to be as grand as an ocean liner; now she realised it was nothing more than a shabby little ferry.

As the boat cut through the choppy waters of the loch, they clung to the guardrail, taking deep breaths to reduce seasickness. Marion was sure the scenery would have looked breathtaking if it weren't for the blinding rain blowing straight into her eyes. The worsening weather forced the family to find indoor activities over the following days. They visited the Museum of Marmalade, where John spat out the preserves on the floor, then a ruined castle, taking a tour of the dungeon.

A guide, dressed in a black cloak, showed them around the subterranean vaults, relating the history of the castle while in the character of a medieval executioner. The performance was subject to John constantly querying the guide's knowledge of historical facts and laughing at his attempts to frighten the visitors with stories of historical 'ghosts and ghoulies'. The other members of the group coughed and shared glances while Mother simpered apologetically. Neither she nor Dad seemed to have the courage to stand up to John.

'You're spoiling everything,' Marion whispered. 'Why can't you stop being so horrible?'

'Why can't you stop being so ugly and stupid?' he spat back at her.

'I just don't know why Dad lets you get away with being like that.'

'He won't say anything.'

'Why not?'

'Because I know stuff.'

'What do you mean, John?'

'Stuff he doesn't want *her* to find out about.'

Then he gave her a look and tapped the side of his nose that had recently begun to sprout blackheads. What on earth could John know about Dad that he didn't want Mother to find out about? For some reason, Marion was sure it had to involve the time the two of them spent down that awful cellar together. Yet part of her didn't want to know any more than she could face the idea of descending those steep stone steps and nosing around amongst the mould and shadows.

★   ★   ★

If things weren't bad enough in public, Marion hated being alone in the hotel room with him even more. She always went into the bathroom to get undressed, but on more than one occasion John pulled down his pants right in front of her, making her burn with shame. He left the toilet

61

unflushed and farted without caring if she was in the room or not. Complaining made his behaviour even worse; it was as if he enjoyed shocking her.

'But what would *you* like to do today, John?' Mother asked one morning over coffee and grapefruit segments in the breakfast room.

'I dunno, what is there to fucking do in this boring hole?'

Mother's hand went to her jaw as if she'd just fractured a filling. She glanced at Dad, who was staring out the window, his face expressionless.

'I mean, why the hell do we even bother coming here?' John continued. 'We might as well stay in the Northport Grand and play bingo with the old codgers.'

A grey-haired lady in a tweed suit looked at them over her copy of the *Herald*.

So they stayed in the hotel that day, Dad drinking whiskey after whiskey in the bar, while Mother read her tarot cards in the Glen Carrick Room, with its roaring fire and panoramic view of the loch. Marion went up to her room to fetch a book to read; as she was about to go back downstairs, she saw John standing with his back pressed against the door, blocking her way.

'I know, why don't we play a game?' he suggested with a malicious glint in his eye.

The 'game' consisted of John making Marion do increasingly ridiculous and humiliating things. He made her touch her toes fifty times until she nearly fainted from lack of breath, then eat toothpaste until she threw up. She crawled on the floor like a dog while he prodded her with a walking stick he'd found in the lobby. He said if she didn't do these things, he would stuff Bettina down the toilet.

Marion thought at least by playing his game she might draw off the dark energy, and he would turn back into the old John who had helped her with her homework and played gin rummy with her, sometimes even letting her win, but it soon became apparent his nastiness was in never-ending supply.

★ ★ ★

After dinner on the final night, they went to the bar to listen to Mrs Galloway sing. Marion thought she looked elegant in a white shift with a tartan sash, her long brown and silver hair piled up on top of her head. A smiling Canadian couple, round as pumpkins and wearing matching Fair Isle sweaters, said good evening as they sat down at the table next to the Zetlands. Mr Galloway played the piano while his wife sang in a swooning soprano of banks and brays, lasses and laddies and rye.

As soon as John began to snigger. Marion got a sharp feeling in her throat.

Mother slid a cigarette from the gold-and-green packet with shaking fingers, and Dad lit it for her.

'Please stop it.' Marion muttered.

'Rubbish,' said John, loudly enough for the Canadian couple to stare at him, their smiles hollowed out into little cavities of shock. Mrs Galloway kept on singing.

'John — you bugger,' hissed Dad.

Then John cupped his hands to his mouth.

'Shut up, you ugly old trout!'

The singing finally stopped, and the room fell quiet. Mrs Galloway's fishlike eyes peered at them from beneath drooping lids.

Dad grabbed John's arm, pulling him abruptly to his feet, then Marion jerked her head backwards, feeling the slap across her brother's face as keenly as if she had been struck herself; in fact, she would have preferred to have taken the punishment. That way the horror would have stopped there. As John rushed out of the room, Mother got up to go after him, but Dad told her to sit down and finish her drink. So the three of them stayed and listened to the rest of Mrs. Galloway's performance, which had tentatively started once again.

An hour later, Marion went back to her room, fearful of what might await her. When she turned on the light, it took a minute for her mind to reassemble the broken-up jigsaw before her. Furniture had been overturned, things smashed, beaks and feathers, mongoose fur sawdust, and tufts of woolly stuffing were scattered everywhere.

John wasn't there. His coat, boots, and that old satchel he didn't like anyone to touch, were gone. Could he have run away? Might he never come back? For a moment this thought filled her with joy. She would be free from the awful anxiety of never knowing what he would do next. If she waited until morning to tell her parents that he had run off, that would give him a chance to get far away, perhaps so far no one could ever find him. Wouldn't that be the best for everyone? She went over to the window and pulled back the heavy tartan drapes. The sight of the loch and its glittery black nothingness filled her with dread. What if he'd gone out in the dark and fallen into the water? She realised then that her love for her brother was separate from herself, something that could not be reasoned with nor controlled, a hungry animal that clawed at her heart. He had to be found. As much as he enraged and hurt her, losing him would cause even greater pain.

After several minutes' knocking on the door of the Balmoral Suite, Dad, wearing his red dressing gown and pungent with whiskey, answered the door. Marion spluttered out her story in such a confusing mess of severed heads and sawdust that it took several minutes for him to understand exactly what had happened. She waited in the corridor while he got dressed.

When he returned in his tan overcoat and driving gloves, he pinched her cheek and said:

'I'll find him, Chuckles, you go wait with your mother until I get back.'

Mother was lying in the middle of the four-poster bed, the bottle of medication within easy reach on the nightstand. It looked to contain about half the number of pills that they had retrieved from the restroom floor. Marion lay down on the bed next to her.

'Are you worried about John?' she asked.

Though Mother's eyes were open, she did not seem to be fully awake. Marion reached out and gently took hold of her hand. The older woman flinched and made a funny squealing noise, like a cat does when you accidentally step on its tail, then shook free of Marion's grasp. Careful not to touch her again, Marion closed her eyes and tried to sleep.

★ ★ ★

It was almost morning by the time Dad returned. He and Mr. Galloway had found John on *The Maid of the Mist*, stowed away with a supply of shortbread and bottled Highland Spring water. It was hardly as romantic as running off to sea since the ferry didn't go anywhere except back to the small pier. He would have spent the rest of his life sailing around the loch in circles.

John was already in the car when they left the hotel. His face was dark with engine smut from the boat, and his eyes had the wary, hunted look of a captured convict. Marion said nothing as she got into the backseat next to him. As Mother approached the car she looked surprised to see him. Opening the rear door, she bent down to speak to him: 'John my love, what are you doing in the back? You know that makes you carsick. Get out and I will sit next to Marion.'

Morning

Marion woke the following morning with a heavy feeling that at first she couldn't explain. Then she remembered that John had been cross with her the previous evening about Judith and the sycamore tree and how he had gone to bed without saying good night. She lay in bed for nearly an hour mulling over her brother's mood; it was unbearable when he got like this, but there was no point in trying to talk to him about it — that always made things worse.

Eventually she forced herself to get out of bed and put on her fleecy blue dressing gown and slippers. While brushing her teeth she noticed one of her molars was nagging a little, and when she spat, there was a tinge of blood in the sink. The possibility of a trip to the dentist filled her with dread.

'Why do things always have to be so ugly and mean?' she wondered, 'why can't they just be smooth and sweet for a while?'

It was nearly a quarter past eleven when she managed to get down to the kitchen for her morning cup of tea. While she was waiting for the kettle to boil she looked out of the window. Around the grey skeleton of the sycamore tree was a promising hint of green.

Holding her cup of tea in her hand, she went out into the garden and walked towards the end of the lawn to look more closely at the tree.

'Those are buds and it's only February too,' she said to herself. 'It can't be dead after all. Judith was wrong.' She smiled, and all of a sudden the ache in her jaw melted away.

A few feet away from the base of tree she noticed a dark space on the turf. That was the place where Dad had burned that box all those years ago. How strange, she thought to herself, that the grass had never grown back.

Marion's Walk

As March progressed and the dense, dark winter became slowly diluted by the promise of spring, Marion found it a little easier to rise in the mornings. Each day she would go to the window and look at the sycamore and, seeing it unbroken, feel relief, as if it were an ailing relative that had survived the night. Then one morning in April she looked out to see sun shining through the branches and a scattering of daffodils around the roots and was filled with a giddy hopefulness, though she couldn't say exactly what it was she hoped for.

For breakfast, Marion had charred toast and some leftover spaghetti hoops that she found in the fridge. After she was done eating she filled a hot water bottle from the kettle and then went into the living room and lay down on the sofa. She placed the hot water bottle beneath her sweater so it rested on her tummy. The wobbly heat felt good, like a living creature pressed up against her. She wondered how it would feel to have a baby in her stomach and how strange it was to think that another person could grow inside your body.

Marion remained on the sofa for nearly an hour, her mind idling from daydream to daydream.

Her brother once said if the human race in general shared Marion's disposition, it was unlikely they would have evolved much beyond the level of jellyfish. Marion had never had any kind of job. Of course neither she nor John *needed* to earn a living, they had 'family money', something that had always surrounded and nourished them, like amniotic fluid. If Marion had been required to support herself, it was difficult to imagine what sort of employment might suit her. She got flustered by the slightest pressure, her memory was poor, and anything to do with money or numbers made her so anxious, she would feel physically sick. Her handwriting was unreadable and her spelling atrocious.

Working in a shop or office was as ambitious for her as becoming an astronaut. She found dealing with people unsettling and she got upset too easily or worried she had offended them for no reason at all. Answering phone calls made her jittery with fear. Dad had always said that she was just too sensitive for the big wide world, and more suited to staying at home, so that was what she had done.

Marion heard the front door open then slam shut. John would be off out to the Royal Oak public house. He usually visited once a week to play chess in the lounge bar with the other regulars. She just hoped he didn't have too many pints of beer, as drink put him in a foul mood.

After a while she switched on the TV, as it was time for the start of the afternoon Heartfelt Production. The film was about an American family, mother and father in their early thirties, boy of ten, and a baby girl, who lived in a large house in some pretty suburban town. Everything in their world looked soft, sunlit, and hazy, and cheerful music played while the family went about their lives.

Then Marion remembered that she had bought some Cadbury Creme Eggs the day before and put them in the fridge. She would have one with a cup of tea when the advert break came on. As soon as she had promised herself the chocolate treat there was no room for anything else in her head, and she found it impossible to concentrate on her film for thinking about the sticky texture of chocolate in her mouth and the sweetness washing around her tongue. It was as if she were a fish caught on an invisible hook that was pulling her towards the kitchen.

The first egg she swallowed in only three bites, standing with the fridge door open, but her treat was over so quickly that she felt cheated and allowed herself to take the second back to the sofa to eat it in front of the TV, but by that time the commercial break had begun, and she felt annoyed because she wanted to enjoy the chocolate during the film, not while watching some silly advert about car insurance. Try as she might, she was unable to wait three minutes for the adverts to end and stuffed the second creme egg into her mouth while a woman on the TV mopped her kitchen with SupaClean. When the film came back on, the little boy was now in a coma in hospital, and the father was being interviewed in the police station; Marion realised she must have missed some crucial plot development while she was in the kitchen and it would be impossible for her now to get back into the programme, so she switched off the television.

As she sat back on the sofa, a dust-laden beam of sunlight squeezed through the gap between tapestry-thick curtains and poked her like an accusing finger.

'Perhaps I ought to go out and get a little bit of exercise. It might do me good,' she thought with that sense of guilt people get from being inside on a pleasant day.

'Don't get up,' said a voice in her head. 'Another film begins in just over an hour.'

'No,' she told the voice. 'Judith is right, I don't get out often enough, at least to leave the house and go for a walk would be something. I can't just lie here all day long — I'll turn into a vegetable.'

★ ★ ★

If you walked right to the end of Grange Road, you came to Northport High Street, then to the promenade and eventually a wrought-iron pier jutting out into the Irish Sea. In the Victorian era, men who had made their fortunes in the cotton trade took their families to Northport to stay in its grand hotels and bathe in the sea. While other northern seaside towns had become run-down in the last thirty years, their hotels filling with asylum seekers and drug addicts, Northport retained its elegant, pastel-coloured charm. One or two celebrity chefs opened restaurants along the front, and the beach won awards for cleanliness and beauty.

As she made her way down the high street, breathing in the sharp, salt-tinged air, Marion felt pleased she had made the decision to get out of the house. Passing Stowe's Tea Rooms, she glanced through the window at customers eating cakes and drinking tea. Years ago she used to go in there with Mother and they would share a plate of chocolate éclairs.

The shop next door, formerly the Beauty Emporium, its window filled with jars of cold cream and opulent bath oils, was now a Bargain Land, where you could buy three antiperspirant sprays for a pound. Next she passed Barbette's Boutique, where Mother used to buy her clothes. They were having a closing-down sale, and a lone salmon-pink suit with a bright red 'Reduced for Sale' sash stood in the window. Marion herself rarely bought clothes; if she desperately needed something, she got it from one of the many secondhand shops in Northport. This was not because she was short of money (though the fabric wholesale business had been sold for a pittance after Dad drowned in the accident, she and John had inherited money from Mother's side), but because dress shops and the women who worked in them intimidated her.

Object, Judith's gallery, stood out from the other shops on the high street. Through the window, Marion saw Judith talking to Greg. He wore a checked shirt, and his full beard made him look like some Victorian gentleman. He was nodding solemnly while Judith pointed at things in the shop.

Then Marion saw the cats made by the drug-dealing prostitute, and thought them just about the ugliest things she had ever set eyes on. The artist had taken two glass cats' eyes, either green or blue, and several wires meant to represent whiskers then stuck them in the middle of hideous lumps of brown clay. The cats were all labelled with names like 'Tufty', 'Nibbles', and 'Gingersnap', and the smallest of them cost £155. Who would be stupid enough to buy something so horrible for that price, wondered Marion, walking away quickly before Judith could see her and pull her into the shop.

★　★　★

The screams of people riding the Shooting Star got louder as she approached the seafront. Marion heard her mother's voice in her head: *Five people burnt to death at the top of the roller coaster when I was a girl. My sister Agnes and I watched them eaten by flames while they were still hanging upside down.* This was just one of the stories that Mother had repeated so many times, it had become stuck in Marion's brain. Just walking past a particular place would trigger the play button, and she would hear the tale recounted as clearly as if Mother were right next to her.

The promenade was choked with families visiting Northport for the day. Even a hint of warm weather would cause these people to hatch from nowhere like bluebottles, then swarm all over the town. Parents led groups of sour-faced

74

children holding inflatable toys like battering rams, and Marion often had to step into the gutter to avoid being barged out of their way. They called out to each other like wild beasts: 'Darren! Callum! Kelly! Hurry up or we'll never get t' beach!' *Where do they get these people from?* Mother's voice demanded, as if they had been ordered in bulk from a wholesaler. *You used to see a much better class of person coming to Northport when I was a girl.*

When she reached the end of the high street, the sight of the dunes shining in the spring sunshine gave her a feeling of bright fear. *There is sinking sand further out that can suck you in before you even know what's happening; no one would come to help you for fear of getting trapped themselves. Many years ago a woman and two young children lost their lives because they ignored the warning signs.* Sometimes Marion wondered why Mother chose to live in Northport at all, when everything about the seaside was so fraught with peril.

Mother had even more horror stories to tell about the amusement arcade on the pier. *Those places are just child traps run by perverts who want to lure you in. There was the little boy who went to play on the slot machines while his mother listened to a brass band at the pavilion. They never saw him again, but someone found his left shoe washed up by the tide.* It was up to your imagination to fill in the gory blanks as to how the shoe had become separated from the boy. Despite these warnings, John and Marion would sometimes sneak off to stare in wonder at the penny cascades and fruit machines, unable to resist the twinkling music and pretty lights that indeed seemed designed to entice a child to some dreadful fate.

Then she saw the Museum of Wax and shivered. Really she couldn't understand why that seedy old place had stayed open all these years. Who on earth went in there? The last time she had visited the museum had been with her brother just before he had gone off to Oxford. A sudden grey cloud swallowed the sun and the air chilled. On the horizon were more clouds. Marion suddenly wished someone kind and capable would grasp her hand and lead her home. She turned around and began to make her way back.

Before she had got even halfway home, the rain came sloshing down, soaking into her trousers and sweater. *What is wrong with you, Marion,* demanded Mother's voice, *would it have been any trouble to slip your raincoat into your shopping bag?* She stepped into the doorway of Tyler and Co. Estate Agents to shelter from the downpour. Surely no one would mind if she waited there for a couple of minutes, would they? Perhaps by then the rain would blow over. As she was standing there, she noticed a listing in the window:

Flat 5
OCEAN VISTA COURT
Two bedroom luxury flat with seafront
balcony. £250,000

As she studied the photographs of the flat interior, a confetti-burst of happy memories filled her head; it was the flat where her beloved aunt Agnes used to live.

There was the large bright living room with the balcony overlooking the sea, the spare bedroom where she had slept when, as a child, she was allowed to stay over. And there was the kitchen where her aunt had shown her how to make French toast and fruit trifle with tins of mandarins and orange jelly. Of course the flat had changed; black and white tiles and a fancy modern shower replaced the old avocado bathroom suite, and the carpets were all beige rather than peach shag, but it was still recognisable from all those years ago.

As she was staring at the listing, a handsome young man in a suit, his fair hair falling into a long fringe, came out of the shop.

'Hi there, I'm Simon,' he said, 'can I help you?'

Marion hesitated — what should she say? It seemed strange that he should come out of the shop to speak to her like that. Perhaps he was angry with her for using the doorway to shelter, but his smile seemed friendly.

'I was just looking at that flat, the one with the balcony overlooking the beach.'

'Oh yes, a very well-appointed seafront property — they don't come up very often, you know. Would you like to see it? I've got some free time right now if you're interested.'

Marion didn't really know why she agreed to go and see the flat; perhaps it was because she was too timid to refuse. Only minutes after she had gone to shelter from the rain she found herself sitting in Simon's spotlessly clean car on a seat that was comfier than an easy chair. For a moment, remembering her mother's warning against getting in cars with strange men, she felt a twinge of fear, then immediately reproached herself, don't be so silly, what would a handsome young chap like him possibly want with you? And anyway he works for the estate agency, so he isn't really a stranger.

★ ★ ★

During the short drive Marion's stomach turned to ice; it was the first time she had visited Ocean Vista Court since she was a child. She must be careful not to get emotional and make a fool of herself in front of the estate agent. Then the moment Simon opened the front door and she walked inside the hallway her nervousness melted away. The carpets felt soft beneath her feet, and the summery colours of the wallpaper and furnishings seemed to glow with some wonderful energy that warmed her bones and cleared away the dense, grey feeling in her head.

'Can I go out onto the balcony?' she asked.

'Of course.' Simon found the key for the French windows and opened them. As she stepped out she saw the rain clouds had blown away and the wide flat sea glimmered like tinfoil in the afternoon sun. She breathed in deeply, feeling exhilarated by the view. A woman was playing with her dog on the beach. Marion remembered how her aunt often let Bunty, her poodle, off the lead so she could race across the sands when they went walking. Aunt Agnes was so different from her sister; she didn't see danger and ugliness everywhere. Life was one delightful adventure to her; she played Maria in the Northport Players production of *The Sound of Music* and went on wine-tasting holidays to Provence with her French-conversation group.

To the left you could see the pier, teeming with tourists. This was where Marion and her aunt spent hours looking in the little shops and kiosks that sold souvenirs. Aunt Agnes loved to buy her niece presents. Marion would pretend these little trinkets had magical properties; a bar of scented soap could make an ugly person beautiful; the little pixie in the snow globe would come alive at night and protect you from evil spirits; a teddy bear was really a prince who had been enchanted by a witch.

'So what do you think, then?'

Marion realised she had been so distracted by memories of her aunt she had almost forgotten Simon was there.

'It's lovely.'

He paused. She realised she was expected to say whether or not she was interested in buying it. Even the idea of Marion buying a flat herself was too silly to imagine, and she felt suddenly guilty at having wasted his time.

'I — do like the flat,' she stuttered, 'but of course — I — will have to think about it. I mean, it's a big step, isn't it?'

The young man's large eyes filled with

sadness, and his lower lip dropped very slightly. Marion was shocked by how genuinely upset he seemed and how much disappointing him, in turn, pained her.

'I might decide to take it in the future, but for the present . . . ' Not knowing what else to say, she trailed off.

'Perhaps if you give me your details, then I could let you know if there is any change in price, or if any similar properties come on the market?' he asked hopefully.

'Yes — yes — of course.' To Marion's relief, Simon seemed satisfied with this, and she gave him her address and number to tap into his nice modern phone.

Despite living in a popular coastal resort, the Zetland family rarely visited the beach, and when they did, the main purpose of the trip, as far as Marion could tell, was for Mother to remind herself how much she despised it. On these rare outings, Mrs Morrison, the family housekeeper, was invited as both guest and servant to the event. She would arrive to work early and spend an age slicing and buttering to prepare for the picnic. Mother liked egg-and-cress sandwiches that John complained smelled like farts when you first opened the Tupperware containers. Meat paste for Dad, even though Mother thought it common. Around ten thirty in the morning the Bentley would be loaded up for the ten-minute drive to the seafront.

Mother would be dressed in her two-piece wool suit, scarf tied around her hair and clear-framed sunglasses. Dad always wore a suit and polished shoes. Even on sunny days Marion and John were forced to keep their coats on for fear the easterly wind might permanently weaken their young bones. Mrs Morrison dressed, as always, in her stiff nylon overall, her thick legs, mottled like raw sausage meat, bare.

It was Marion and John's responsibility to help Dad set up 'camp'. First the tartan blanket, always a little crusty with stains of previous picnics, was used to lay claim to a plot of suitable beach. Folding chairs with tight springs and metal frames that could snap shut on a child's small pink fingers if you weren't careful were brought for the adults to sit on. A series of striped canvas sheets attached to wooden posts marked the perimeter of the camp; their supposed function was to provide shelter from the wind, but they were really there, Marion thought, to separate Mother from the 'rough types' who frequented the beach.

Mother did not paddle in the sea or walk along the sand enjoying the sunshine on her face. The only pleasure that she derived from visiting the beach was in disapproving of her inferiors; yet in order to enjoy this activity, she was required to place herself in proximity to them. Anyone who played cricket, listened to popular music or allowed their dogs or children to run free might fall victim to her disdain. She often peered over the windbreak, cigarette in hand, to criticise overly large backsides and sagging stomachs in a voice loud enough for the person to hear, while Marion cringed with shame.

As Dad preferred to stand, Mrs Morrison would be offered a folding chair, though the offer would need to be repeated several times and refused before she sat down and got out her knitting, a long, brown tube-shaped thing that she had been working on for as long as Marion had known her. If this was a sleeve, then the garment consisted of nothing but sleeve.

When they were little, Marion and John would be forced to ride the donkeys. Even though this was supposed to be a treat, Marion dreaded it. The donkeys were nasty stinky things with terrifying teeth, not cute and cuddly like the storybook animals she adored. And she was frightened of the grubby little men in caps with small, tough hands that plonked you on the seat, then smacked the donkeys' bums to set them off hurtling down the beach, leaving you fearing you would be thrown headfirst over a pair of moth-eaten grey ears and break your neck.

Once they got settled, the picnic hamper would be opened and its contents unpacked and passed around with ritualistic formality: gilt-edged plates and cups with indelible stains around the rim, a crusty pot of gentleman's relish, a fruitcake with icing that fought your teeth to see which was strongest, strange little forks and spoons that resembled scientific equipment, and enough sandwiches to bury a man.

While they were eating, Mrs Morrison would commence her favourite topic of conversation: Mr Morrison. A man who appeared to have no profession other than undergoing surgery on one part of his body after another. She would relate with pride how his ailments continued to baffle modern science as if by refusing to either die or be cured he had outwitted those smart-aleck surgeons. Mrs Morrison would lower her voice when describing the more X-rated elements of Mr Morrison's treatment, while Marion, perched on the edge of the tartan blanket weaving its fringe into plaits, strained to listen to the gory details:

'They split him open like a kipper.'

'He's had it all taken away, down there, you know.'

Sometimes the words were so dangerous that Mrs. Morrison could only mouth them, and then point to body parts, while Mother responded by raising her eyebrows in what could have been either surprise or disbelief.

While the women chatted, Dad and John were allowed beyond the perimeter of the camp to survey the beach. As John got closer to puberty she would sometimes overhear Dad whispering little comments to him about the girls in their bikinis.

'That one needs sorting out.'

'What you wouldn't do to that, lad, if you got the chance, eh?'

'That doesn't leave much to the imagination, does it, son?'

'I'd show her what for.'

'She needs a good seeing to.'

John would say nothing, just stand there watching the girls, his cheeks reddening in the wind.

One year a group of teenage girls, the type Mother would think common because of their loud giggling and bright makeup, formed their own camp close to the fortress of windbreaks and tartan. When they then switched on a large portable radio, a look of disgust wrinkled Mother's face.

'Philip, go and tell them to turn down that racket,' she said to Dad.

Dad whispered something to John, and the two of them went off in the direction of the girls, while Mother leaned in to hear the details of Mr Morrison's most recent 'ectomy'.

Marion watched Dad lean over to chat to one of the girls. She was the plainest of the group with short mousy hair and must have been fifteen or so, perhaps a little older than John. Then she was distracted by Mother scolding her for straining sand through her fingers. 'Don't touch that stuff, Marion, it's full of dogs' business and God knows what.'

When Dad returned, he was alone. An hour or so later John appeared, looking flushed and smirking in his nylon windcheater. Mother asked him what the devil he'd been up to. John replied he'd been looking for oysters, then shared a wink with Dad.

'Oysters? On Northport Beach? I've never heard of such a thing,' Mother replied.

Mrs Morrison shook her head, then wound up the never-ending sleeve and shoved it into her bag.

Later that afternoon Marion glimpsed Dad under the South Pier giving the mousy-haired

84

girl a couple of ten-pound notes. He then licked his thumb and wiped it across a fresh graze on the girl's forehead. For some reason this sight made Marion shiver and cross her arms over her yet-unformed twelve-year-old bosom.

At the end of the picnic there would always be food left over.

'Why don't you take all this for your Sharon and the kids?' Mother would say to Mrs. Morrison in a soft, patronising tone.

This was Mother having a dig. Mrs Morrison's daughter was a single mum with two kids both to unknown dads. Mother was letting her know that despite being allowed to sit on a folding chair and drink tea from a gold-edged cup with a picture of a quail on it, she was beneath them. Mrs. Morrison would pucker her mouth defensively and shake her head as though she would rather let the kids starve than eat leftovers.

The Tree

'Simon, you're just a young man. Why do you waste all your free time with me? You should be going out to pubs and discos with people your own age.'

'But I love spending time here, Aunt Marion,' said Simon, resting his head on her lap as they sat next to each other on the big white leather sofa. 'I feel so happy just being with you.'

Running her hands through his thick blonde hair, she felt a warm glow of happiness.

'I'm the luckiest woman in the world to have you as a nephew, Simon.'

'And I'm so lucky to have you as an aunt. Since my parents were killed in the car crash, you were the only one I could turn to.'

★   ★   ★

Marion was pressing John's shirts in the face-wardrobe room while daydreaming about Simon, the young man from the estate agency. In the fantasy she lived in her aunt's old flat on Ocean Vista Court and Simon had called round to visit. They ordered Chinese takeaway and ate it while watching television together.

'An accident waiting to happen — ' Suddenly her dream was shattered by a sharp female voice coming from the garden at the rear of the house. Marion, still dressed in her nightgown and holding the hot iron, went over to the window. Judith, in a green waxed jacket, was standing by the sycamore tree talking to someone. A burst of steam from the iron scorched Marion's cheek. Judith must have jumped over the wall from her own garden. If John saw her, he would have a fit. She would have to be got rid of immediately.

'It would only take a good gust of wind to bring that branch down. It could fall on anyone,' she heard Judith say. After quickly pulling on a pair of trousers and tucking her nightgown into the waistband like a blouse, Marion rushed downstairs.

Opening the back kitchen door, Marion came face-to-face with Greg, Judith's lover. He was a full head taller than Judith and wore a lumberjack shirt and bobble hat. His beard was a muddy-brown colour, and he had a silver ring through his nose and some other bits of metal in his eyebrows. In his eyes was the look of a boy who had been caught stealing.

'Marion,' said Judith, who was standing behind him wearing skinny jeans and Wellingtons with little skulls on them. 'I didn't know you were home. I was just showing Greg the tree.'

'Judith, you can't be here right now. This isn't a good time. I'm busy,' said Marion, trying to sound stern.

'Doing what?' Judith snorted, amused by the idea that Marion could ever be busy. 'I'm sorry, but this is important. You don't seem to understand that tree is dangerous.'

She held out a leaf that was speckled with ugly red marks. Marion felt the tree had let her down somehow, pretending to be healthy, only to make her look a fool in front of Judith. Then, noticing a knotty, tumourlike lump beneath one of the branches, she felt a stab of guilt. Judith turned to Greg, demanding support.

'You can see what I'm talking about, can't you?'

'Well, yes — I mean — ' From his appearance, you would have expected Greg to speak in a booming, manly voice, but instead he sounded whiny and girlish. 'He is quite an old chap — looks a bit unwell, I suppose . . . ' He trailed off, then went over to the tree and began picking off little bits of bark as though they were scabs from a wound.

I don't care if the tree is sick, I won't let her bully me, Marion said to herself. She can't just walk in someone's garden and start bossing them around like this.

'Even a fool could tell the thing is rotten through and through.' Judith kicked the trunk. 'Did you mention getting it removed to John yet? It's been months since you said you would.'

'No, John is very busy, I didn't want to bother him. You know, I really think you both should go now. I promise I will ask him, though.'

Then Marion heard something. It was coming from the grate in the back wall that let air into the cellar. Very faint, echoing sobs. A chill came over her. This is it, she told herself. They are going to find out what is down there. This is how it will end.

Judith and Greg were both staring at her. Surely they could hear the sound too? They are going to call 999 on their mobile phones. Within minutes the police will arrive and break down the cellar door. Marion realised she almost wanted them to hear the noise; wouldn't it be a relief to end all that dreadful secrecy?

'Why don't you just go and get your brother now, Marion, then we can sort out this matter once and for all. Go and get John,' ordered Judith.

'I can't,' she said weakly, and then moved so she was standing in front of the grate, as if this might block the noise.

'But why not? Isn't he home? When do you think he will be back? We might as well come in and wait.' She began to walk towards the house and seemed ready to barge in through the kitchen door.

The sobbing got much louder, almost like screeching, the sound of someone terrified to the point of hysteria. Marion felt as though she were standing on the deck of a boat rocked by surging waves. The smell of bleach and drains filled her nose. She remembered feeling the same way that awful day in the wax museum with John. Suddenly everything before her eyes went silvery white, and the boat capsized.

When her vision cleared, she found herself lying on the sofa in the living room, Judith and Greg looking down at her. They made her stay there for several minutes with her feet higher than her head. Greg, who appeared to know about first aid, said she needed to do this to get the blood supply back to her brain cells.

'Please don't tell John,' she kept repeating. 'He

89

will be so angry with me.'

Judith was holding on to Greg's arm, as though afraid all the tangled wires, crumpled newspapers, and various broken odds and ends that cluttered the room might suddenly swarm and attack her. Judith couldn't have been in the house since Lydia was a child, and things had gotten much worse since then. They must think we are animals to live like this, thought Marion. It seemed pointless to even try and explain or apologise. Though Marion felt embarrassed at Judith seeing the inside of the house, she decided she didn't care a fig what Greg, with his pierced face and girl's voice, thought about it.

'I'll be quite all right,' she insisted. 'You should go. Please.'

'Marion, you need to go and see a doctor — you might be having a brain hemorrhage or God knows what,' said Judith.

'I'm quite sure I'm not, Judith. Really, I will be fine — it's just that I didn't eat any breakfast.'

'That sounds like a reasonable explanation to me, Jude, I'm sure she will be fit as a fiddle after a cup of sweet tea and a piece of toast,' said Greg, looking desperate to escape.

★ ★ ★

Later that afternoon, Marion lay on the sofa watching a film about two young gymnasts who were molested by their coach, then went on to win Olympic medals after testifying against him in court. She found it hard to get involved in the story; the girls wore rather too much makeup for her liking, and Marion couldn't help feeling they had perhaps encouraged the coach. She also felt sorry for the coach's wife, who was pregnant and kept getting harassed by the press all the time during the trial.

Before the film had finished, Marion turned off the TV and lay on the sofa staring at the island of yellow damp that had been mysteriously spreading across the ceiling for the last few years. Her neck was hurting from the angle she had been watching television, and for some reason it was impossible to move the cushions into an arrangement that made her comfortable; eventually she found a position that supported her aching back, but then she needed to go to the toilet. When she returned, the pillows had all moved, and no matter how much she wriggled about, she couldn't get settled again.

She began to think about the crying noise coming from the cellar. Why had the person been so upset? Were they in pain? Surely if one of them became ill, then John would call a doctor. Perhaps they were missing home, it must be difficult being so far away from one's family, unable to even make a phone call. It seemed strange that neither Greg nor Judith had heard the crying. Was it possible she had imagined it? Could she be going mad like Great Aunt Phyllis, her grandmother's sister, who had spent the last years of her life in a mental asylum?

Mother said Phyllis had been quite a normal sort of person to begin with. She had worked as a store detective for years at Boots and in her spare time she liked to go ballroom dancing and

91

had even won prizes. Then she started going funny in her mid-forties. She would accuse people of trying to steal things in the street. She once accused a man of pinching his own Jack Russell and then tried to make a citizen's arrest — grabbing him under the arm and attempting to drag him to the police station. When she and John were children, they had been taken to see her in the institution. Marion remembered her as a silver-haired skeleton strapped up in a highchair, screaming like a baby for her jam pudding.

Then it occurred to her how close *they* were, just a few feet below, separated by floorboards and carpet. Living and breathing, their heads just as crammed with thoughts and feelings as her own. The idea of them hearing her movements and thinking about her gave Marion this peculiar itchiness beneath the surface of her skin. It was impossible to imagine how their lives could be anything but awful, yet what could she do about it? And if she was powerless to help, wasn't it better not to know what things were really like down there? Compassion for the visitors struggled with the desire for ignorance, producing in Marion a paralyzing anxiety that she could only relieve by striking her temples with her knuckles as if physically expelling the verminous thoughts from her head.

House of Wax

The everything-at-stake anxiety that filled the Zetland household during the time John was studying for his entrance exams to Oxford University was similar to that of a country on the verge of war. Marion was forced to become even more silent and invisible than usual; now she had not only Mother's nerves to worry about, but also the possibility of disturbing the peace needed for her brother to absorb the huge quantities of knowledge demanded by The Exams.

The Exams: in her imagination, they were old and terrible gods that could make someone's greatest dreams come true or doom them to a life of misery. John carried a book with him at all times, poring over heavy tomes about science or history in the bath or at meals. If the exam gods looked down and saw him wasting a single moment of revision time watching telly or reading a comic, they would punish him with failure, and since there was no hope of Marion achieving anything, his failure meant failure for the entire Zetland name.

In the evening after school he sat at his desk surrounded by textbooks. These dry manuals with their big sums and long words frightened Marion. She felt sure if she even tried to put all that information into her own weak brain, like dangerous chemicals stored in the wrong containers, they might cause it to explode.

Following Physics Part 1, his first exam, he came home with a red face and his shirt soaked through with sweat.

'How did it go?' Marion asked. She admired her brother with the asthmatic fervor other girls felt for movie stars and pop singers.

Instead of answering, he threw his leather book bag down on the floor and stomped upstairs.

'Marion, go and see if he's all right,' Mother instructed her, and she followed her brother upstairs fearfully.

'Well, that's sodding that, then,' he exclaimed, then threw himself on his bed so the springs twanged like a banjo. 'I buggered it up. I'm done for. I'll have to go to bloody Durham instead with all the other Oxbridge rejects.'

'But you revised absolutely everything that could possibly be on the exam. You did your best and you couldn't have done more. I'm sure it will be all right,' said Marion, trying to soothe him.

'How do you bloody well know?' he snarled, making her back away. 'Did you mark my question on the Doppler effect? Do you even know what the Doppler effect is?'

Of course she did not, so she went up to her hot attic room and prayed for him. 'Please, God, let John go to Oxford. It doesn't matter what happens to me. You can make me a cripple if you like; I really don't mind. In fact, I would probably get fussed over more if I was in a wheelchair.' Then she regretted thinking the last bit, as it made her becoming a cripple not so much of a sacrifice.

She prayed each day until his results came. When John won his place at Oxford all four of them were, for once, united in celebration. Dad took them out to dinner at Axendale Golf Club. They ate beef Wellington washed down with real champagne. During the meal they made bets about where John's brilliant future might take him. No one dared suggest he take over the family business. As a verified intellectual, he couldn't be expected to concern himself with things so mundane as nylon mesh, rayon, and twill. Mother decided John would become a politician, maybe Chancellor of the Exchequer, because he was good with numbers. Dad disagreed, politicians were a bunch of crooks and liars, he should become a scientist and make some great discovery.

'Find a cure for the common cold, that's what people want, or, better still, for baldness,' announced Dad, picking beef Wellington out of his teeth with a toothpick, then pointing it at his audience for emphasis. 'I'd invest money in a scheme like that.'

Marion hoped whatever he did, her brother would become famous. She saw him travelling all over the world meeting presidents and kings of exotic lands. People would write books about him and perhaps even ask her what it was like to be the sister of a great man. One day he would be knighted by the queen. Sir John Zetland. No one ever suggested what Marion might become, her future was of no importance whatsoever, but she was more than happy to let her brother have the limelight.

Marion drank two full glasses of champagne during the dinner; then, as they were about to leave, she felt horribly sick. She clasped her hands to her mouth, but a small amount of yellowy broth slipped through her fingers and dripped onto the regal-red carpet of the club house foyer.

While she emptied the remaining contents of her treacherous stomach in the ladies' toilets, Mother stood guard outside the door.

'You had to ruin his day, didn't you?' she muttered. This seemed to be addressed not to Marion, but herself, as if in fact she were at fault by giving birth to a daughter who would eventually grow up to spoil a superior child's success by vomiting.

★ ★ ★

Just before the beginning of his first term at Oxford, John took his sister to the Dish of the Day on the promenade. It was rare for John to take her out for a treat like this, and as they walked into the café together and asked for a table, Marion felt tipsy with happiness.

The waitress came to take their order. John knew right away that he wanted steak pudding, chips, gravy, and peas, but Marion couldn't decide between fish and chips or chicken in the basket; she liked both yet it was vital to choose the perfect meal to accompany the precious time she was spending with her brother.

'Marion, just decide what you want, or you get

96

nothing,' said John, snatching the large plastic menu from her hand.

'Scampi,' said Marion.

As the waitress walked away, Marion almost cried out that she had changed her mind, she wanted the chicken instead, but if she did, John would get mad at her. How perfect chicken in the basket would have been, so golden and tasty nestled in its sweet little wicker basket. Why had she said scampi? She hated scampi, those nasty chewy fishy things. The funny little word had just jumped out of her mouth like a frog before she could stop it. Then her spirits crumbled entirely when John got out a book from his jacket pocket. On the cover was printed a title that Marion didn't know how to pronounce and a picture of a man standing on top of a mountain. She would have swapped any meal for him to pay her just a little bit of attention. Didn't he know how much it would mean for him to talk to her instead of reading?

You should be satisfied a brilliant person like your brother has been nice enough to waste his time taking a dummy like you out to lunch, said Mother's voice in her head. So she made do with sitting there, looking around the café, trying to enjoy just being out and in his company.

Even though it was a warm day, her brother was wearing a tweed jacket and his brand-new college scarf. Marion thought he looked very much like an Oxford student already. Perhaps when he was living in college, he would invite her to stay with him from time to time. She might even be introduced to some of his brilliant

97

friends. Marion imagined him having a friend called something like Toby or Peter. He would have thick blonde hair swept to one side and speak with an upperclass accent like Anthony Andrews, the star of *Brideshead Revisited*, her favourite television show. He would wear those beige trousers with a nice blue shirt open at the collar or a navy blazer for more formal occasions.

She imagined meeting Toby/Peter for the first time in John's rooms. They would be in some old stone building overlooking one of those court-yards with funny names. Quadrangles, that was what they were called. Everyone would be drinking sherry, she might be sat in a window seat, perhaps John had forgotten to introduce her to his friends because John could be forgetful like that sometimes, and Toby/Peter would ask who she was. 'That's just Marion, my silly little sister,' John would say.

But Toby/Peter would be intrigued by the thoughtful way she looked out at the quadrangle and the 'mysterious air' that Marion felt sure she had become expert at assuming. He would ask her out to go punting followed by a picnic. She would be his partner at the end-of-term college ball, then one day John would be best man at their wedding.

Her daydream was interrupted by the waitress bringing their order. With a glistening plate of gravy-covered food before him, John put his book down on the Formica tabletop.

'Freederick Neetchee. Is it any good?' said the waitress, twisting her neck to read the title of the book.

'Nietzsche says that God is dead, and it's okay to murder people if you feel like it,' John said, shaking the vinegar bottle vigorously over his chips.

'I like Harold Robbins myself,' said the waitress, then drifted away to serve another table.

Marion cut into a piece of scampi. The yellow crust fell away, leaving a slimy grey thing, like a blind eyeball, staring up at her from the plate.

'What do you mean by that, John? That it's all right to murder people?' asked Marion.

'This bloke Nietzsche says that there isn't a god, so there aren't any rules about morality and stuff, you have to make them up for yourself, and then you become like superman.'

He took a slurp of Coke up through his blue-and-white-striped straw and followed it with a burp.

After their meal, John wanted to see the Museum of Wax. When Marion visited it with Aunt Agnes, she felt the waxworks were staring at her and became convinced they moved around when no one was looking. But she didn't tell John she thought the place was creepy; the important thing was that they were spending time together. At the entrance of the museum was a wizened, little old man in a red gilt-trimmed uniform, who Marion thought looked like one of those toy monkeys that play the cymbals. When John paid the money, the monkey man put his cigarette behind his ear to count out the change.

They went inside and came face-to-face with the queen and Prince Philip, both looking outraged to find themselves in the lobby of such a scruffy museum with its flyblown chandelier and threadbare red carpet. Next to the royals were the prime minister and someone who John said was the American president from twenty years ago. On the other side of the room stood the Beatles, Mick Jagger, and an Elvis who appeared to be screaming in pain.

The next room contained scenes from history, including the first man on the moon and the death of Nelson. The one after that had scenes from famous films, Marilyn Monroe getting her skirt blown in the air and a bald King Kong, whose fur had been almost completely devoured by hordes of hungry moths.

Marion and John were the only visitors that day in the Museum of Wax. Perhaps because no one else was there, John started fooling around in a way that was out of character. He stuck his head right up Marilyn's skirt and then swapped Churchill's cigar for a piece of the rock they had bought on the pier. Though she was happy that he was having a good time, this behaviour made Marion nervous, and she wished he would stop before someone came in and caught him messing about.

At the end of the tour they came to a curtained doorway. Above it was a sign that said *Dungeon of Fear*, the letters written as if they were carved into stone. Just the thought of what might lie behind that thin green curtain made her shudder.

'Come on, Mar, let's have a look in there,' said John.

'It says you have to be eighteen or over, John, and I'm only seventeen. We'll get in trouble.'

'Oh, don't be such a baby.'

He grabbed her hand in his; though well cushioned with flesh, his grip was as powerful as a strongman's, and she had no choice but to let herself be pulled through the curtain. Inside the Dungeon of Fear there was a smell of pine disinfectant that didn't quite hide the gloomy stench of drains. It was much colder than the rest of the museum. The lights were a dim greenish colour, and the creepy singing of ancient monks echoed around the bare brick walls.

They stopped next to a stark-naked woman with red lips and long black nylon hair. She was tied to a stake that stood in the middle of glowing embers; ribbons of yellow and orange celluloid covered her pubic hair and bottom. The sound of crackling flames and screams played from a speaker.

Marion studied the sign in front of the display:

Witchcraft was common in 16th- and 17th-century Europe. Disciples, most often women, would celebrate the 'Witches' Sabbath' in order to worship the devil and gain demonic powers that could be used against their enemies. Since the Catholic Church had deemed the use of witchcraft heretical, around 200,000 witches were tried, tortured and burnt at the stake. According to folklore, once a pact was made with Satan a mark would appear on the witch's skin; if you look carefully you can see that the witch in our display has a mark above her right breast.

Marion saw the red claw mark on her chest; around it the 'skin' had been applied in crude greenish-pink strokes, and little bubbles had formed beneath the paint so it looked like she had goose bumps.

John pointed at the witch.

'What do you think of those tits, Marion?'

'It's horrible, John, I don't like this,' Marion said, putting her hands over her eyes.

John sniggered. Marion almost wanted to cry when she realised part of his enjoyment was coming from the fact that she hated this place.

'The nips look like a pair of dried figs,' he said, and then he grabbed her arm and pulled her along to the next display. A murder victim was lying on the cobbles of a Victorian alley, guts spilled out like tinned spaghetti, while a caped man stood over her, wielding a knife.

Marion read the display:

Jack the Ripper was a serial killer active in London in 1888. Murders attributed to Jack the Ripper involved prostitutes who lived and worked in the slums of Whitechapel. The women's throats were cut prior to evisceration and the skill evident in these crimes gave rise to the theory that the killer was a doctor.

Next they came to a man with a moustache standing over a woman lying in a bathtub. The woman's head was completely submerged. Flowing brown hair veiled her face and her long pale legs stretched straight out of the water, feet resting on the edge of the tub.

George Joseph Smith murdered his three 'brides' between 1912 and 1914. Bessie Williams, Alice Burnham, and Margaret Elizabeth Lofty were all found dead in the bath.

The final display was called the *Prisoners in the Cellar*. At the end of the dungeon there was an area surrounded by bare brick walls. Three women, dirty and emaciated, were lying on filthy mattresses, their arms and legs chained to the wall. This part of the museum was even gloomier than the rest, and Marion had to squint to read the description:

In the 1960s a German man called Otto Benz snatched three young girls off the streets of Hamburg, then kept them prisoner in his cellar for ten years. His wife, who lived with him in the house above, claimed to have no knowledge of the women. The bodies of the three victims were only discovered by a building worker years after Benz died from liver cancer; it was presumed they succumbed to starvation after their kidnapper was hospitalised.

Looking at the display, John's face got shiny and red like when dad let him drink a bottle of brown ale.

The smell, the strange lighting, and the sight of those poor girls chained to the cellar wall, their sticklike bodies, rotten teeth, and thin straggling hair made Marion feel woozy. She tried to turn away from the scene, but John held on to her arms from behind, forcing her to look.

'I want to go, John, I don't like it in here,' she said.

'Don't be such a bloody wimp, Mar. They're not real, they're only wax models.'

'But John, it's horrible.' Suddenly everything before her eyes went cloudy-white as if the room had filled with smoke. As she slumped against John's body she felt something hard brush against her buttocks and lower back. It was as if some swollen, sluggy parasite had attached itself to her brother and was now attempting to attack her.

When she came to, she was sitting on a stool by the entrance with the attendant standing over her. He was wound up to the limit of his clockwork fury, yammering on at John for taking her into the exhibit. 'She must have had a nervous fit. That's what it can do to you. There's a reason it says eighteen or over — you two are lucky I don't call the police.'

'What if he tells Dad?' Marion had asked as they walked home down Northport High Street.

'Don't be daft,' he growled at her, 'the old bugger won't tell, he would get in shit for letting us sneak in.'

Marion was mortified with herself for fainting. Now she was sure John would never invite her to visit him in Oxford, and she wouldn't be going

104

to any balls with Toby/Peter. John spent the next few weeks shut up in his room, even eating his meals there. Mother said he must be preparing for university, studying hard so he would have a head start on the other students, but Marion knew the real reason. It was because of what had happened at the wax museum. He had revealed some hidden part of himself to her, and now he felt angry and ashamed.

A Warning

Thursday afternoon at 2 p.m. Marion turned on the TV, straight after the advert for Safemore's Stairlifts, gentle piano notes played over the image of Brendan O'Brian, dark haired and handsome, leaving a white cottage and walking through woodland by the banks of a stream and finally arriving at a cliff top. The camera closed in on Brendan's face as he gazed at the sunset, jaw tilted upwards, eyes filled with love and compassion. Then the title in green-and-gold Celtic lettering appeared on the screen: *Beyond with Brendan O'Brian*.

Brendan appeared in his pastel-decorated studio before his rapt audience of mostly middle-aged or elderly women, his hand pressed to his forehead, waiting for the first communication 'from beyond'.

Suddenly he opened his eyes and enquired in his charming Irish brogue if anyone knew a J, someone whose name began with J, he was unsure if this was the first or last name? A forest of hands went up. The J left too soon, apparently, leaving a whole heap of money troubles behind. A lady in a blush-coloured blouse waved her arm furiously, it seemed she knew precisely such a J. Brendan moved closer and placed a hand on her shoulder.

Holding the microphone near the woman's grief-stained face, Brendan asked: 'Was it James?

No, then Jack?' The woman shook her head and whispered, 'Jerry.' Jerry, Jerry, of course, repeated Brendan. Jerry wanted her to know that he was awfully sorry for all the trouble she had had over the will, but he was doing fine, his psoriasis had cleared up almost completely on the other side, and he had just passed his pilot's licence.

The woman's eyes brightened.

'Yes, Jerry did have psoriasis — he had suffered from it since he was a boy, and I remember once when we were sitting in an airport together he remarked how impressive one of the pilots looked, leading his crew across the concourse in his smart uniform — '

'Well, my dear, you will be happy to know that his greatest ambition has been fulfilled,' said Brendan triumphantly while the audience clapped.

'I'm leaving his love with you.' Then Brendan made a gesture as if he was handing the woman an invisible present.

It struck Marion as a little odd that pilots would even be required 'on the other side' but it was uplifting to see the poor woman's grief eased by Brendan's message.

Then Brendan asked if anyone knew a K who liked to dance the fox-trot. One of the few men in the audience, a bald chap with a chubby face, put up his hand.

'Yes, that will be my sister Karen.'

Brendan took his hand from his forehead and made a gesture as if throwing an invisible ball at the man.

A flutter of admiring 'ooh's went around the studio.

'When did she pass, sir?' asked Brendan.

'A year ago. She was knocked over by a drunk driver. Only thirty-one.'

A collective gasp of empathy came from the audience.

'Karen has something to say to you.' Then Brendan closed his eyes and once again pressed his hand to his forehead. His face scrunched up as if he was concentrating on something hard.

'She says keep practicing the cricket with young Thomas. One day he'll play for England.'

The man nodded in recognition and the audience clapped.

'And something else: Have you been having a bit of trouble with your tummy, sir?'

After glancing around self-consciously, the man nodded.

'I don't want to frighten you, but Karen says you need to see a doctor about that, right away. *Right away*,' he repeated.

A shadow darkened the man's face just before the camera cut back to Brendan. At that point the programme went to break, and that ad with the 'mature lady' who sits staring out the window all day long watching her grandchildren play in the yard, then suddenly gets the confidence to join them on the trampoline when she discovers 'Peels Pliable Pads', that Marion found so distasteful, came on screen. She turned the sound to mute, then lay back on the sofa. She closed her eyes and imagined herself to be walking along that cliff top with Brendan O'Brian.

Perhaps they might find a bench to sit down

108

on and he would take hold of her hand, and look directly into her eyes, silently communicating his affection. Marion hoped the spirits would respect their privacy at this moment and not attempt to interrupt such exquisite intimacy with their messages about psoriasis, missing legal documents, and such. At that moment a crash from the hallway, and the sound of John letting out a cry, interrupted her fantasy. She got up from the couch and found her brother sitting on the lower stairs, his face bright red and beads of sweat covering his forehead. At his feet was the completed model of the Avro Lancaster Bomber, one of its wings broken off.

'John, John, oh my goodness, did you fall?'

Instead of replying, he stared at the ruined model, his clenched jaw trembling.

'Oh, what a shame,' said Marion, kneeling to pick up the pieces of broken plastic.

'Don't touch it, Marion. Leave it, just get away, get away!' he growled, rubbing his left arm vigorously.

Using the stairs for support, he tried to stand, but as soon as he let go of the banister he pitched forward, smashing the remains of the model into shards beneath his feet. When John bellowed out loud, she did not know if it was because of the Lancaster's complete annihilation or his own physical suffering.

Marion moved to catch him; her brother's frame was so heavy, she was unable to stop herself falling backwards, and the two of them ended up flat on the hallway floor. Using every ounce of her strength, she lifted him up again,

109

then managed to support him into the dining room and get him sat down on a hardback chair.

'What's wrong, John? Do you want me to get the doctor?'

'Nothing's wrong, Marion,' he said, trying to catch his breath. 'I just had a funny turn.'

'What does that mean, a funny turn?'

'It means you should mind your own bloody business, woman, now leave me alone, will you?'

As he swung out his arm to swat her away she flinched in alarm. Then, feeling the sting of tears behind her eyes, left the room. As she went through the hallway she couldn't prevent herself from stamping her foot on the pieces of grey plastic and grinding them hard into the floor with her heel before going back into the living room and sitting down on the sofa. Brendan O'Brian was mutely swinging his arm in the air as if throwing the invisible ball at a young woman in the audience. Marion picked up the remote control and switched off the set, her mind in too much turmoil to concentrate on television.

In the Night — 2

Marion woke at three in the morning, her heart racing. She had been dreaming about Bunty, her aunt's dog; she was barking outside the bedroom window, pleading to be let in. Then Marion realised a real dog was barking out in the street; it was Mr Weinberg's Pomeranian. Really he shouldn't let it out at this time in the morning. It was a disgrace. The pain in her hip was worse too, and it had spread to her lower back. Lying in the darkness, unable to get comfortable, her mind soon filled with troubling thoughts. Why had John fallen like that? Was he sick? What would it mean for her if he got ill? What would it mean for *them*? John always seemed so strong and invincible, it scared her to see any signs of physical weakness, but what frightened her most of all was the rage he used to mask that vulnerability.

She heard John open his bedroom door and then stomp downstairs. What was he up to at this time? Was he feeling unwell again? She got out of bed and put on her father's old blue-and-red tartan dressing gown and matching slippers. Putting her hand in the right pocket, she touched a little nest of dried Kleenex. She took it out and used it to blow her nose. She could hear John fussing around in the kitchen downstairs.

After using the toilet she went back to bed. She switched off the light, but her head was too squirmy with thoughts for her to go to sleep, so Marion lay in the dark watching the quivering shadows cast by the poplar trees outside her window and waited for the dog to begin barking again.

'If anything happened to John,' she said out loud, 'I think I would die. I couldn't cope with all the bills and money things. I even forget which day the rubbish bins are collected.'

'You would cope somehow. People manage. People who are blind, people who have no arms and legs live by themselves and get by perfectly well,' said Neil.

'But I can't live alone.'

'You wouldn't be alone, Marion, you have me.'

Neil

'Unless I can see exactly where they are and what they are doing, having people in the house makes me jumpy. I can feel them skittering around like bugs,' Mother would say with a shudder. Since she couldn't stand them being at home all day long during the school holidays, as children, Marion and her brother spent much of their free time at the warehouse of Zetland's Fine Fabrics.

John studied his science books in the conference suite, while Marion wandered up and down between giant stacks of rolled fabric, pretending they were the walls of some ancient castle or deep ravine. The workmen in their dull blue overalls were ogres, and she had to hide from them to escape being captured.

Neil came to work in the warehouse when Marion was fifteen. She remembered exactly the first time she saw him, that gangly frame that was too big for the blue overalls clinging on to a roll of grey underlay like a drunken dance partner. The other workers were always making fun of him, as if an ability to move rolls of fabric with ease gave them superiority.

Unlike the other workers, he didn't stand around smoking in the loading area on his break, instead he sat on the pallets reading a book, holding his long, strawberry-coloured fringe out of his pale blue eyes. His lips were full and pink like a girl's, and he bit his fingernails, revealing wrinkled strips of newborn skin. This proof of his sensitivity made Marion heady with tenderness.

The first time he spoke to her Neil offered her a cheese-and-onion crisp, then told her about his plans for the future; he was going to study languages at Durham University, but before that he intended to fulfil his dream of travelling to America and driving all the way from one coast to another. During another break-time conversation she found out that his mother was a nurse and his father an accountant. Afterwards she imagined herself attending dinner at their house, being formally introduced to his parents as Neil's girlfriend.

'Such a nice, polite girl,' his mother, who always dressed in her nurse's uniform, even for dinner, would say. 'Did you notice how she cleared her plate so thoroughly? Not like those fussy girls who ruin their health with fad diets.'

'So modest and well-spoken,' the father, who always wore a suit and glasses, would respond. 'Not like those teenage girls who dye their hair green and listen to rock music.'

'She will make a perfect wife for Neil,' the mother would declare.

Halfway through the summer, Neil was offered a job as a tour guide in Spain and left the warehouse without saying goodbye. Marion blamed the warehouse men for his departure and invented violent deaths for the worst of the bullies as punishment: Big Phil was crushed by rolls of red velvet and Smithy burnt to death in a fire. She comforted herself with dreams of

114

running away and travelling with Neil on the coach, sitting next to sunburnt holidaymakers and listening to him talk about the history of bullfighting and flamenco dancing, how to change money and whether or not they could drink the local water.

From then on, like a cutting taken from a plant, a separate version of Neil flourished inside Marion's head. Imaginary Neil provided her with comfort when she was miserable, and company when she was lonely. She often spent hours at a time, lying in the bath or on her bed, creating a fantasy world where the two of them lived their lives together.

They went on holiday, took long walks through forests, and climbed mountains. They had a big white wedding where doves were released into the sky and they ate a cake with five tiers. Sometimes they had children; sometimes she gave names to the children, like Alex and Stephanie. Then Alex fell off a horse and had to be in a wheelchair. Then she changed the story so that Alex wasn't in a wheelchair but Stephanie got abducted and she and Neil had to go on a TV news conference and ask people for help finding her.

'I just want to die,' she exclaimed. 'How can we go on without her?'

'We have to be strong for Alex's sake. Don't worry, I know we will find her,' said Neil, because he was always so good at reassuring her when she was upset. Then Stephanie was found, and they were all happy again because she hadn't been interfered with or anything like that. It turned out she had just lost her memory after bumping her head, and then been taken in by a kindly old woman who had looked after her for a while before sending her back home.

★ ★ ★

Marion lay in bed listening to the doorbell ringing. It was late morning but she was still tired after a sleepless night. Was the doorbell always so loud? It rang so rarely that Marion couldn't remember. She put on her dressing gown and went to the top of the stairs, afraid to go farther down in case the person outside could see her through the stained glass panel in the door.

Briing — briing.

Why wouldn't they go away? Surely someone collecting for charity or delivering a parcel would have given up by now.

Then a loud clattering shook Marion's bones; the person was rattling the letterbox. She would have to answer, or they would never leave her in peace. Steeling herself, she crept down to the hallway. A shadowy shape was hunched behind the glass panel. When she opened the door, she found Mr Weinberg standing on the step, his ancient face creased with anger. He was wearing a hat and overcoat even though it was a sunny day. A blob of egg yolk stained his collar.

'Vy didn't you answer the door?' His accent was a thick soup of German and Northport. He looked at her dressing gown. 'In bed at nearly eleven o'clock?'

'No — no — not in bed — I was busy doing something,' insisted Marion, affronted by the accusation despite it being true. 'Is there something I can help you with, Mr. Weinberg?'

'Have you seen Polly? My little dog, she is missing.'

'Your dog? No, I haven't seen her.'

Mr. Weinberg was trying to push his way into the house, but she stopped him by keeping her weight behind the half-opened door.

'She ran away yesterday morning ven I took her for valk. Maybe she is in your garden.'

'No, no she isn't.'

'How can you be sure?' Eyebrow hairs, thick as electrical wiring, poked over the top of his huge glasses. 'Did you check already, before I came? You have psychic powers? Perhaps that is vat you were doing when I ring the bell. You get psychic message that Mr Weinberg's dog is missing, so you think I go and look for it before he comes even.'

Anger heated the soup of his accents, so Marion found it almost impossible to understand what he was saying. Even though Mr. Weinberg was being really quite rude, since he was elderly, she had no choice but to be polite to him.

'Well, I haven't looked *yet*, of course, but I will look and I'll let you know if I find him,' she promised.

'*Her* — Polly is girl,' he said, pronouncing her like 'herrr' and girl 'gurrl' in his funny way.

'Her, I'm sorry.'

'Perhaps you should let me check. That vill be the best, I think.'

117

'No, I don't think so. It's not convenient. I promise I will let you know if I see her.'

Then Marion practically had to shut the door in the old man's face to get rid of him. She waited until his hunched silhouette had gone from behind the door before going back upstairs to lie down on her bed and recover.

★ ★ ★

As a child, Marion would often stay with her aunt in the flat overlooking Northport Beach. They would have midnight feasts of crisp sandwiches and fizzy orange pop, feeding titbits to her aunt's poodle, Bunty. Before they went to sleep her aunt would tell stories about when she and Mother were girls. The sisters were taught to play the piano by an Italian lady who had lost a limb during the war. She was called Mrs. Morello, like the cherries, and used to stamp her wooden leg in time to the music. As teenagers the two girls had entered a beauty contest on Northport Pier, but before the judges even made a decision, Grandma Carter arrived and dragged them home by their hair, still wearing only swimsuits and sashes.

One story in particular gripped Marion. It had happened when Mother was just fifteen in the Grange Road house the family still lived in; she had been carrying her newborn brother downstairs when she tripped on the fourth stair from the bottom and fell, crushing the infant beneath her body. The baby had been called John. Mother must have named her own firstborn in

118

honour of him. Marion longed to ask Mother about the tragedy. Did she still feel torn up with guilt? Had Grandma Carter ever forgiven her? Did the poor little baby scream and cry, or just go silent in her arms? But Agnes swore her to secrecy. 'You can't say a word, Marion, not on your life. My sister would never speak to me again if she knew I'd told you that.' And Marion would put her hand on her heart and promise.

⋆ ⋆ ⋆

Bunty's accident happened one Saturday afternoon when Marion was twelve. Agnes had invited the whole family over to the flat for lunch. John, who didn't like visiting his aunt, was in a sulky mood. While they were still in the middle of eating their iceberg lettuce, cold chicken, and boiled eggs, John took a book out to read. Agnes told him quite firmly to put the book away, as it was rude to read in company. Mother, who always seemed a little afraid of John, didn't say anything, but Dad agreed with Agnes.

When John shoved his plate of food away from him, knocking over a jar of Hellmann's mayonnaise, Marion went cold inside. Then he said he had a stomach ache and needed to go to the toilet. After he had been gone about five minutes they heard a funny sound like something heavy being knocked over. Then John came back into the room, picked up a boiled egg with his fork, and shoved it into his mouth whole.

It wasn't until they were about to leave that Agnes noticed Bunty was missing. They searched everywhere for her, then Aunt Agnes went out onto the balcony and screamed. Bunty was lying dead on the pavement below.

Agnes just couldn't understand how it happened. She said she was sure the balcony door had been closed. Even if it had been left open, Bunty was too big to squeeze through the railings, and they were too high for her to jump over. Then Agnes got it into her head that John had lifted the dog over the railings and let her fall. She said it must have happened when he went to the toilet. But John swore he had nothing to do with it. Even when Agnes screamed at him to admit what he'd done, John's face stayed smooth as a saucer of milk.

Agnes said she didn't trust John as far as she could spit. She called him a cruel, nasty little boy and she was as sure he had killed Bunty as if she had seen him do it with her own eyes. These words cut Marion in two. Her brother and her aunt were her favourite people in the world and she wanted them to love each other as much as she loved them.

Mother refused to believe that John was responsible and was furious that her own sister could accuse him of such a terrible thing. After that day, the two of them never spoke a word to each other. Marion was forbidden to visit her aunt or accept the presents she sent at Christmas and birthdays. She cried for weeks and even considered poisoning herself with the bad berries one more time. Then she remembered Dad's promise that the doctors wouldn't bother to pump her stomach if she tried that malarkey again.

★　★　★

One morning over breakfast, Dad read the announcement from his copy of the *Northport Herald:*

'Agnes Carter, Aged 57. Died from ovarian cancer in Saint Anne's Hospice, Northport.'

He said it with the exact same tone of voice he had used to inform them of the closure of the little train that ran from Pleasure Beach to the boating marina. When no one commented on the news, Dad just folded up the paper, then carried on eating his scrambled eggs and black pudding.

Shopping

On Fridays, Marion went out to buy the week's groceries. Unable to drive, she took a wheeled shopping trolley on the two-mile journey to the SmartMart on the edge of Northport Business Park. It would have been much easier for John to take her in Mother's silver Mercedes, of course, but he was always too busy.

'Don't forget the list, Mar,' said John as she was putting her coat on at the door.

'Stop going on at me. I've got it.'

'Are you sure?'

'Yes, I have it right here.'

Marion opened the zip-up pocket of the handbag where she kept her purse, but there was no list. John let out a long sigh.

'I bet I left it in the kitchen.'

She went and fetched the shopping list, and John watched while she put it safely in her bag.

'There are important things on that list, Marion. Now don't lose it again.'

'I know, I know, important things, I promise I won't lose it.'

'You'll forget your bloody head, woman.'

Marion set off on the long walk to the supermarket along roads choked with traffic as people drove to Northport for the May Bank holiday. All the way down Grange Road, up and down curbs and across bumpy pavements, she dragged the trolley so by the time she reached the car park of the SmartMart her arm and shoulder ached as if she had been pulling a plow behind her.

The SmartMart was packed with tourists stocking up on cheap food to eat in their holiday flats and caravans over the weekend. The crowds and bright lights made her dizzy and confused, and it took several minutes of wandering around before Marion found the aisle for jam, only to be dazzled by all the different varieties. One with pictures of lovely purple berries on the label looked appealing, but another kind was fifty pence cheaper. As she was trying to make up her mind, a short, muscular man with a bald head knocked her with his trolley and didn't bother to apologise. Then as she was picking out bread, a woman in denim shorts and flip-flops pushed her out of the way and grabbed five white medium-sliced loaves, throwing them into a shopping trolley already piled high with cheap pork sausages.

She stopped at the cold meat counter to get sliced ham for John's sandwiches. A girl with short brown pigtails poking from under a cardboard hat and a plump figure that bulged beneath her uniform was cleaning a bacon slicer. Marion stood waiting for several minutes, but the girl did not seem to notice her. She wondered if she ought to say something but didn't want to seem rude. The girl must have seen her but needed to finish what she was doing before serving anyone.

Then a tall woman wearing a long white linen dress and pushing a child in a buggy as if he were a small prince leading a parade went up to the counter. The baby was wearing a little sunsuit that perfectly matched the colour of his mother's dress. The plump girl immediately stopped messing with the slicer and enquired what the woman would like.

'Excuse me, I was here before that lady. I have been waiting to be served for several minutes,' Marion insisted.

The plump girl looked at Marion with shocked, round eyes as if she were an ill-mannered ghost that had just materialised next to the deli counter. Then the tall woman shook a cascade of butter-tinted hair and said:

'Just serve her, please, we can wait.' The woman spoke in a lovely, polished voice just like a radio announcer.

'Are you sure, madam?' the girl asked anxiously.

The tall woman swept a gracious hand tipped with coral-painted fingernails towards Marion.

'Honestly, it doesn't matter.'

'Yes, well, what do you want, then?' the girl snapped at Marion. Then the baby's cheeks went red, and he began to make a horrible squealing sound. The woman picked up her child and squished his blotchy face into the crook of her pale, elegant neck.

'That's all right, now, scrumpkin, we don't like rude people, do we?' she said, patting his fat shoulders.

A furnace of rage lit inside Marion. It was so unfair: they were the rude, ill-mannered ones, not her, she had done nothing wrong.

'I — I — d-don't want it any more, you can keep your nasty old ham,' stuttered Marion. 'I — I'm never going to buy anything from this horrible shop again.'

And then something odd happened. Mother would have said Marion 'Just flipped'. Of course, she should have just gone on with her shopping, timidly avoiding the woman and her baby as she went up and down the SmartMart aisles, but as she was about to walk away she noticed sitting on top of the counter a tray of sausages labelled: Organic Pork with Herbs and Jamaican Chilli Dip. Sample trays like this were often left out in SmartMart with things like cheese or wedges of meat pies. Marion was sometimes tempted to try them, but then felt guilty if she didn't buy any.

Marion wasn't sure exactly why she swung out her arm knocking the tray off the counter and towards the woman in the white dress. She watched the little sausages on sticks and dish of red sauce fly into the air and strike the woman and her baby, almost as if someone else had done it. Really, the tray couldn't have hit them very hard, certainly not hard enough to scar that horrid baby's cheek as the woman claimed afterwards. And only a small amount of Jamaican Chilli Dip landed on the pristine dress, leaving a stain the shape of a strawberry on the shoulder.

Sitting in the store manager's office, Marion really felt quite terrible about the whole thing but perhaps not as terrible as she should have done. In fact, although she spent most of her life worrying that something bad was going to happen to her, now that something bad had happened, she was surprisingly calm. While she waited in the small office so stuffed full of filing cabinets and boxes that was hardly big enough to contain a single desk, she heard the woman screaming complaints in the hallway outside.

'I — I want you to call the police right away, that mad woman assaulted my baby and I — she's dangerous, probably mentally ill — people like that should be sectioned or something — you know my husband will be just furious when he hears about what happened to Charlie. He works in local government — he has a very senior position and many of our closest friends are *lawyers*.'

As she was sitting there listening to all of this, she imagined how the nasty woman would like it if something really awful happened to the baby. Perhaps a speeding car might hit little Charlie's pushchair while she was crossing the road? Marion's flush of pleasure was soon replaced by an unpleasant afterburn. It isn't right to blame the child; he can't help what his mother is like. Perhaps he will grow up to hate her. 'I couldn't abide by my mother, you know, such a rude overbearing woman.' Then the woman in the linen dress would die alone in some dingy retirement home wondering why her son never came to visit.

Working at one of the desks in the room was a man in his thirties who, according to his name tag, was in fact the manager of the whole store. As he typed at his computer his face assumed a pleasant smile. He was quite handsome in a soft, rumpled sort of way. He had a double chin and slightly receding brown hair. She noticed he wasn't wearing a wedding ring. Marion knew of course that this hardly affected her, but she did not like the idea of him being lonely, of going back to some small, bare flat and perhaps reheating one of the large variety of frozen meals sold by the supermarket (that he would be able to buy at a discount as a perk of his job); though perhaps bachelorhood might be preferable to being burdened with some overbearing wife like the woman who was now standing in the corridor shouting.

She quite liked just sitting there while he worked. It reminded her of visiting her father at the warehouse when she was a child, crayoning or turning the pages of a book while he sat at his desk writing cheques or making phone calls. She enjoyed feeling as though she was part of something without any demands being made of her.

'Can I get you coffee or a water or anything?' the store manager asked her politely.

'Oh, I'm all right, thank you. That is very kind of you, though,' replied Marion.

Marion judged from his manner and voice that he was university educated. She wondered what would happen if she got up and tried to leave. Would the handsome, youngish manager try to restrain her?

Then they heard the woman outside exclaim:

'If you don't have that crazy fat bitch arrested, I will have *you* fired and sue this bloody shop for negligence!'

At this point the manager glanced at Marion and gave a little shrug. Marion felt a flush of joy.

This gesture let her know that they were allies, co-conspirators against the awful woman.

Then the assistant manager, who had been standing outside the room listening to the woman's complaints, came into the office looking weary. She was a heavy woman in her fifties. Her hands were bedecked with gaudy rings that seemed painfully tight for her thick fingers. Wiping a sheen of sweat from her flushed face, she looked at Marion, then turned to the manager and shook her head. All her gestures seemed exaggerated as if she were performing in a comic play. The manager swivelled round in his chair and leaned back with his hands behind his head in a relaxed manner. The office was so cramped that his outstretched leg brushed against Marion's shin, making her flesh tingle.

'Do you really want me to call the police over this, Jeff?' said the woman in a strong Northport accent.

'I think we can sort it out ourselves, don't you, Linda? This lady hardly seems a threat to me. Perhaps it was an accident, who can say. What if she apologised and offered to pay for the garment to be dry-cleaned?'

Linda looked at Marion with an expression of pantomime sternness.

'Would you be prepared to do that?'

'Of course, that seems reasonable, but how much ought I pay — '

Marion took a wad of notes from her worn purse. Mother had always told her to carry a bit of spare cash in case of emergencies, and this, she supposed, was an emergency. Linda and Jeff were clearly quite surprised by the amount she held in her hand.

'You must have a couple of thousand quid in there, love. What if someone stole it?' asked Linda, her brows raised and eyeballs bulging.

'Well, I suppose if they did, I could just get some more out from the bank,' Marion replied.

Jeff and Linda exchanged looks that Marion did not quite understand.

'Tell you what, dear, give us a couple of hundred, and I'll see what she says,' said Linda.

Marion handed over the money. A few minutes later Linda returned and said that although the woman had accepted her money, she did not want her apology, and Marion was free to go. Marion realised suddenly that she was sorry the little drama had ended so soon and that she would have to leave this office and the company of Jeff the store manager.

★ ★ ★

It was difficult to chat with Mother, as even the blandest subjects might upset her. 'White carnations make me think of Uncle Tom lying in that hospital bed while the tumour ate him alive,' she would complain if flowers were mentioned. Or if someone said they were packing to go on holiday, she would announce: 'Suitcases remind me of all those poor Jews being sent off to the camps, they used to show films of their luggage piled up, packed ready to go off to their deaths.' And the conversation would be brought to a juddering halt.

Dad wasn't much of a talker either. If someone started chatting to him, he usually picked up a newspaper or switched on the television in defence. Since her parents spent most of their married life in frigid silence, it seemed odd that after Dad's death, Mother should became obsessed with the idea of communicating with his spirit, even insisting that Marion accompany her to weekly sessions of a spiritualist congregation at Northport Cultural Centre. The hall was let out to all different kinds of groups and societies, and each Thursday as the spiritualists arrived they would be met by Lycra-clothed women chugging water from plastic bottles and wiping hair from their sweaty faces after the 'Trim and Tone' sessions.

Marion loved these evenings. For once she felt young and lively compared to the stale, misshapen souls who went along because the only people who ever loved them now resided on what was referred to as the 'other side'. Toothless Mr Bevan had been devastated by the loss of his mother despite the fact she had lasted to the age of ninety-seven, and he would gasp as if stuck by a dagger each time someone made reference to her favourite type of cakes, which happened to be coconut macaroons.

Bea King was an actress who regularly appeared as an extra in pub scenes of soap operas or on the jury of legal dramas. She always wore long colourful caftans, and her face was surrounded by a vapour of red frizzy hair. Dark crusts of stage makeup gathered in the lines above her mouth when she dragged from her cigarette and talked about her only son, Michael, the product of a brief fling with a Nigerian jazz drummer, who had died of a heroin overdose.

Jean Page's husband Barry had been crushed in an industrial dough mixer. Jean then lost all poor Barry's compensation money to a confidence trickster who took her to bed, then persuaded her to invest every penny in stocks and shares that didn't exist. She was desperate to contact Barry so she could apologise for not being able to afford new trainers for the kids or the catalogue payments on the colour TV that would soon be repossessed.

There was Miss Anderson, a tiny lady with a foreign accent, who always wore odd dresses with laced bodices and frilly collars. These get-ups might have been the national costume of her homeland, though no one ever bothered to ask where that was. Her face, round and squishy like an unbaked bun, made it hard to guess her age; she could have been anywhere between forty and seventy. She didn't seem to want to speak to anyone in particular; instead, like a volunteer prison or hospital visitor, she was interested in hearing from departed who might have no other friends or family that cared enough to try and make contact.

Each week a medium would guide the sessions. Sometimes it was Chris Shelby, a huge, cantankerous woman with cropped platinum hair and flamboyant taste in cardigans, who would strut across the floor pinching the bridge of her nose as if the sprits were blocking her sinuses. She always lost her temper if a message came through that no one understood, and Marion was sure that people often lied about knowing, for example, someone called Theodore who had been killed in a skiing accident, just to keep her happy. She once, rather shockingly, told Mother that Dad understood her need for physical love and would forgive her if she found another man to satisfy these needs, confirming Marion's suspicions she was making it all up.

When Chris didn't turn up, Bea or Mr. Bevan would attempt to make contact, but usually without much success. Bea would work herself into a trance that involved a lot of swaying to music and pungent incense that gave Marion sneezing fits. Once during a session she collapsed, and Mr. Bevan had to lay her down at the back of the hall with her feet propped up on a stack of yoga mats. Mother maintained this nonsense was all an act designed to get attention and that Bea couldn't talk to the dead any more than she could make a squirrel understand Chinese.

Marion liked Mr. Bevan best. At break times she helped him pour tea into the white plastic cups and set the bourbon creams out on paper plates. Mother would say, 'No more than two biscuits, Marion,' but he always let her have the broken ones at the end of the packet.

When Mr. Bevan took his turn as medium, Marion would wring her hands anxiously, willing him to succeed. The same audience that responded obediently during Chris's sessions sat in awkward silence when Mr Bevan took to the stage. While proffering vague, spluttering messages from beyond, the only reaction he got was coughing and scraping of chairs. When finally his energy and confidence were sapped dry, he would admit defeat, muttering feebly, 'Nothing seems to be coming through. Perhaps we should call it a day.'

Once he asked if anyone knew someone called Sally. The back of Marion's neck prickled when she heard the name; perhaps it was Sally, Dad's secretary who had died with him in the accident. She put her hand in the air, but Mother gave her a good slap on the leg, so she took it down again before Mr Bevan noticed her.

'I have a girl called Sally here,' he had called out in a voice as flimsy as a stray thread. 'Does anyone know her? She wants you to know it wasn't an accident. He did it on purpose.'

Mr Bevan's eyes searched the room desperately, but since there was no response, he was forced to give up.

'Oh dear, things don't seem to be going too well, do they? Maybe I should call it a night, then.'

Sally

On weekends Dad sometimes took the two siblings on trips to Frank's Yard, a local wrecking site. The reason for these trips, according to Dad, was educational. He would walk them around the yard, stopping by the gaping wrecks of vehicles and point out such things as pistons, crankshafts, and carburettors, then explain the workings of the internal combustion engine. If they came across a car that had been smashed in a road accident, Dad would stand looking at it, just whistling and shaking his head.

'That thing must have gone up like dry kindling.'

'D'you think anyone was trapped in it? John would ask, his eyes shining with excitement.

'Doesn't bear thinking about, does it? Being cooked alive in a burning heap of metal.'

Dad said it was criminal the amount of decent stuff people threw away. He and John found an old movie projector that they took back to the house to repair.

'What have you brought that filthy thing home for?' Mother cried.

They carried it down the cellar. Marion never knew if John and Dad got round to fixing it or not, but if they did, they never asked her to watch films with them.

What Marion liked most about Frank's Yard were the wrecked fairground attractions: An octopus with only five of its eight legs remaining. Some rusty little bumper cars shaped like mice with big sad eyes. A ghost train that was itself a ghost. Horses from a merry-go-round with big scary teeth.

At some point during the visit, Dad would go and chat to Frank in his cabin. Frank was a skinny little man with a bald head and stubble on his face that looked like dirt. You wouldn't have thought he was at all the kind of person a smartly suited businessperson like Dad would want to mix with, but Frank and Dad knew each other as boys when Frank's father managed the fabric warehouse.

He had a grown-up daughter called Sally. She'd sit on a stool in the cabin, dressed in dirty jeans and men's work boots. Marion didn't think that Sally was pretty, at least not like a storybook-princess; she had this birthmark on her left cheek that resembled the icky patch that forms when piece of fruit has been left resting in one place for too long. Yet there was something about her that made you want to stare.

Perhaps it was because Sally never stayed still. She was always wiggling her bum from side to side on the stool, taking a puff of cigarette, giggling, then wiping her mouth with the base of her thumb, her little tongue flicking out as she removed a speck of tobacco with her fingertip, then tying and untying her oil slick of black hair with a silver bobble. These tiny movements were mesmerising like those of a thief creating a distraction while they snatch your wallet. Dad was always watching Sally, waiting for an

135

opportunity to light her cigarette or catch her arm if she slipped, giggling, from the stool.

One day they went to the yard and found Sally alone in the cabin doodling love hearts on the margins of a racing paper. She said Frank had gone to Blackpool to pick up some old roller coaster cars. Dad stayed drinking coffee in the cabin with her, while Marion and John played on the fairground equipment.

A while later Dad came over to tell them Sally needed cigarettes, so he was going to take her to buy some in the Bentley. Since they would only be gone half an hour, the two of them should wait here.

Marion and John went and sat in the mouse bumper cars and made noises like they were crashing into each other. Then Marion felt something scuttle over her foot. When she looked down she saw a real mouse, trapped in the foot well of the bumper car. Shrieking, she jumped out.

John laughed and then spent ten minutes trying to kill the mouse by throwing stones at it while the poor little thing raced around in a panic. Marion thought that was funny: a real live mouse trapped inside a pretend one. John made her throw stones too, but she didn't really want to hurt it, so she missed on purpose and was glad when it finally found a way out through a hole in the metal shell.

When the sun disappeared behind a mountain of twisted metal, they went back to look for Dad. The cabin was locked, and the parking lot empty. Together they wandered around the dump.

'What're we going to do?' Marion asked her

brother. She wanted to take hold of his hand but knew that would make him angry.

'We'll just wait here, stupid. Why, are you scared or something?'

'No, just hungry. Do you think it's time for dinner yet?'

'You're going to have to wait a bit, fatso.'

John went off to find a place to go to the toilet, leaving Marion alone. Everything seemed spookier in the falling light. The octopus became a giant hand grabbing at the sky, loose bits of metal creaked in the wind, and the skeletons sitting in the ghost train glowed eerily.

He seemed to be gone for an age. She called out. 'John, what're you doing?'

Then her brother jumped out from behind a fake tombstone and shouted 'boo' right in her face.

Marion screamed and stumbled away from him. She lost her balance, falling backwards onto a pile of scrap, then felt something sharp stick into her hand. When she got up, the palm was wet with blood.

'You stupid idiot, why did you have to do that?'

'It wasn't my fault,' she protested. 'You jumped right out at me.'

Then John did something weird; he grabbed her wrist and licked the cut. His tongue felt rough and warm and in a funny sort of way she liked it.

'You have to do that to stop it going bad. If that happened, they'd have to take off your whole arm.'

He gave her a handkerchief to wrap round the

137

cut. Miraculously this treatment stopped the bleeding.

'How did you know to do that?' asked Marion.

'I read a book about survival skills,' said John dismissively. 'Just don't tell Dad.'

'Why not?'

'Because you don't have to open your fat mouth about every damn thing, do you?' he yelled.

When they saw the white glare of the Bentley's headlamps staring at them through the gates, Marion nearly burst with relief. They heard Sally laughing as she struggled with the padlock.

On the way home Dad stopped at Murphy's chip shop and bought them a fish supper each. Being allowed to eat on the backseat of the car made the two of them feel like kings — Dad normally had a fit if Marion even tried to nibble so much as a fruit gum on that sacred calfskin upholstery. While stuffing lumps of delicious fried potato into her mouth Marion saw something glint in the darkness. Sliding fingers greasy with chip fat down the back of the seat, she pulled out Sally's silver hair bobble, a few strands of black hair still attached. She was about to remark on her find, then remembered John's words about not opening her 'fat mouth about every damn thing' and slipped the bobble around her wrist before carrying on eating.

A few months later, Dad gave Sally a job at the warehouse. She swapped her jeans and work boots for miniskirts with long rainbow-coloured socks and had her long hair cut in a Prince Valiant bob that cunningly hid the birthmark.

★ ★ ★

Dad's office above the warehouse was filled with the dry, pleasant smells of new cloth and freshly sharpened pencils. Through the windows you could look down at workmen moving giant rolls of fabric below. While Dad talked to clients on the big black telephone, twisting his fingers through its long curly cord, Marion would sit in a corner, turning the floppy pages of sample books, flooding her mind with colours and patterns.

Regatta Stripe made her think of aristocrats drinking champagne on boats with pure white sails; Bermuda Mirage — a man bleeding to death on a sandy beach; Turquoise Duchess — an ageing yet beautiful woman putting on diamonds to meet her young lover.

Sally shared the office with Dad, and as far as Marion could tell, she did nothing all day but read fashion magazines and apply cherry-scented lip gloss that came from a small bottle with a roller at the end.

When Marion grew bored of the sample books, Sally would lend her magazines. They had titles like *Girl Trend*, *Jacey*, and *Modern Chic* and were far more exciting than the fabric sample books. Even the adverts fascinated Marion. Her favourite was for deodorant. In the picture a girl in a white dress rode a horse along a country lane, with a wistful expression on her face. Marion longed to be that girl. The horse would be called Jester and she would ride him every day to visit her best friend, Anna, who was

139

slowly and beautifully dying of consumption.

Girls wrote to the problem pages wanting to know if their breasts were normally shaped or if they could get pregnant by sitting on their boyfriends' laps; there were detailed diagrams of female parts that showed you how to put in a tampon properly and where pubic hair was meant to grow on the female body. To Marion the business of becoming a grown-up woman seemed terrifyingly messy and she wished her body could be as clean and changeless as a plastic doll's.

Sitting on a floppy book of damask swatches, she studied articles about how to make your eyes look bigger by putting a darker colour in the socket and highlighter on the lid, then curling your lashes with tiny little tongs. She learned that vertical stripes made you look thinner, and girls with short necks and round faces ought to wear their hair long and straight to give the illusion of length. Marion believed if she followed all these rules to the letter, then she'd be just like Sally.

The men in the warehouse were always whistling at Sally. She didn't seem to mind, but Dad got furious when he caught them doing it. He would tell them they were a 'bunch of uncouth buggers', then threaten to fire the lot of them and see how they liked that. John said Sally was a flirt and knew how to twist men around her little finger. He pretended that he didn't like her, but Marion knew he'd stolen one of her woollen mittens and kept it hidden in his sock drawer.

After Sally had been working at the warehouse

for a few years, she started dating a sales rep called Owen. Dad didn't like his secretary going out with this charming Welshman, who visited the warehouse extolling the virtues of stain-resistant velour. He claimed it was 'unprofessional'.

One day, Marion saw Sally hurrying down the metal staircase that led to Dad's office, black mascara streaks staining her cheeks. When Marion asked what was wrong, Sally told her that Mr Zetland demanded that she finish with Owen or risk losing her job. Sally, of course, chose Owen over Zetland's Fine Fabrics. A week later she was showing off her diamond engagement ring and telling everyone she had found a job as a receptionist at a solicitor's firm.

Each evening Dad came home from work with a dark look on his face and snapped if you spoke to him. Just before Sally's notice was up, he announced that he had to go on a business trip to Scotland to visit the suppliers at Highland Tartan Mills. He needed someone to take minutes, so Sally would have to go with him. Dad and Sally were on their way for lunch with the tartan suppliers when the majestic Bentley swerved off a bridge and into a river. An Australian backpacker who was hiking in the area dove into the fast-flowing water but couldn't open the car doors and nearly drowned himself trying to save them.

Marion imagined the two of them trapped underwater, hair twisting about Sally's face, Dad, his black moustache stretched into a scream, while the Australian banged on the windows of the Bentley, watching them perish. Yet it was impossible for her to accept that the accident had actually happened. She ought to feel devastated, but death, like algebra and French verbs, was something her brain just refused to grasp, leaving her wondering if she might be too stupid to grieve.

John took leave from his new teaching job at Broadleaf Academy to make arrangements for the funeral.

'That Sally was no good,' he said to Marion. 'She drove Dad to this.'

'What do you mean?' asked Marion. 'Sally wasn't driving the car, Dad was.'

John made one of his 'for goodness' sake' huffing noises and went off without saying anything else, leaving Marion with a head full of jigsaw pieces that refused to fit. Certainly Mother couldn't help her make sense of it all. She refused to speak to anyone and spent her days sitting up in bed, fervently dealing tarot cards like a gambler on a losing streak. It was John who dealt with the detectives that came all the way from Scotland. They talked to him in the living room for more than three hours, while Marion tried to listen at the door.

'They can't prove it wasn't an accident. There's no evidence,' he told Marion after the police had finally left.

'But who says it wasn't an accident?'

'Her dad, of course. That bugger Frank is trying to put the squeeze on us, but he won't get a penny if I've anything to do with it.'

After things had calmed down, and John had returned to Broadleaf Academy, Mother overcame her dislike of touching people to hook

Marion's arm with her dry fingers and say: 'You won't leave me, will you, Mar, not ever?'

'Don't worry, Mother,' she replied, full of happiness at being needed. 'I'll stay with you.'

Mother never spoke about Sally or how strange it was that the car had just gone off that bridge on a fine day in broad daylight. If anyone asked her about Dad, she told them that he was a wonderful and devoted husband who had been ripped away from her in the prime of life. Mother knew how to turn a blind eye to things.

Lauren Hargreaves

John had taken the job teaching chemistry at Broadleaf Academy, a mixed boarding school, straight after graduating from Oxford. If Mother had been disappointed by her son choosing to waste his talents on teaching when he could have been earning a fortune working for some drugs company or becoming a member of parliament like she wanted, she hid it well enough. For fifteen years he earned a reputation as a solid and well-respected member of staff, and it seemed likely that he would have remained at the school until retirement if it hadn't been for Lauren Hargreaves.

There were two things that Marion knew for certain about John's dismissal from Broadleaf Academy: the girl's name was Lauren Hargreaves and John had never laid a finger on her. *Never laid a finger* — even those words troubled Marion. Where did the girl claim fingers had been laid?

At nearly forty with his reputation in ruins, he was forced to leave his flat on the school campus and move back home to live with his sister and ailing mother. Late one night he got terribly drunk and went into Marion's room, where, sitting on the edge of her bed, he blurted out his story between glugs of whiskey:

The girl was a barefaced liar — everyone knew that. She'd already been kicked out of

144

three other schools and was always up to no good — getting caught sneaking into the boys' dorms or drinking cider. His only crime had been in allowing her into his flat on campus. And why had he done that? To give her extra tuition, of course, because she was falling so far behind. To help the ungrateful little bitch. But would anyone believe him? Not a single one of those bastards stood up to support him, did they? Not even his chess buddy Tony Boyle, head of Physics. Not even Bob Phillips! And to think he had bloody well covered up for him, hadn't he? When that cash went missing from the legacy fund!

Marion should have been flattered that he confided in her, instead she found the unexpected display of intimacy frightening. Each bit of the story felt like something long and sharp being pushed into the soft pincushion of her brain.

After a while his words became too slurred and tearful, and she wouldn't have been able to understand him even if she'd wanted to. All she could make out was something about a fruit knife, a school porter, and the girl wandering the grounds with a torn blouse and bloody knee.

Whatever had or hadn't happened, it seemed that nothing could be proven against John. Even Lauren's parents, who divided the year between the slopes of Colorado and the Côte d'Azur, didn't seem particularly inclined to believe their daughter. All they cared about was avoiding a public scandal, and they agreed not to involve the police so long as John was removed from the school.

It was a small blessing that at least they managed to hide the awful business from Mother. She never even asked why her son had moved home. In the years since Dad's death, a diet that consisted almost entirely of warm milk and sleeping pills had sent her so far downhill that sometimes Marion wondered if she even knew who John was. Mother died just six months after John lost his job. Secretly Marion was grateful to Lauren Hargreaves. She did not know how she could have coped all alone in that big old house without her brother there to keep her company.

Noise from the Cellar

It was a warm summer night and Marion had opened a window to let some air into the stuffy dining room. While she and John ate their dinner of tinned ravioli the sound of voices could be heard coming from outside; Judith must have people over. She heard a loud shriek of female laughter, and then an unfamiliar male voice said: 'Go on, I dare you to show it to Jude, she's never seen one before.'

It occurred to Marion that Judith had not mentioned cutting down the tree since she and Greg trespassed into the garden some months ago. She must have forgotten all about it. John was using a slice of white bread to mop up sauce from his plate when a loud banging came from the cellar door. The commotion sent a bullet of panic right through Marion's chest. She looked at her brother.

'What is happening, John?'

John got to his feet and closed the window, shutting the drunken voices from the garden.

'Get in the living room, right away, shut the door and stay there until I tell you to come out!' he ordered.

'Yes, John,' she answered timidly, afraid of his rising anger as much as the noise from the cellar.

Her heart hammering, she went into the next room and closed the door.

'Don't think about them, you silly old girl,' she

said out loud. 'Let John deal with it. Just don't let them into your head, and it will all go away.'

Then she heard a female voice scream something, it could have been 'help us', but she wasn't sure, since the voice was so muffled. This was followed by the sound of furniture being knocked over.

'Don't listen to it!' she told herself, rapping her knuckles hard against her temples. Then she switched on the television and turned the volume up as high as it would go. The programme was about gardening. A man with a beard was advising the viewers how to prune clematis plants. She turned the channel, a young woman in a silver dress was singing a song before a panel of judges. As she forced herself to concentrate on the program Marion's breathing became steadier.

'It's all right,' she told herself. 'John will deal with it, everything is all right.

★ ★ ★

She woke in the middle of the night with the vague sense of having had an important dream, but when she tried to remember it, the dream remained forever beyond her grasp. It seemed these days she couldn't get through a night without waking three or four times, and usually it took forever to get back to sleep again. According to the glowing green hands of the clock, it was 3:15 a.m. The heat in her room was heavy and dark, pressing down on her body, filling her mouth and nose, making it difficult to breathe.

'Help us.' She could have been wrong, but she

was almost sure that was what the voice had said. 'Help us.'

On her way downstairs to get a glass of water, she passed her brother's room. His door was closed, but she could see a band of light shining through the gap below. Muttering came from within. She stopped by the door to listen:

'Never any peace — these women never give me any bloody peace. What am I to do with them? Tell me that? I try to do my best for them, but what thanks do I get? What thanks? All I want is a little bit of love and comfort — is that too much to ask for?' Then came the huge and terrible sound of him sobbing.

At that moment the urge gripped her to go into his room and tell him she would no longer stand him having the visitors down there. That it was wrong and he must let them go immediately. The whole affair was making her sick with worry. She put her hand on the doorknob and was about to turn it, then stopped. Whenever she thought about defying him, an invisible brace tightened around her chest, making it difficult to breathe. What was she afraid of? John had never raised a hand to her, yet sometimes he looked at her like she was a drowsy fly he could crush between finger and thumb anytime he wanted to.

The Box

Mrs Morrison the housekeeper had been cleaning John's room when Marion heard her scream. The look on her face when she came out carrying the cardboard box, you would have thought she'd just witnessed a murder. The housekeeper went straight into the front room where Mother was having morning coffee and reading the *Telegraph*.

Mrs Morrison's gruff voice was easier to understand from the other side of the heavy oak door, Marion picked out *filth — indecent — disgusting* from the muffled flow. Mother's speech, warbling and reedy as the call of a waterbird, was harder to decipher. Before the door handle had finished turning, Marion had scampered away and found another vantage point beneath the dining room table.

She caught the bitter odour of cigarette smoke and then saw Mother's polished grey heels click rapidly down the parquet floor and stop by the telephone nook.

'And she thinks she can lecture me about decency, Philip,' said Mother, letting a nervous flurry of ash fall onto the parquet floor.

'What with her Sharon having those kids by different fathers and not one of them sticking around a minute after they were born.' She spoke loudly enough to make sure that Mrs Morrison in the living room could hear too.

Marion crept upstairs to look for John, but he was nowhere to be found. Knowing that both Mother and Mrs Morrison refused to go down there for fear of rats and spiders, he was probably hiding in the cellar. Thirty minutes later Dad arrived home from the warehouse. Sucking on a boiled sweet she had found, still wrapped, beneath the dining room table, Marion listened to his conversation with Mrs Morrison.

'Come on, Peg, you know what teenage lads are like. He's got a healthy curiosity about things.'

'What I saw wasn't healthy, Mr Zetland,' declared Mrs Morrison, her voice upper-class with indignation.

'Just let me deal with it.'

'Mrs Zetland informed me that as of today my services would no longer be required.'

Dad's sigh was long and low, like the air being let out of a bicycle tyre.

'Come on, don't be daft. You're like one of the family. I'll call Dr Dunkerly, get him to bring her something. She'll have forgotten it all by tomorrow.'

Then Dad plucked something out of his wallet, put it into Mrs Morrison's hand.

Marion folded the wrapper of the boiled sweet very tightly and squeezed it between the floorboards.

'When I am grown up with a husband and children, I will come back and find this and remember how things were when I was a child,' she vowed to herself, then scrambled out from beneath the table.

151

Through the dining room window Marion watched Dad place the box near the wall of ivy at the far end of the garden. She just caught the sound of him whistling something cheery as he went down the back steps to the cellar.

Marion slipped out through the kitchen door. It was a damp, heavy day and the pitter-patter of fat raindrops flattened her hair. Slowly she approached the box, each step feeling like a sin as her black patent 'indoor shoes' pressed into the mud and specks of mire freckled her white socks.

The lid of the box was loosely folded, 'Walkers Cheese and Onion Crisps' printed on the side in faded blue letters. She reached out cautiously, nervous its wicked contents might fly out and strike her in the face. With one hand, she gently moved a ragged flap of cardboard to one side. The shapes and colours inside screeched at her. Stark white thighs, a gash of red like raw minced beef, a dark nest of hair, a twisted mouth.

As she ran to her bedroom, maggoty thoughts hatched in Marion's head. That woman — how could she breathe? Involuntarily she clawed at the collar of her polo-neck, imagining what it must feel like to have someone pulling a black leather strap around your throat. What kind of person would allow their photo to be taken with no knickers on? The most shocking thing of all was the picture being inside the heads of Mother, Dad, and Mrs Morrison, their normal thoughts struggling to find space around it. And John. How on earth could anyone actually *want* to look at something like that?

From the way Mrs Morrison carried the box, it looked heavy. There must be dozens of magazines in there. She gasped at the thought of hundreds and hundreds of women fixed in everlasting torment, a world of shame and terror contained in that old Walkers Crisps box.

Peering through the bedroom window, she saw Dad standing by the box with a plastic bottle in one hand. He poured liquid onto the soggy cardboard and then lit a match. White smoke plumed out of the opening, shrouding the sycamore and the rosebushes, until the whole garden was filled with mist. By the time it cleared, the box had transformed into a pile of silvery ash. The pictures in Marion's head, however, remained unburned, and when she closed her eyes, they were brighter and sharper than ever.

Brendan O'Brian

Marion felt a flush of excitement when she saw the poster sticking to the wall of Northport Library. Tuesday the eighteenth of July. The idea that she might go along entered her head, but she immediately shooed it away. Then she saw one wrapped around a lamppost and several more stuck to the walls of the little brick shelters along the seafront, next to posters advertising comedians and musical groups.

One morning as she was picking up the post, Marion noticed a blue flyer lying on the hall floor.

Brendan O'Brian World Famous Medium
8pm Tuesday 18th July
Northport Community Hall

The name Brendan O'Brian filled her with girlish yearning that she found impossible to repress. The very same Brendan O'Brian she had watched for so long on television. Was this a sign meant especially for her? No, it was silly to think that, they pushed them through everyone's letter box. Yet she had a strange feeling that she was meant to go. After all, the spiritualist church meetings she had attended with Mother had always been so interesting. Perhaps this was what she needed to break out from her dull life: to meet people and begin to live.

Where else could I go? Surely not to a pub by myself, she thought. Judith had suggested French lessons, but that would bring back all the shameful humiliation of school. And it would be so nice to do something different for a change. She might make a friend, a respectable, middle-aged woman like herself or even a kindly old lady who was desperate for companionship. She knew the idea of meeting a *man* was ridiculously far-fetched. And even if she did, the type of male that frequented this sort of thing was unlikely to be suitable.

Then she heard Mother's voice warning her that she would have to walk past Albert Park alone after dark. *Something awful could happen to you, Marion, you could be robbed or worse. Don't you remember that poor girl who got dragged into a van by two men while she was walking by the park late at night?*

Marion's mind flip-flopped constantly in the days leading up to the event. Eventually at 6:30 p.m. on the evening of the meeting she decided she would go and rushed upstairs to find a decent outfit. A state of panic gripped her when she realised there was almost nothing suitable in her wardrobe. Eventually she settled on the drab black suit she had worn for her parents' funerals, with a grey wool jumper underneath. It was far too warm for July, but at least it looked respectable.

After spending so long deciding what to wear, Marion was left with only twenty minutes to get to the meeting. It was eight fifteen when she arrived at the community hall, all sweaty in her layers and blisters forming on her heels from running. How she hated to be late! The white pillars framing the entrance looked elegant from a distance, yet close up they were shabby off-white and scarred with badly spelled graffiti. Jezus is dea was scribbled in a green marker pen that must have dried out before the writer got to the end.

There was no one to buy a ticket from in the lobby, so the meeting must have already begun. Feeling guilty for not paying, she crept into the darkened hall and sat near the back. There were about fifty people in the audience, most of them elderly or middle-aged women, one or two men.

Brendan O'Brian seemed older and plumper in real life than he did on television, and his dark hair had turned grey, but Marion supposed the series might have been filmed some time ago.

He wore soft black training shoes and a grey velvet tracksuit that made him look rather like an otter. When Marion arrived, he was in the middle of talking to a lady with a long silver-and-black ponytail sitting in the front row. Her head was bowed, so Marion couldn't see her face. It seemed he had made contact with her daughter who had died of breast cancer. The woman's shoulders began to rock backwards and forwards when he announced that her daughter was there every night when she read bedtime stories to her granddaughter, Casey.

'I'm leaving her love with you,' he said to the bereaved woman, then held out his hand as if presenting her with an invisible package. The same gesture he'd make on the television show.

He began to pace around the room, waiting for the next spirit visitor.

'Does anyone know a T?' he called out to the audience. 'He liked to feed the birds.'

A thin blonde girl shot up her hand, the bangles on her arm making a loud rattling noise.

'My great uncle Terry, he sometimes fed the ducks in Albert Park.'

The spiritualist performed the familiar gesture as though he was throwing an invisible tennis ball towards the girl.

'He's saying that you won't pass the first time, but don't give up. Can you tell us what that means to you, my darling?'

She smiled elatedly as though she had won the grand prize in a raffle.

'That's right, that's right. I'm thinking of taking my driving test.'

'Well, you might need a few more lessons, love. And practice those three-point turns,' said the medium in his jolly Irish brogue.

Laughter rippled through the audience. Marion liked the little Irishman, and she could tell that the rest of the audience liked him too. Everyone was desperate to receive a message; it meant you had been singled out by some greater power, that you were special. Being out and amongst other people made her happy, yet the feeling was tinged with regret at having missed out on so much in life, staying in alone for so many countless evenings when other people were doing things like this, going to plays and musical concerts, eating in restaurants or just chatting to each other at parties.

The medium spoke to several more people. Some of the messages were tragic: 'Alan said the pain was so great at the end that passing came as a relief.' Or sometimes funny: 'Sheila wants you to stop planting hydrangeas in the front garden, she can't stand them. They remind her of her mother-in-law.'

Then the medium went silent for several minutes. The atmosphere became tense with expectation as everyone waited for the next message. Finally he spoke: 'The lady I have with me is singing a song that we all know. She's got a good voice too, not quite Julie Andrews but not far off.' And then he began to sing, 'The hills are alive . . . ' Marion knew at once it was her aunt, but for some reason she was too afraid to put up her hand.

He scanned the room, like a store detective looking for a shoplifter, and then his eyes stopped on Marion. As he moved down the aisle, getting closer and closer to the row she was sitting on, her pulse began to throb. She lowered her head, hoping he would walk past, but the medium stopped right next to her seat.

'What's the matter, Marion, don't you want to say hello to your auntie?'

She looked up and stared into his kindly brown eyes.

'Agnes knows that it was you who did it,' said the medium.

'I — I d-don't know what you mean,' stuttered Marion.

Then he said quite simply, as if he were stating her name: 'You are evil.'

The hall fell silent — everyone was looking at

Marion. Her mind swam with confusion. Why had he said this? Could he really see something inside her, a dark stain that was invisible to everyone else?

'I — I can't be evil,' she said. 'I am nothing. I am nobody.'

He put his hand on her shoulder. She felt as though all the life in her body was being drained through that hand and if he held on for long enough, she would die. Looking down at her, like a priest giving the last rites, he said softly:

'You are the kind of evil that comes from nothing, from neglect and loneliness. You are like mould that grows in damp dark places, black dirt gathered in corners, a fatal infection that begins with a speck of dirt in an unwashed wound.'

With all her strength, she pushed the little man out of her way and stumbled along her row of seats towards the exit. A man in a shabby grey suit sitting halfway down the row refused to move his knees out of the way to let her pass.

'Will you please move?' asked Marion, nudging his long legs with her bag.

A woman with cropped black hair and eyeliner that extended into devilish upward flicks, whispered to him, 'Did you hear what he said? Evil — *she* is the one.'

The man stretched his legs out further, as if to deliberately keep her prisoner.

'Please let me pass, will you! You must let me pass! I have to get out of this place!' The man's mouth gaped in shock as Marion kicked at his skinny shanks, making the trouser bottoms flap. She forced her way through, knocking over the woman's handbag so loose change and clumps of used tissue rolled onto the floor.

'Well, look at that, will you?' said the woman groping for her things in the dark space beneath the seats. 'Not an ounce of consideration for anyone.'

Other people turned to glare at Marion as she made her way out of the theatre. She heard the word repeated around the hall like the tweeting of birds in an aviary. *Evil — she's evil — evil.*

'I saw her sneak in,' hissed an elderly lady in a purple turban between applying a greasy coat of lip salve to her wrinkled mouth. 'I don't think she even had a ticket.'

★ ★ ★

All the way home her heart was hammering as if she were being pursued by a rapist. What a horrible man, she thought, how dare he make those accusations when he doesn't know anything about me? She crawled into bed without even taking off her clothes and lay shivering with shock beneath the blankets. Over and over again the scene played in her mind: Why had he said those things? Why had he chosen her? She felt raw and broken as if she had been publicly whipped.

The memory of all those people staring at her was the worst thing. Not a single one of them had come to her defence. Surely no one could have believed him? It was all a sham, she reassured herself. That girl was in on the act, she didn't really have an uncle who liked to feed birds. Mediums had all sorts of tricks and ways of finding out information about people. Nearly everyone had an aunt, and the song was a lucky guess. Brendan O'Brian probably wasn't his real name. He would be one of those Irish gypsies who went around the country deceiving decent, honest people. I should report him to the authorities for saying those things, thought Marion. I could sue him for slander.

The morning after the encounter with Brendan O'Brian, she awoke feeling drained and with aching muscles as she might after a bout of flu or some physical trauma, but her mind was calm. The incident had confirmed that in a world full of people who took pleasure from hurting others, she was better off staying at home. It had been a mistake to try and break free, this was where she belonged, where no one could touch her. As she wrapped the covers around her body, the bed seemed more comfortable than usual, and seeing as it was only quarter past nine, she decided to spend a little longer sleeping.

@coppelia
Sept 15th
Hi Adrian it is good for me to hear from you again so soon To write you it is good practice for me in English. It is of course my dream to visit your wonderful country one day! At present I am working in city many miles from home, because there is no work in my village, except chemica factory and even then you must know some people to get job.

I am work as waitress in a place called the Kitty Kat Klub. Guys from the local mine come in

161

to get drunk and have fun with the girls. They are mostly not so bad, sometimes I feel sorry for them. I want to say: Don't spend all your money here you should send to wives, but then if I did my boss Ivan would get so mad!! Last week he threw one girl out into snow wearing just her g-string and high heels. For what reason? She was supposed to be on diet and he caught her eating potato pancakes!

My friend is Katya one of the dancing girls (in the bar she has to go by the name of Roxanne because there is already one Katya). All day she dances until some guy picks her, then they go into back room. I do not do this work, I am decent girl, I only serve drinks! Sometimes Ivan he asks me to be dancing girl but I refuse.

xxx

Sept 29th

How are you Adrian, what is the news from England?

My heart is sore from missing mama and my beautiful baby back in village. Baby is so cute, her name is Varvara. Already I think she can be ballerina and mama is playing Tchaikovsky music to her while she dances. When I was young girl I dreamed of becoming ballerina but then papa got sick and there was no more money for classes.

I am determined to work hard and save so that Varvara can do whatever she wants. Maybe she will be doctor rather than ballerina or even just ordinary person, I do not care so long as she is happy.

Love and kisses Alla xxx

Oct 11th

Dear Adrian It is so cold here today. I wish I had
money to buy new coat but I must send
everything back to mama. The same guys come
in Kitty Kat Klub all the times. Maybe they are
beginning to get bored with me as they do not
give so many tips. Maybe I am getting old, even
though I am only twenty-two, that is quite old
compared to some of the girls, Natasha is only
sixteen and she is giving private dances in the
back room.

I hate to ask you this and hope you do not
think I am taking advantage of our friendship but
PLEASE PLEASE if you hear of any job
opportunities in your wonderful country you let
me know. I feel you are my very good friend.

Love Alla

xxxx

Nov 1st

Dear Adrian

Something very bad happened to Katya. She
was kidnapped by one of the guys from the Klub
Kabana. This is also club for dancing girls, many
of the girls leave Klub Kabana to work here at
Kitty Kat because the guy who runs it is very bad
man who beats the girls.

The boss got mad with Ivan for stealing his
girls and as revenge he takes Katya. They keep
her blindfolded and tied up for three days. When
she is let go they had cut her face and now she
cannot work anymore. It is horrible and the
police will do nothing because they say she is
prostitute. Ivan says I must take Katya's job or he

163

will fire me. I am very scared. I do not know what to do. Please can you help me Adrian?
Alla
xxx

Marion had been picking daffodils from beneath the sycamore tree at the end of the garden when she heard the child crying. It was only months after Mother's funeral, and she had thought of taking some to the grave, but when she looked closely, she saw the petals were tinged with brown and little black bugs were crawling around inside the bell-shaped flower. *For goodness' sake, Marion, you could at least go to the trouble of buying something from a decent florist, rather than giving me those rotten old things.* After casting the tainted blooms away, she peered over the garden wall and saw a little red-haired girl. Though not very good at guessing the ages of children, Marion thought the girl must be about four.

'What's the matter? Why are you crying?' she called out. The child looked up; her mouth was open and ragged with pain. She scowled at Marion, mucus dripping from her lower lip. 'I'm sorry, I didn't mean to scare you, I just wanted to make sure you were all right. Have you hurt yourself? Where's your mummy?' The child looked down at a small felt mouse she was holding as if it might have the answers to these questions. 'Is your mummy inside the house?' 'Ummy hurt gar — ' said the girl through sobs.

'I'm sorry, what did you say?'

'Mummy hurt gar!' she shouted.

'Your mummy hurt you?'

'Ooooooooooh — ' Then she let out a long squeal of frustration. A fat globule of spit fell from her lip, forming a dark patch on her green dungarees. The girl wiped her face with the felt mouse and took a shaky breath.

'Mummy hurt car — Daddy has to pay to make better.'

'Oh, I'm sorry.'

'Dey're fighting.'

'I see.'

'An when car got hurt — I got a sore arm.'

The little girl held up her left arm. Marion saw a dark bruise.

'But don't tell Daddy,' she whispered, and put her finger over her mouth.

'All right, I promise I won't.'

Then Judith came out of the house, looking like a French prostitute from the 1920s, her hair in a lopsided black bob, red lipstick, leather miniskirt with fishnet tights. Marion waved at her over the fence.

'Hello there, I'm your neighbour, Marion.'

Judith ignored her, so Marion tried again. 'I think your little girl is upset.'

With barely a glance in Marion's direction, Judith snatched up her daughter and went back into the house.

A few weeks later she appeared on Marion's doorstep with Lydia. The little girl was holding a pink lunch box in one hand and sucking on a raw, unpeeled carrot in the other. Unlike the last time they met, Judith was smiling and apologetic, her words came out in a giddy torrent: 'Margaret, isn't it? Hello, I'm Judith, I'm so sorry we haven't had a chance to really meet until now, but we've been so busy, what with the move and everything. I was wondering if you could do me the most enormous favour. This is terribly cheeky of me, I know, but if you're not busy, could you watch Liddy for just a short while?'

Judith patted her daughter's head as if she were an unfamiliar, yet friendly dog who had just wandered up to her.

'You see, I'm in the middle of something of a crisis — do you know Patric Mulvane the sculptor? Of course you don't, but he does fantastic things with bird skeletons — well, I'm supposed to meet with him, as a potential client, anyway I won't bore you with the details, but her father promised to leave work early and take care of madam here — but he hasn't turned up — I'd be so grateful.'

'Marion.'

'Sorry?'

'My name is Marion, and yes, I'd be happy to watch her.'

Lydia came into the house, without saying goodbye to her mother. She handed Marion the carrot, still warm and moist from being sucked, then went into the kitchen. After sitting down at the kitchen table, she opened her pink lunch box, took out a drawing pad, and some felt-tip pens, and began drawing pictures of neat little houses.

Marion was filled with wonder as if a baby unicorn had trotted into the house. She sat down cautiously so as not to frighten her away, then watched as she drew pictures. It was difficult to believe something so perfect could exist; perhaps some magical toy maker had created her in his workshop, painted that tiny mouth with sugar-pink enamel and modelled those blue eyes from sapphire-coloured glass. Next to the child, Marion felt like a storybook ogre with her big, messy body, clumsy movements, and rough, blotchy skin.

After a while the girl got bored with her drawing; she pushed the pictures away and began kicking her legs beneath the chair.

Marion spoke in a whisper. 'Why don't you come upstairs with me, I have something exciting to show you.'

The girl looked cynically at Marion, and put a finger in her mouth, dragging down her lower lip.

'What is it?'

'A secret, something you can't tell anyone else about.'

Lydia followed Marion up the stairs right until they came to the attic.

When she first saw all the teddies, nearly a hundred piled on the bed, Lydia's eyes swelled with amazement. She charged across the room, jumped onto the bed, and then began tossing the toys in the air and whooping with glee.

'So many teddy bears, I love them all! How did you get so many?'

'Some of them belonged to me when I was a little girl, and the others didn't have a home, so they came to live here.'

Marion lined the toys up in rows, and Lydia pretended she was the school teacher and they were the children. Then the bears were the audience in a theatre while Lydia put on one of Mother's old hats, a silk scarf, and what must have been several thousand pounds' worth of jewels to sing 'Three Blind Mice' for them. Marion clapped and cheered with delight. At eight o'clock that evening, when Judith came to collect her, Lydia sobbed and pleaded with her mother to be allowed to stay longer.

'If you act like this, I won't let you come and visit Margaret ever again,' Judith said. The look of distress in the little girl's eyes gave Marion a glow of pleasure.

From that day on Judith brought Lydia round to visit Marion at least once or twice a week; perhaps a babysitter cancelled at the last minute, she had to go out on an important errand, or even, 'Lydia just begged me to let her come over, Marion, you know how much she loves playing with you.'

Marion bought special food, things that Judith herself would never have allowed the girl to eat: crisps, chocolate, gummy bears, and fizzy drinks. During the summer months they went to the beach for picnics. While most adults seemed to lose patience with children and their fanciful, repetitive games, Marion never got bored playing with Lydia. It fascinated her to watch the child as she went about arranging her toys and chatting to herself, a look of concentration on her chubby pink-and-white face. She had felt such love for the little girl, she almost wanted to

168

gobble her up alive.

She once overheard Judith and Lydia's father talking while drinking wine one evening on their patio.

'We really don't know anything about these people, Jude — do you think Lydia should be spending so much time there?'

'Oh, Duncan, don't be so bloody paranoid, they are both as harmless as old carpet slippers. He does have the air of the disgraced scout leader about him, took early retirement from some public school, but I should imagine he's only interested in boys; anyway, he spends all his time down the cellar playing with his train sets. Lydia never sees him. I admit she is a bit loopy, but quite sweet, never had a child of her own and desperate to love someone else's.'

If John was around during Lydia's visits, he would pull faces that she found terrifying or grab hold of her and tickle her tummy until she went red from screaming. John, of course, was only trying to entertain her, he just didn't understand that girls didn't like rough play, so Marion tried her best to keep Lydia out of his way.

Lydia was five, sitting at the dining room table eating lunch, when she asked:

'Why do things grow up? Why doesn't everything stay little?'

'I don't know,' said Marion. 'I suppose because the little things need big things to look after them.'

Lydia picked up a piece of cheese on toast from a plate decorated with fairies and goblins dancing in a woodland glade. The design was entitled Midsummer's Eve and came from a collection of six that hung on Marion's bedroom wall. The others were Christmas, Whitsuntide, Easter, All Hallows' Eve, and Twelfth Night; the plates were collectors' items and meant only for decoration, but since Lydia liked them so much, Marion let her eat off them from time to time.

'Marion, are you big or a little girl?'

'I'm a big person, of course.'

Lydia chewed thoughtfully on her toast.

'But you don't have anyone to look after.'

'Well, I suppose I have John. We look after each other.'

'Is he your husband?'

'No,' laughed Marion. 'He's my brother.'

Lydia's sweet face hardened into a strangely grown-up expression.

'I don't like him. He's scary like an ugly smelly wolf.'

Marion was shocked. Should she say something? Tell her off for being so rude about a grown man? But she could never bring herself to get cross with Lydia. Marion remembered that Dad had always called her 'young lady' when she was in trouble, for some reason.

'That's not a very nice thing to say, young lady.'

'Make him go away, then we'll be able to play games without anyone messing things up.'

'I can't do that, he's my brother, Lydia.'

Then suddenly Lydia picked up the plate and threw it on the floor, where it shattered into pieces.

'Oh!' exclaimed Marion. 'Lydia, why did you

do that? You know how precious that plate was to me?'

The child stuck out her bottom lip defiantly.

'It was a silly plate. You're too old to have things with fairies on them.'

The sight of the lovely broken ornament made Marion feel as if something sharp had lodged into her heart. And to think the other plates had lost a brother. The set would never seem the same again. In that moment she loathed Lydia, even though she knew it was wrong to hate a child. While she was picking up fragments from under the dining room table, Marion saw a glint of something shiny between the floorboards. Rubbing her finger across it, she remembered stuffing the sweetie paper there when was young. After several minutes had passed Lydia slipped off her chair and peered under the table.

'What are you doing?'

'Nothing,' snapped Marion.

'I'm sorry I broke it.'

Marion lowered her head and put her hands over her face. I won't let her see that I am hurt. I won't let a child know she has done this to me, she told herself.

'It doesn't matter. I don't care about the stupid plate.'

'Then why do you look so sad?'

'I-I'm not sad at all, Lydia.'

'Don't tell fibs!' scolded Lydia in a mocking voice that made Marion's ears hurt. 'You were crying. I can tell.' She fought the urge to grab Lydia by her pale arm and drag her back to her mother.

'I was just thinking about things, aren't I allowed to do that? About when I was a girl.'

Lydia slid under the table and positioned herself cross-legged opposite Marion, then she reached out and pulled her hands away from her face.

'Were you sad when you were little?'

Marion sighed.

'Sometimes I was sad, yes.'

'Was it because of John? Because he was nasty to you?'

'No, it wasn't. Not because of John.'

'Then why was it?'

Marion felt the anger rising again. She knew she shouldn't be cross with Lydia but she couldn't help herself.

'I don't want to talk about it. Now, you be quiet, miss, or I shall give you a good slap, do you hear me?'

Lydia's small face went pale with shock, but she didn't move; instead, the two of them stayed sitting beneath the table saying nothing until Judith rang on the doorbell to fetch her daughter.

★   ★   ★

Despite the breaking of the plate, Lydia carried on coming to the house to see Marion. For her eleventh birthday, Marion bought her a Beach-time Boogie Babe, even though Judith had deemed the toy with its long blonde hair and skimpy bikini 'an offensive stereotype of femininity.'

'But you will have to keep it here, of course, so

172

she doesn't see it,' said Marion, pouring her a glass of Coca-Cola, then emptying a giant bag of pickled onion flavour Monster Munch into a bowl.

Lydia pushed a Monster Munch into her mouth and crunched. 'Love you so much Em, you're the best. You're never too busy to do stuff with me, Mum is always on the phone to clients or going to look at some ugly pictures, she hardly notices me.' Marion swelled with happiness. No one had ever thought her 'the best' before.

Once, a year or two later, Lydia arrived in tears after an argument with her mother.

'Mum is such a bitch, she always blames Dad for making her unhappy, but she's the one that always starts the arguments, he just gets stressed because she's wasting all his money keeping that stupid art gallery open. She is trying to make him go to counselling meetings with her where they have to talk about why they fight all the time. She wants me to go too. I know why they argue, it's because she's such a pain in the arse. She won't let me watch TV, she says if I am bored, I have to read a book or play my violin, I hate that stupid violin. Why doesn't she play the damn thing if it's so much fun?'

Marion wondered if she ought to defend Judith, but she secretly enjoyed hearing Lydia say these things about her mother.

When Duncan moved in with his twenty-five-year-old blonde mistress who wore saris and had a pierced tongue, Lydia ran to Marion and clung to her, sobbing.

'I don't blame Dad for going, I hate her, I hate

173

her, I wish I could leave, I wish I could come here and live with you! Can't you ask her? Or maybe I could just run away and hide in your spare room, she wouldn't even know I was here. You could bring me snacks and then at night I could come down and watch telly with you.'

Marion was half tempted to agree to Lydia's plan, in fact, she had often fantasised that Judith would be killed in a road accident or die of a fatal disease and she would be allowed to adopt Lydia. 'How good and generous Marion is to look after that poor young girl,' people would say. There was obviously the problem of Lydia's father, but in her fantasy he rejected Lydia too, and only Marion could save her from the orphanage. When Lydia was older, they would open a gift shop together called Pleasant Surprises on the seafront that sold pretty things like decorated pillboxes and scented soap.

★　★　★

As the years passed Marion was shocked how quickly Lydia grew from a pretty child into an attractive young woman with a taste for shorts and miniskirts that showed off her long slender legs. There were occasions when John looked at the girl in a manner that made Marion uneasy.

'Really,' she would think to herself a little angrily, 'if I were her mother, I would *never* let her go out dressed like that. How much prettier she would look in a nice long skirt perhaps with a bright floral pattern. But it isn't my place to say anything to Judith . . . '

174

After Lydia started college at sixteen, she visited less and less. One day Marion saw her on Northport Pier with two other girls. They were standing by one of the kiosks, laughing and joking around. They all wore tiny shorts and long loose T-shirts decorated with delicate sketches of flowers and fairies. A pretty girl with long dark hair put on a huge pair of novelty sunglasses and began walking like a duck while Lydia and a blonde girl laughed. Marion caught Lydia's eye and was about to wave, then Lydia turned away quickly and began looking at a display of postcards. That cold, grey feeling of being ignored reminded Marion of her days at Ladychapel, and she quickly walked away.

She tried telling herself that Lydia was a teenager, and teenagers didn't want to waste their time with adults. And yet it was around this period that Lydia became much closer to her mother. Judith seemed to relish complaining to Marion about Lydia's neediness. 'She's getting so possessive,' Judith would moan. 'She doesn't even like me dating men. She wants me to act like some repressed, 1950s housewife. Then we could bake cakes and get our nails done together.'

When Judith spoke about Lydia like this, Marion would ache with envy. How wonderful it would be to have a vibrant young daughter to share pleasant experiences with. She saw the two of them in a sunlit kitchen putting trays of pretty cupcakes into an old-fashioned oven. They

wouldn't even care if they left them in too long
and they came out black as coal. Laughing, they
would throw them away and start another batch.

Laundry

The little travel alarm by her bedside (why did she have a travel alarm, she never went anywhere?) said 10:15, but the heavy weight of dread that pressed down on Marion stopped her from getting up. It was Monday. Monday was a bad day because of the laundry.

Eventually she gathered the strength to push off the weight and forced herself to get out of bed and go into the bathroom. After washing herself she sat for several minutes on the edge of the bath thinking about what she had to do. I don't know why you get so worked up about this, she said to herself. All you need to do is gather the dirty laundry from the baskets in your and John's bedrooms and then stuff it all in the big washing machine. And then when it is done, leave it to dry in the face-wardrobe room. That was the simple part. What filled her with dread was washing the third basket that contained the things belonging to the visitors.

Of course she could have refused to do *their* laundry, but that would have meant bringing up the matter with John, and if they were never mentioned, it was easier to pretend that they weren't really there. Sometimes she would even think to herself: How could there possibly be *people* living in the cellar of our house? John is only going down to meddle around with his tools, to try and fix all those old broken things he

177

brings home. Then laundry day would come along, reminding her that they must indeed exist, and she would be once again overcome with a brittle, cold feeling of fretfulness.

She always tried to deal with their things as quickly as possible, piling them into the washer, then dragging them out again, trying not to look too closely at anything. But every now and then something fell on the floor and she would have to pick it up. And once you looked at whatever it was — perhaps a pair of panties decorated with blue butterflies, a pink flower-patterned T-shirt that almost seemed small enough to belong to a child, or that yellow silk bra with wire poking out through the ragged lace trimming — then a picture got stuck in your head, and you couldn't help wondering about the person it belonged to.

Even if you did manage to get it all done without really looking at anything, it was impossible to ignore the smells; sometimes they made her feel quite sick. And that would start her thinking about other things, such as *how they went to the bathroom and washed themselves*. She seemed to remember there being a sink in the cellar and drain near the steps at the back. One supposed foreign people, especially if they were poor, might be more accepting of such primitive 'facilities', yet conditions must be unpleasant, inhuman almost. What if one of them decided they would no longer put up with the situation and wanted to leave, would John allow it? How could he stop them? She heard that voice again: 'Help us, help us!' 'I can't help you!' Marion wanted to shout.

178

'Please leave me alone.' Then she rapped her knuckles against her temples to chase the cries away.

★   ★   ★

By late afternoon when the laundry was all clean and dried, Marion decided to reward herself with some Choc Mint Chip Cookie Melts, a kind of biscuit with a soft centre, while she watched her afternoon TV programmes. She opened the packet, put several on a plate, and then took them along with a cup of sweet tea into the living room.

The film she watched was about a single mother who had cancer. The woman's teenage daughter kept getting in trouble for taking drugs and going out with the wrong sorts of boys. Despite the girl's terrible behaviour, the mother, who had lost most of her hair to chemotherapy, stayed calm and serene and wrote a letter to the girl that was only to be opened after her death. At the end of the film the girl read it and then scattered the mother's ashes over a cliff. She made a beautiful speech asking for her mother's forgiveness and declaring that she was going to college to study medicine and hoped one day to be able to help cancer patients like her mother.

By the end of the film, Marion had eaten the entire packet of biscuits. Feeling drowsy from an excess of sugar, she went upstairs to her room to lie on her bed. Surrounded by her teddy bears, she closed her eyes and began to daydream.

She imagined that she lived in America in a little white house with a beautiful green lawn.

Neil was her husband, and together they had a family of three children. One of these children suffered some misfortune, a rare debilitating illness perhaps. She saw them receiving bad news from a kindly doctor who was bald and wore spectacles. To tell them the news, he took off the spectacles and rubbed his furrowed brow.

Then she looked into Neil's eyes and saw fear that exactly mirrored her own, and they grasped each other by the hand. After months or perhaps even years, the doctor with the furrowed brow would tell them that thanks to their devotion as parents and the hard work of the fine doctors and nurses in the hospital, the child was showing signs of improvement. One perfect summer day the child would be allowed to return home from hospital. Marion and the other children would make Welcome Home banners, then there would be a barbecue in the garden. While the healthier children leapt into the pool, the recovering child, possibly still in a wheelchair and wearing clothes that were rather too warm for the time of year, would smile bravely at his loving parents.

'As long as we all have each other,' Neil would say, 'that is the important thing. Of course there will always be troubles along the way, but together we can survive anything.'

In the same way a starving man might swallow rags to stuff his belly, Marion found it was possible to fill the emptiness inside her with daydreams, and for a brief moment before dozing off to sleep, she experienced something similar to the warm, sated feeling of being part of a family, of loving and being loved.

★ ★ ★

One sticky, overcast day in the middle of August, Marion was dragging her shopping trolley across the car park of the SmartMart when she saw him. It felt like being shot with an arrow. Of course she recognised him immediately; hadn't she thought about him every single day for the last thirty-odd years? The strange thing was, real Neil didn't look at all like *her* Neil. If anything, he was more handsome. She had given imaginary Neil a potbelly and a balding head. This version had got better with age.

He had to be in his late fifties, but he looked ten years younger, suave like the lead actor in a TV show, someone who might play an ambitious politician who is cheating on his wife. His hair was gingery grey, and he wore neat beige trousers and a polo shirt. With him were a pretty teenage girl and a lanky boy of about twelve. Both the boy and the girl were tall, loose limbed, and had their father's red hair and freckles that looked like chocolate chips in vanilla ice cream. The children were smartly dressed in shorts and pastel T-shirts. Marion thought they were the cleanest-looking people she had ever seen in her life.

The boy said in a lispy-posh accent, 'Dad, you are so embarrassing — I can't believe you told that guy you used to be in the Olympic rowing team.'

Neil replied in a voice only slightly scratched by the years: 'Well, it was worth it to get a discount on that case of Shiraz, don't you think, matey?'

181

'And when you actually signed your autograph for him,' the girl squealed, 'I thought I was going to pee myself laughing.'

As the three of them were piling groceries into a shiny, plum-coloured car, Marion walked past with her head down. Imagine if he saw her in those stretchy black trousers and old jumper with stains on the cuff? She would die on the spot. Just as she was passing, Neil let the trunk slam shut. As he stepped backwards, his warm, strong back collided with Marion's hunched shoulder.

'Oops, gosh, sorry,' he said, then turning round to face her, 'are you okay?'

Marion made an odd moaning sound, then immediately lifted her hands to her face. As she hurried away, she heard the young girl say:

'For God's sake, Dad, you're such a clumsy oaf, you nearly knocked that poor old lady over.'

Marion managed to keep all her emotion tucked inside until she had reached the safety of her attic room. When she finally let go, the sobs came out in big shuddering waves that shook the bed and sent many of her friends bouncing onto the floor. She imagined the mother of those perfect children was probably some manicured beauty, the type that never had a hair out of place. She could see them all at home now standing around some very clean and modern kitchen, hugging one another and laughing while a healthy meal of whole wheat pasta and organic vegetables simmered on the cooking range.

After she was done crying, Marion went to Mother's room and sat in front of the big dressing table. The girl had called her an old lady. She knew she didn't look good for her age — she hadn't looked good at any age — but it cut deeply to hear it said out loud. Putting on her reading glasses (her distance glasses were practically useless; she badly needed a new prescription), she examined her reflection. What the girl said was true. In Marion's youth, her face had been a pillow of featureless pink flesh, not pretty perhaps, but firm and robust; now the skin had become coarse and grey, and her flesh sagged. Could anything be done? Perhaps she should wear makeup like Judith suggested or go on a diet, but food was the only pleasure she had, and would it really make much difference? If she bought some new clothes, she might look better, but she hated going clothes shopping; the assistants were always so rude to her.

She had always been plain, but now she was old and plain; it seemed doubly unfair to have aged prematurely when so little had happened to her. How had she got worn out so quickly? She felt like a little girl inside, and yet she was an old woman on the surface, an old woman with the experience of a child. Most old people at least had memories, they had been married, had children, gone on holiday with their families, danced at parties with their lovers, had successful careers, while she had done nothing. But was it really her fault? Try as she might, she did not see what she could have done differently.

Marion went back to her own room, scooped up the teddies that had fallen, and lay on her bed. She tried holding the bears in her arms, but that only made her feel worse, an old woman comforting herself with children's toys. It was too pitiful for words. She imagined Neil and his beautiful children seeing her like this. If anyone knew what her life was, they would turn away in horror. Another person would kill themselves rather than endure her life. If only she had been able to break out, but it seemed she was surrounded by an invisible barrier that separated her from the rest of the world, and no matter how hard she struggled, she could never fight through.

She could find out where Neil lived, go to the house, then wait until they were all asleep and burn it to the ground. This thought, like a shot of strong spirits, gave Marion a measure of comfort, but the feeling was soon replaced by self-revulsion. No, I mustn't think things like that, she told herself, Neil is a good man. He deserves to be happy. If she didn't have a loving family, it was her own fault for being stupid and lazy and ugly, for being the sort of person other people didn't want to be around.

When she tried to bring into her mind the old Neil, the one that had lived in her head for so many years, it suddenly occurred to her how silly that was. If she hadn't locked herself away in a world of fantasy, might she have had the courage to go out and find someone and have children of her own? A real man, even if he was someone plain and dull like her?

When it was time to get up to make dinner, Marion could no more move than if she were trapped in the sinking sand on Northport Beach that Mother used to warn her about. Just after nine o'clock there was a knock on the bedroom door. John came in holding a glass of cordial.

'Marion love, what's up?' For once his voice was full of concern.

'I don't feel well,' she said.

'Do you need the doctor?'

'No, not like that.' She turned over so he could see her swollen eyes.

'Oh.'

He set the cordial on the bedside table and sat down on the edge of her mattress.

'You get that from Mother, you know. Remember how she used to lie in her bed for days on end. Perhaps you do need to see the doctor. They make special pills that can help.'

Mother had taken the pills to create a pillow around her, but in the end that pillow had smothered her.

'No, I don't want pills.'

'But they might make you feel better, Marion.'

'But things wouldn't actually *be* better, would they? So wouldn't *feeling* better be a sort of a cheat?'

'Does that really matter so much?'

The pills had made Mother limp and drowsy all the time. All it took was one too many of those little white discs and she dozed off in the bath, her head slipping beneath the warm lavender-scented water. Before she could manage to wake herself, she drowned.

John put his hand on Marion's arm. Perhaps he meant to comfort her, but it felt as though he was holding her down. She froze, then pushed her brother to one side and jumped out of bed.

'No, I don't want to be like her, lying there all day doped up, like something floating in a tank. I don't want that! I'd rather have anything than that!'

★ ★ ★

It was almost twenty years since Mother had gone. Marion found it hard to believe how quickly time had passed — especially since so little had happened in that period. Twenty years. Some women had raised a child to adulthood in that time.

Marion could never have organised Mother's funeral by herself; all those stressful phone calls to make and confusing forms to fill in. How she feared forms. It was so hard to get the letters in the tiny little spaces, and then nervousness at getting something wrong would cause her to make mistakes over the simplest things, such as spelling her own name. She would have to keep starting over with a fresh one until a pile of crumpled error-filled paperwork lay in front of her.

What would she have done if John hadn't been there to deal with everything? Of course everyone assumed Marion to be incapable of handling all the arrangements because she was so distraught, but in her heart she knew this wasn't exactly true. Marion couldn't say that she had loved her mother or even that they had ever gotten along particularly well. Yet her death created an unsettling emptiness.

Marion's adult life had always revolved around

Mother's demands and wishes:

'You need to go to the shops to buy me some new nylons, the sixty denier so my veins don't show through, not the thin ones. Call Dr Dunkerley about my prescription. Remind Mrs Morrison to clean the brass door handles. Today we should go to Stowe's for a cream tea.'

And now that Mother was gone, she hardly knew what to do with herself other than lie on her bed, aimlessly sorting through the contents of her mind as if it were an old sewing box full of tangled threads, foreign pennies, and rusty needles. No matter how many times she went through these odds and ends, she couldn't find any grief. There was plenty of worry for what the future might hold, sorrow for the missed opportunities in her life, but apart from that, nothing but useless nonsense. Was there something wrong with her? She had cried buckets when Katie-Lynn Tavish had been wrongly accused of smothering her baby in *Prayers for an Angel* and had wept when Jerome the blind boy had to go live in a home because his grandfather died in *No Memorial of Love*, so why couldn't she cry for her own mother?

The body was cremated at Northport Crematorium. Apart from John, herself, and Mrs Morrison, the only other guests were the members of the spiritualist church. During the service Bea had wailed rather than sung a jazzy lament that went on for nearly thirteen minutes, by which time the minister was looking at his watch. When finally he was forced to put a stop to the performance because other people were waiting outside for the next funeral, Bea collapsed in hysterical sobs. Marion thought it was strange that Bea should be so upset, since presumably Mother could still attend the Thursday-evening meetings if she wanted to.

After the funeral everyone had gone back to Grange Road for tinned salmon sandwiches and tea prepared by Mrs. Morrison. Miss Anderson appeared veiled in black lace, with a plate of some glazed swirls of confectionery that were hard as plaster of Paris when you bit into them. Bea and Jean Page showed an inappropriate degree of admiration for the grandeur of the house and kept picking things up and scrutinising hallmarks as though they were professional auctioneers.

At one point Mr Bevan ushered Marion into the kitchen, saying that he wanted to have 'a quiet word alone with her.' He told her she should treat Northport Spiritualist Congregation as if it were her family and that they expected her to continue attending meetings.

Marion had always liked Mr Bevan, yet the way he held her hand while stroking the inside of her wrist with his thumb made her uncomfortable.

'I've always been very fond of you. It's a mystery to me why no man has ever made you his wife,' said Mr. Bevan.

As he spoke, little bits of spittle escaped his toothless mouth. Then he reached out and tickled her under the chin. Marion moved away from him slightly, just enough, she hoped, that he would realise that she did not like being touched by him, yet without hurting his feelings.

'You know you don't need to hold it all in, love, all that emotion. You don't need to be brave in front of us. You can have a good cry if you want to.'

'I don't feel like crying. Really I don't,' she protested.

This didn't stop him.

'Go on,' he urged, 'Just let it all out, let it all out, girl.'

Then, as the old man pulled her into a hug, she felt his hand reach around and press her bottom against his hips. Mr. Bevan's eyes were closed, and his tongue lolled out from between toothless gums. As she turned away, her left breast was gripped by a bony hand that squeezed hard. Marion felt as if the old man were trying to milk her.

Hot and nauseated, Marion rushed away and locked herself in the guest bathroom. While the other mourners were still gobbling sandwiches, she fumed at herself for ever being nice to him, getting anxious when the spirits failed to turn up for his sessions and pitying his little flat in the Senior Shelter that had an alarm in the bathroom so he could get help if he fell. Had this kindness led him to think she would be interested in some kind of romance? He must be at least twice her age, and to behave like that at Mother's funeral made it all even worse.

Marion waited until everyone had left to go back downstairs. Mrs Morrison was in the kitchen cleaning up sandwich crusts and dirty teacups left by the mourners. As she rinsed the

189

brown sludge of tea leaves from the great Royal Doulton pot, the housekeeper declared she would be retiring.

'I kept going as long as I could, for your mother's sake, but I'm not a young woman myself. Ken and I are buying a flat in Málaga.' Ken was Mrs Morrison's new beau, whom she'd met salsa dancing after Mr Morrison finally succumbed to the surgeon's knife. 'I'd rather be lying by the pool drinking a cold Heineken than spending my old age as a nanny for two grown-up children.'

The Envelope

Marion was lying on her bed reading *The Tale of Pigling Bland*. The story made her feel so sad. Those little pigs being sent off to market by themselves and then poor Pigling Bland having to deal with that nasty farmer who wanted to eat him; really it was just awful. She hoped that things turned out well for him and Pig-wig when they ran over the hills and far away. Pig-wig did seem rather foolish, though. She worried that silly girl might end up leading Pigling Bland astray. As she put the book back into the little shelf by her bed she heard John's heavy footsteps up the stairs. He was calling her name angrily.

Marion froze. What had she done wrong? What could have got him so worked up? Then he hammered on her bedroom door so hard, it must have chipped the paint.

'Yes, John, what's the matter, love?'

The door opened and a single eye and livid slice of her brother's face appeared in the gap.

'Where's that bloody envelope?' The words came out hard and fast like machine-gun fire.

'What envelope?'

'I left an envelope on the dining room dresser. It's gone.'

'But I haven't seen it.'

'Marion, it had foreign currency in it,' he said sternly. 'A lot of money. You must have seen it.

191

Who else has been in the house that could have taken it?'

Her mind began to churn. Had she seen it? Perhaps she'd put a letter in the rubbish by mistake? Could she be so stupid as to do something like that and not remember?

'I'll come and help you look for it, John.'

She spent an hour rushing from room to room, searching in a mixed-up backwards and forwards manner that meant she kept looking in one place repeatedly while missing other spots altogether. All the time John followed her around, like a police inspector waiting for her to confess.

'Have you checked all your pockets, John?'

'Marion,' he roared, 'that envelope is not in my bloody pockets. I left it on the damn dresser, and you must have moved it.'

'But I'm sure I didn't, John, I'm almost completely sure,' she said, going through the bathroom cabinet, taking out each bottle of expired antidandruff shampoo and athlete's foot remedy one-by-one, then replacing it. There were so many places it could be, she felt as though this searching would never end and she would carry on like this for the rest of her life. When she tried to go into John's bedroom, he stopped her.

'I don't want you nosing around in my private things,' he told her.

'But you might have left it in there.'

'I know damn well I haven't.'

On their third visit to the kitchen she remembered she had not checked in the cabinet above the sink. When she opened it, the pile of junk mail fell out and scattered across the floor. Marion got down on her knees and began searching through all the flyers and envelopes while John loomed over her.

'For God's sake, woman,' he said, shaking his head so hard his jowls waggled. 'Look at all this bloody mess. No wonder everything goes missing in this sodding house.'

Then he began to tremble and struggle for his breath. He put his hands on the kitchen table to steady himself.

'Are you all right?' asked Marion.

'It's you,' he panted, 'you've worked me up into this state, you silly woman, don't you see that? Now get me some water.'

John seated himself at the table while Marion hurried to the tap.

'Why don't you rest down here and I will carry on looking?' she said, handing him a glass.

He nodded and drank greedily, spilling some water down his chin and onto his shirt.

Without John following her around, she was able to go into his room.

The room was decorated with faded brown and yellow wallpaper. A greasy-looking satin quilt covered the high double bed. Along one wall was a bookcase with hundreds of volumes about science and things she didn't understand. From the ceiling hung the model planes, all facing in the same direction like a flock of dark birds frozen in time. An album containing a collection of cigarette cards with the faces of cricket players on them that John collected as a boy lay open on the dresser next to his bottles of cologne and brilliantine.

Between the two windows was John's desk and modern computer. There was something about this great block of a thing, with its enormous dark screen like a giant robot head, that made her feel it might come alive and attack. Pinned on the wall next to the computer was a map of the world and around it several pictures of smiling young women. Who were these women and what was John's connection with them?

Marion went over to the desk and, being careful not to disturb the computer as it hummed and whirred in its sleep, opened the top drawer. Inside were several pieces of cheap women's jewellery. She picked up a tangled chain. A few long blonde hairs had been trapped in the fastener, and its silver butterfly pendant was spotted with something dark red. Thinking it might be dried blood, she shuddered and let it drop back into the drawer.

John shouted from downstairs:

'Marion, what are you doing up there?'

Quickly she closed the drawer, then picked up a pair of trousers that he had left draped over the bedstead.

Turning one of the pockets, she found two fifty-pence pieces and some mints stuck to a wrinkled cotton hankie.

When she reached into the other pocket, she pulled out an envelope. It wasn't sealed, and a dark wad of oily notes slid out. She glimpsed a name, Violetta Dada, and part of an address, a long row of numbers and a street name, Prospect Georgy something or other.

When Marion returned to the kitchen, John snatched the envelope from her and began counting the money. She wanted to tell him what a fool he had been, that it had been in exactly the place he said it wouldn't be, that she had been right all along, but she knew this would send him into an even worse rage.

'You were right, John, it was on the dresser all along. Hidden under a place mat. I can't believe we missed it.'

'What did I tell you, Marion? You keep this place like a pigsty. A bloody pigsty.'

When he said 'pigsty' the second time, a little fleck of spit flew from his mouth and landed on her cheek. Outraged and humiliated, Marion wiped it away with the back of her hand.

★　★　★

For dinner that evening they had tinned macaroni and cheese. Marion had left it in the pan without stirring for a few minutes too long while trying to reach a fork that had fallen between the fridge and the cupboard. She failed in retrieving the fork and wondered how long it might stay there. Perhaps until after she and John were dead and the house had been sold?

Scraping the macaroni out of the pan, she saw little brown and black lumps of singed pasta amongst the yellowish mush. I don't care, she said to herself. I hope he gets a bad stomach. Her nerves were still jangling from all the drama earlier that day. John should have apologised for shouting like that and accusing her of losing the

195

stupid envelope. He hadn't even thanked her for finding the damn thing. He snapped at her so often these days, and his temper seemed worse than ever. And she was furious with herself for not standing up to him. Marion took a mouthful of macaroni and chewed, the black bits gave it a nasty bitter taste. John poured a glass of cordial for her.

'Nice macaroni, Marion.'

He obviously felt guilty and was trying to get on her good side. She wanted to ask who was this Violetta and why was he sending her money, but part of her was scared of knowing. After dinner, Marion went into the living room and sat down on the sofa as far away from John's end as possible. Placing her own cushion, the red velvet one, behind her back, she threw his cushion, the large blue one, onto the floor as a small gesture of protest.

To watch television, John and Marion sat in the same places they had watched *Magpie* and *Tiswas* from as children; Marion on the right side of the sofa nearest to the bay window at the front of the house, John on the left closest to the door. When Dad had been alive, he had sat in the big brown leather armchair to the left of the fireplace and Mother had sat opposite him in the smaller velvet-covered chair. Those chairs were always empty, and it never occurred to John or Marion to sit in them.

John came into the living room with a tray of tea and biscuits and set them down on the table. He picked up his cushion from the floor, then sat down and turned on the TV. They watched a documentary together about a little girl who lived in a very poor village in India. The girl had a horribly deformed face, and all the people in the village feared her, calling her the demon girl. She couldn't even leave her hut because other children would throw stones. Then an aid worker found out about the girl and contacted his brother, a surgeon, who lived in England.

The surgeon agreed to perform reconstructive surgery for free, and the documentary makers paid for the girl along with her father to fly to England for the operation. After the operation was completed and the bandages had been removed, the surgeon showed the girl her face in a mirror. Though she wasn't pretty, she did look at least relatively normal. When her face was healed, the girl said to the surgeon, 'You have killed the demon and brought me to life.'

When Marion noticed there were tears in her brother's eyes, she melted and immediately forgave him for shouting earlier. He was not such a bad man, really; he had a good heart deep down.

After the documentary, they watched the news. There was a story about one of those hot sandy places where people are always shooting and blowing one another up. They showed a small child who had had one of his legs blown off by a bomb. Marion felt overwhelmed by a sense of pity as the boy stared into the camera with terrified brown eyes. Then she reminded herself that these things happened all the time, people suffered, that was the way of the world, and one had to accept it or go mad from thinking about it.

Then there was a piece about treatment for cancer patients. Marion didn't like stories about illness; it reminded her of Aunt Agnes dying alone in the hospice. It also made her scared that she would get ill herself and one day die in one of those terrible places. But she watched anyway because John thought the news was important.

When the news was over, John switched off the TV and she began clearing the tea things. As she was about to take the tray through to the kitchen John stopped her.

'Sit down, Marion,' he said. 'I want to talk to you about something.' Then he got a serious look on his face. 'We will have to make another trip in a couple of weeks. To pick someone up. I'm expecting another visitor.'

For once she stood up to him. Marion said no, she couldn't take it, not again, her nerves would just fall apart. She wouldn't go with him to meet another girl. But John was so much better at arguing than she was. He had a clever way of putting things that always made it seem like he was right, whereas trouble addled Marion's tongue and her words came out jumbled like the ravings of a madwoman.

He had a special feeling about this. From the messages she wrote, he sensed that she could be the right one, the girl who would love him when she got to know him. A girl he might marry, perhaps start a family with. Would his own sister deny him that? He needed to love and to be loved. He insisted that the girl would get suspicious if he turned up to collect her alone. She was more likely to feel safe in the presence

198

of a mature woman. Apart from everything else, he had sent this girl a lot of money, for a passport and for the cost of her journey. All that would be wasted if they didn't go to pick her up.

But what about the others, wondered Marion, hadn't he felt the same way about them? And what would happen to them now? They were people, he couldn't just hoard them away like those broken toasters and radios he never got round to fixing. Instead of answering her, John slipped into one of his dark moods. Each time he came into a room, she felt the temperature drop. Sometimes she caught him staring at her, and Marion would imagine a tiny version of herself trapped in the great dome of his balding head, crazily fleeing from flames and monsters. Bit by bit his moodiness sapped her resistance, each slam of a door or stamp on the stairs making her weaker.

★   ★   ★

One morning while she was cleaning the bathroom, she heard a loud crash. The weight of dread she carried at all times got heavier as she made her way downstairs. On the living room floor, in front of the fireplace, were several pieces of broken china. She looked up to the mantelpiece and saw the glazed white lion with bulging black eyes that had sat in the same spot all of Marion's life was gone. Mother said it had been made in the Orient nearly a thousand years ago. When she was a child, Marion would stare at the lion for hours, then close her eyes; when she opened them again, she would be certain that its large head had turned slightly or one of its paws had moved.

John had broken it because he knew she loved it. As she gazed at the sharp white shards lying in the hearth she wondered what would be next. The milkmaid figurines with their pink cheeks and tiny rosebud mouths? The crystal jug with silver medallion that bore the arms of George III? It would be impossible to hide them all away from him. Picking up a dagger-shaped piece of china in her hand, she squeezed until a drop of blood oozed from her palm. How could anyone do this? How could he be so cruel?

The next day she found a headless shepherdess lying at the bottom of the stairs, a pale hand still clutching her crook, a baby lamb looking up forlornly at where its mistress's sweet face used to be. The day after that it was a Japanese vase adorned with the story of two lovers and then the silver teapot with tiger paws dented beyond repair. Each time she found another precious object destroyed she felt like something inside her own body had been smashed.

Mother's voice echoed in her head:

This is your fault, Marion. This wouldn't happen if you just agreed to do what John wanted. You shouldn't upset him. You know what he is like when he gets upset.

But I can't, Marion insisted. I can't do it, and I'm upset!

Mother's only answer was to purse her lips and roll her eyes upwards.

One morning John came up behind her while she was making tea in the kitchen and picked up the Paddington Bear mug she had used since she was twelve years old.

'All you have to do is sit in the damn car, Marion,' he said. 'Even you can manage that, can't you?'

She accepted that that there was no point in trying to stand up to him; he was too strong-minded for her. And he knew that she couldn't live with being hated. If she did as he said, just sat there and said nothing, waited until it was over, that wouldn't be so bad, would it? She would do this to make him happy. Anything for a quiet and peaceful life. As soon as she had made the decision to help him, the weight became a little lighter.

'All right,' she declared. 'I'll do it.'

John placed the bear mug down on the work top.

The relief lasted until the night before they were due to pick up the new visitor. Marion lay awake all night, imagining stories on the news about a middle-aged brother and sister luring young foreign women to England then imprisoning them in a cellar. She heard Mother's voice in her head:

No one cares about these girls. They've got nothing. That is why they come to this country. John can help the poor unfortunate things. He can give them an education and protect them from the evil men who want to use them.

But what about their families, she wondered. Someone must miss them and wonder what happens to them?

Their families don't want them, no one does, replied Mother. *Think how lucky you are, Marion, to have been born in England to a good family who took care of you. To have a decent home and financial security.*

★ ★ ★

When John tapped on her door at 6:30 a.m., Marion forced herself out of bed and into the chilly bathroom, where silverfish were still slithering around the sink. Her limbs felt cold and strange, as if they didn't belong to her at all but were attached instead to some stiffening corpse that she was forced to clean and dress. After managing to get herself down to the kitchen, she made a cup of tea and some toast, then sat there unable to eat or drink a mouthful.

John's appetite was untroubled by nerves. He stuffed eggs, sausage, and bacon into his mouth with one hand while holding the newspaper in the other. He was wearing the black suit and tie that he had worn for Mother's funeral. Marion, nervously picking at fuzz-berries that decorated the sleeves of her coat, wondered if she should have put on something smarter.

John had spent the previous afternoon carefully wiping the ghost-grey paintwork of Mother's Mercedes with a soft yellow chamois in preparation for the journey.

It took several hard turns of the ignition for

them to get it going. Marion had her fingers crossed inside her coat pockets in hope the car would refuse to start at all and they wouldn't be able to make the trip; but after several minutes of mysterious grinding and screeching it lurched forward down the gravel driveway and onto Grange Road. The car radio was tuned to a station called Casual Classics. 'One of our listeners' favourites now,' said the presenter in a syrupy voice. 'This is the Queen of the Night aria from *The Magic Flute*, to set your day off to a great start.' John whistled along to the music as he drove.

August 2nd

@violetunderground
Hi Adrian thanks for adding me!
Here some things about me:

I am a girl called Violetta of course! It is my dream to be famous designer and to make red carpet dress for very famous actress. Perhaps Scarlett Johansson she is my favourite actress of all. My favourite designer are Versace, Burberry and of course Chanel. I am always drawing pictures of clothes I would like to design, I am very good artist you can see my pictures on tumblr page.

For the present I am working in big hotel. My best friend is Irina, we are both chambermaids. We have to make beds all day long and it is very hard work. Some people are kind and leave tips, but others even very rich people leave nothing then block toilet with their nasty rich people poops.

The girls on reception are bitches. They think they are better than us chambermaids. The worst is Ariana, she has a long nose and cross eyes. One day I came to work through the front entrance because I was late and she reported me to Maria and I lose an hour's pay. Maria the head house-keeper is a super witch. We have to put these little tiny bottles of shampoo and shower gel in rooms each day. Hundreds and hundreds of them. Before we are allowed to go home Maria searches our bags to make sure we don't steal any.

Last month Irina found a human pinkie finger in the waste bin of Pendragon Suite. Maria told her to flush it down the toilet because the hotel people do not want police making trouble. We think maybe some gangster cut off the finger because the guy owed him money.

Lots of love
V
/<3
xxxx

August 10th
I am so tired tonight I can hardly write anything to you. And I must sleep on the floor of Irina's room because mama no longer wants me at home. One time Irina's brother came into bathroom while I was in shower and took piss right in front of me. I couldn't even say anything and just stood there wanting to scream. Tomorrow a hundred more beds to change and toilets to scrub. A thousand little tiny bottles of shampoo. How many more bottles of shampoo until I am rescued?

August 19th

Dear Adrian, when will I see you in real life? I have many times been looking at your photographs the one of you looking handsome on a boat is my favourite but also I like Adrian skiing and Adrian playing the guitar for his friends while drinking wine and eating what I think perhaps is potato chips. I wonder if soon you will play your guitar just for me? That is my greatest dream come true. You are so handsome with your blonde hair that is so thick and sticking up, your healthy pink cheeks, and your blue British eyes.

Why can't we talk on the phone sometime or Skype? Are you too shy? That is okay I do not mind, I like it when boys are shy. Did you ask your aunt about the job again? I don't care if pay is not much good — I will work just to sleep in a bed and eat. I will even sleep on floor and not eat a lot, maybe some chocolate though, English chocolate is so good, a friend gives me one time from holiday!

August 29th

Did you forget again to ask your aunt and uncle about the job? You are always forgetting things and I have to remind you! I am angry with you Adrian. No, I was joking, of course I am not really angry! When you don't email for a few days I am scared you are bored with me and sometimes I feel you are my only friend in the whole world. Adrian. I think about you so much. If I am to be your girlfriend I promise not to be annoying and ask you for things all the time. I will be a good little mouse. I think the English girls they will hate me for stealing you. Why don't you have an English girlfriend? Maybe you do and you are just pretending. Sometimes I get scared that you meet a pretty and nice English girl and you forget about me and I don't get anymore messages.

You are so much nicer than the boys here, all they want to do is smoke drugs and talk about stupid motorbikes.

Sept 10th

I received your letter and money today. Angel Adrian I will pay you back in a thousand kisses when I see you. Thank you thank you thank you. I am a little scared because I haven't been to foreign country before, I will be a little lost girl and you will be the prince who is rescuing me.

Now I will tell Maria and all her little bottles of shampoo to go to hell.

Tell your aunt and uncle I don't mind to do any job and I know good English and I can work very hard. I am good at cleaning things, being polite to people, mathematics, fashion, cookery and historia. I would like very much to learn to drive a car. I think if you will teach me I can learn things very quickly and I know you will be a good teacher and not get angry if I make mistake!

I will meet them as agreed on the 27th. They will be parked in the silver Mercedes car in the park of McDonald's near to the port. I hope they are very nice people. It is just a little disappointing that you will not be there to meet me yourself. Since you are going to be on the ski trip until end of month — then we will be

together and able to have some fun times I hope.
All my love and kisses
Violetta
xxxx

It was almost six years ago when they had gone to collect the first visitor. John told her he needed to meet someone arriving on a ferry at some port hundreds of miles away. He said she was a young woman who didn't speak very good English and that she would be staying with them for a while. The news sent Marion into a spin. They had never had a visitor staying in the house before.

'But who is she, and how did you meet her? Is she going to be staying long? I suppose we could put her in Mother's room, but I would have to change the bedding, and there is water leaking in near the front window. Will I have to buy foreign food or will she eat what we eat?'

But John wouldn't say anything more about the guest, and when she quizzed him, all she got was silence and black looks. It wasn't until a few days before they were supposed to make the trip that Marion said she wouldn't go with him unless John explained exactly what was going on.

Her brother confessed. He said he had met Sonya through an internet chat room, and they had been corresponding for several months. Marion was shocked when he told her that he had posed as a twenty-one-year-old university student called Adrian Metcalf. He showed Marion the emails and photographs that he had sent to the girl. The photographs came from the Facebook page of one of his former sixth-form pupils at Broadleaf Academy; they showed a handsome blonde youth on a yacht with his arm around two friends, playing the guitar at a party and skiing. The boy, he told her, was now deceased. Walking home late after a New Year's Eve party, he had slipped on ice and fallen into a freezing cold lake.

Marion couldn't believe what her brother was telling her. How could a good, decent man like him be capable of lying to a stranger?

'You have to tell her the truth, John, immediately,' she insisted.

'Marion, you don't understand, we're in love,' John replied.

'How can she be in love with you? She thinks you're someone else.'

'You don't realise how lonely I am, Mar. I feel like I'm dying inside.'

'Then why don't you be honest with her, John. Come clean. Send her a real picture of yourself, that lovely one you had taken in your good suit for the Oxford reunion bash. You never know, perhaps she'll still want to come over and stay with us.'

'Look at me Mar, what young woman would want an old fella like me?'

Then John went down on his knees and began to cry, his face twisting up.

She had seen that stricken look on his face the day they found Sir Isaac Newton in the middle of Grange Road, his thin, tabby body mangled by a car. Nine-year-old John having befriended the stray displayed an unusual degree of tenderness towards it, buying tinned tuna and condensed milk from his own pocket money, yet Mother had refused to let him keep the 'filthy creature' in the house on the grounds of its extreme ugliness and the likelihood of it carrying disease.

'I just want to find a nice girl who'll love me and give me children,' he said. 'You know, this Sonya comes from a very poor background. She grew up in an orphanage and has no family. Perhaps if I am kind to her, she won't mind that I'm older.'

*　*　*

Lying awake for many nights, she went over it all in her head again and again; of course it was wrong to bring the girl all this way on false pretences. The whole business had to be stopped. She just wouldn't accept it. Then she would think of the look of suffering on John's face when he told her how lonely he was. Wasn't there a chance that the girl might see past his baldness and potbelly and perhaps appreciate him for his intelligence and decency? And if the two of them married and started a family, wouldn't that be wonderful? Certainly there was no longer any chance of Marion herself becoming a mother, yet she yearned to have a child in the house, a little person who would call her Auntie Mar, someone she could take for walks on the beach and play games with.

She loved her brother, he was her only living family, and wasn't it her sisterly duty to make him happy? Of course she had doubts about what he was doing, who wouldn't have? But if she refused to help him, what would happen then? Might he go away and leave her alone in this huge house, wandering from room to dusty room, imagining footsteps and whispers that were not her own? How long before she went quite mad with only teddy bears and ghosts to talk to?

Finally she said to him:

'Please, John, you must promise me this: that you will behave like a gentleman towards the girl. And if she refuses to accept you, if she says she doesn't want to stay here with us, then you will pay for her to go back home?'

And John had agreed.

★ ★ ★

When Marion first set eyes on Sonya's round, pale face with those large terrified eyes, she was shocked how young the girl looked, perhaps no more than seventeen. She was shaking with exhaustion and too shy to speak when they picked her up at a McDonald's restaurant near the port. She wouldn't let go of her suitcase, a battered old thing that had been decorated with stickers of horses and ponies like something belonging to a little girl. When she asked about Adrian, John said that Adrian was their nephew and she would meet him when they got home. Marion was too afraid to say anything all.

As soon as they got back to Grange Road, John sent Marion upstairs so he and Sonya would have time to talk alone. She lay on her bed with her stomach tightened into a fist. It seemed almost impossible that this young woman and her brother could fall in love, yet Marion did her best to persuade herself that with time and patience, John might win her heart. She recalled *May to December*: a Heartfelt Production in which the heroine, a young Victorian kitchen maid, rejected a reckless stable lad in favour of a kindly squire with white, muttonchop whiskers who could offer her a good home and financial security.

The next morning when Marion went downstairs, she found John sitting in the kitchen alone.

'John, what happened? Where is she?'

'Marion, I don't know how to tell you this — but Sonya is an unsuitable sort of person.'

'What do you mean?'

He picked up a slice of Marmite and toast.

'She's a prostitute. It seems I have been the victim of deception. This young woman has already slept with dozens of men.' He tore at the toast with his teeth and then licked melted butter from his lips. 'She offered to perform acts that I wouldn't dream of describing to you.'

Marion felt her neck and face become fiery hot.

'Is she still here? You have to get her out of our house.'

'I can't. Not yet. She brought drugs with her on the ferry. She wants me to sell them and give her the money. Of course I refused, but then she threatened to go to the police and say that we kidnapped her.'

John looked at her with such an awful expression in his eyes that Marion thought her

211

heart was going to stop.

'I don't understand. She seemed like such a sweet young girl. We have to go to the police at once, John, we have to tell them the truth.'

'No, they won't believe us. Not after what they think happened at Broadleaf.' And then his mouth twisted into a peculiar smile. 'You'll be in trouble, too. We both went to get her, didn't we?'

Marion imagined herself being arrested and then taken to prison; it would be like school again but a hundred times worse. Nasty, rough women making fun of her, calling her names. And she would never be able to sleep if she had to share a room with others. She would most likely drop dead from the stress of it all; in fact, it would be better to die.

John told her he would keep Sonya in the cellar for a few days, just until she calmed down, and then he would send her back home.

★　★　★

A week later when Sonya still hadn't left, Marion demanded to know what was happening.

'I've come to a decision, Marion,' John announced, looking as excited as he did when he was a teenager and got accepted into Oxford. 'She is going to stay with us for a while. I'm going to educate her, to improve her English, to teach her science, mathematics, literature. This way she can aspire to be something more than a just whore or a criminal.'

'She's going to live with us? In this house?'

'Yes, but she'll have to stay hidden. In the

cellar. I've made it quite comfortable for her. The young lady has everything she needs.'

'But why does she have to stay down there?'

'The people who gave her the drugs are looking for her. She worked for a gang of very dangerous men, and if they find her, they'll kill her. They'll probably kill us too, for protecting her.'

Marion was terrified. What choice did she have but to trust her brother? She had relied on his judgment her whole life.

'John, it doesn't seem right — her living down there — just how long will she stay?'

'Until it's safe. You mustn't tell anyone, though. Not a soul. And I don't want you going anywhere near her — '

'Why ever not?'

'Girls like Sonya can be very clever and manipulative, Marion, someone as softhearted and unworldly as you would be no match for her. That little lost kitten has come from the streets. In the past she's had to protect herself — you know I found a knife in her pocket?'

Marion recoiled, feeling her plump flesh shrivel as though the blade was already being pressed against it.

'Of course the poor soul can't be blamed for being that way,' John continued in his soft, cajoling tone. 'I want to help her, to teach her to trust people again. But that will take time, like taming a feral animal. Until then you promise me you won't go down there?'

She nodded solemnly like a child vowing not to run out into the busy road lest she be struck by a car.

John kept the cellar locked, but Marion would have been afraid to go down even if he hadn't.

★ ★ ★

Then, six months later, John announced they were going to pick up another girl. Of course Marion had said no, she would have nothing to do with it, but her brother insisted. The girl, who was called Alla, he said, if they didn't help her, she would end up working as a prostitute for a criminal gang. According to him, they made these girls do dreadful things, and many of them became drug addicts or killed themselves if the gang leaders didn't beat them to death. If she came here, he could help her get an education and a good job. They were saving this girl's life, how could she refuse? Weeks of arguing and sleepless nights left Marion exhausted and confused. Eventually John wore her down and she agreed to go with him to meet the girl.

And Alla had been so different from Sonya; though only in her twenties, she had had the jaded eye of experience. Tall and glamorous in her fur coat, winding manicured fingers through her long blonde hair, she had looked Marion up and down with a smirk as she identified the older woman as someone of no significance.

The girls had to stay down in the cellar. He said that was very important. People were looking for them, perhaps watching the house. They couldn't even risk being glimpsed through a window. But did they have to stay hidden all the time, every minute of the day? And could

214

they possibly want to stay down there? Wasn't that even worse than anything these so called 'gang members' might do? She had so many questions, yet whenever she challenged John, darkness would fill his eyes and the air would become so thick, it was impossible to breathe.

Truth be told, Marion was a little relieved that the visitors remained down in the cellar. She had always been shy of people. Company made her anxious, and she had never learned how to make small talk. The girls would probably giggle about her behind her back, making fun of her clumsy body and scruffy clothes.

★ ★ ★

The inside of the Mercedes had a damp, mildewy smell from being locked in the garage for months. A silky cobweb that covered the wing mirror clung on until they reached the coast road, then blew off into the wind. By the time they were on the motorway, driving along between green fields and trees, Marion began to feel a little better. It was a sparkling autumn day, and just being in a car and away from Northport was such a novelty, she realised she was almost enjoying herself.

They passed a wrecking yard. The top of a crooked ferris wheel poked over the wall.

'There's Frank's place,' said Marion excitedly. 'Remember when Dad used to take us there?'

John just shook his head and grunted in reply.

It was nearly half past one when they reached the McDonald's car park, half an hour before the girl was due to meet them. As they waited, John kept looking at his steel watch. Condensation from their breathing began to build up on the windows of the car, and Marion wiped hers with the sleeve of her coat and peered through the glass for signs of the girl. Three children, their tummies and bottoms sticking out aggressively, followed a large woman with a drab blonde ponytail across the car park and into the low, redbrick restaurant. Even inside the car, you could smell the sweet, rancid odour of fat coming from the building. Marion's back began to ache, and her mouth was dry. She wriggled her toes to get some life back into them, but it didn't make them any warmer.

John kept flexing his fingers and cracking his knuckles. Perhaps she isn't coming, thought Marion. Once they had come to this car park, waited for hours and hours, but no one arrived. John became a dark tornado of fury, ranting about all the months of preparation wasted, not to mention the money he had sent. He had called the girl all the names under the sun, saying she was a vile, thieving bitch and what he would do to her if he ever caught hold of her. His driving on the way home had been so reckless, she was surprised they weren't killed.

Marion was afraid even to suggest the same thing might have happened again. After they had been waiting nearly an hour, she finally dared to speak.

'John, you don't think she might have missed the ferry — '

'Why don't you leave the bloody thinking to

me?' he snapped. 'She'll be here.'

The wriggling anxiety inside her grew claws and teeth. She tried to breathe, but her chest was too tight. She wanted to get out of the car and run, as if she were being kidnapped. What if she went into the restaurant and told everyone what was happening? Would they even believe her?

'I — I think I'm going to be sick.'

'Oh, for God's sake — '

'I'm sorry — '

She opened her car door and heaved. Of course she hadn't eaten, so there wasn't much to bring up — just some clear liquid that formed an egg-white froth on the dark grey tarmac of the car park. Luckily, no one saw, and when she was done, she wiped her mouth and closed the passenger door.

'What the hell is the matter with you now?'

'I can't help it, it's my nerves. I just want to go home, John,' she said shakily, then buried her chin in the collar of her coat, unable to look directly at him.

'Marion, just — just pull yourself together.'

'I can't, John, I can't, I don't want to do this.'

'We are helping these girls,' he reasoned. 'If they didn't come to us, then God knows what would happen to them.'

'But if we are helping them, then why do we have to lie?'

'Because some people don't know what's in their best interests. Other more intelligent people have to make decisions for them.'

'But still it doesn't feel right to me.'

'I don't care what it *feels* like to you.' The

word 'feels' came out long and slippery, giving her the shudders. 'You'll do what I bloody well tell you, you stupid bitch!'

He slammed his hand against the dashboard in the way that someone hits an object rather than the person they really want to hurt. Marion's eyes began to sting. She tried to stop her face from crumpling, but it was impossible. If he saw her crying, that would only make him angrier, but John knew her so well, he could sense tears long before they were pouring down her cheeks.

'Oh, for God's sake, don't start the bloody waterworks now.' He sighed.

'I'm sorry — ' But Marion could not stop herself.

John forced a gust of air from his mouth.

'All right — I'm sorry for shouting at you. Just try and calm yourself down.' His voice became gentler.

Marion searched inside the glove compartment for a tissue but found only a single beige leather driving glove, supple as living skin, a pair of scratched sunglasses, and an uncapped tube of hand cream encrusted with grit. John gave her a clean white handkerchief from his pocket, and somehow the fact he was being kind to her made Marion feel even worse. She rubbed her eyes with the handkerchief and blew her nose. If the girl was coming, then Marion wished she would please hurry up, so they could get all this over with and be back home as soon as possible. She closed her eyes for a moment, filling her head with thoughts of her aunt's flat with its soft

218

pastel light and cosy furniture; she imagined herself lying on the sofa while Agnes cooked something nice for supper.

She could hear her singing 'My Favourite Things.' Marion began to hum the tune in her head.

'There she is,' said John suddenly. 'That's her, Violetta.'

Marion opened her eyes. A young woman with long black curly hair, dressed in a short denim skirt and wedge heels, was walking down the slip road and dragging a large wheely suitcase made from shiny pink plastic behind her. The girl's legs were thinner than Marion's wrist, and it seemed impossible that they could support even that tiny body.

The girl had to skip up onto the sloping grass verge to avoid a red car that was heading towards the McDonald's drive-through lane. Her suitcase got stuck on the curb, and the driver of the red car beeped, even though he had more than enough room to get round.

Violetta. To Marion the name sounded gypsy-ish. You could see the raspberry-coloured lipstick and glint of hoop earrings across the car park.

The girl glanced in their direction but didn't seem to register the car. There were no other vehicles in the car park aside from a white painter and decorator's van and a massive red Land Rover. Still the girl seemed hesitant and began to drift towards the McDonald's building.

'What's she bloody well playing at? I told her to look out for the silver Merc,' said John. 'You'll have to go and get her.'

'No, no I don't want to.'

'Just get out and wave at her.' John jabbed the soft flesh of her upper arm. 'Then she'll know we're here to meet her.'

Legs stiff from sitting in the same position for so long, Marion got out of the car and waved at the girl. Violetta stared back blankly, then began dragging the suitcase towards them.

'You are the family of Adrian?' she called out in a strong foreign accent.

Though she was small, there was something fierce about the girl. The way she looked at her made Marion feel the way she did around animals; that they were working out the best place to bite or scratch.

'Yes, yes that's right,' said Marion.

Violetta wedged the pink suitcase onto the backseat of the car, then got in next to it. She looked about eighteen, nineteen at the most; her perfume of sickly sweet chemicals stung the back of Marion's throat.

'I have had to walk so far in the rain and then I am nearly killed by cars. It was almost impossible to find this stupid McDonald's. I do not know why you could not come to meet me at the proper place when I get off the ship.'

'It's a ferry, not a ship,' corrected John.

'Ferry — ship — who cares — it is the same.' Violetta made an angry huffing sound, then bounced back heavily in her seat. 'Adrian is not here?'

'No, no, Adrian couldn't come,' John said briskly, 'didn't he tell you in the message?'

'Yes, but maybe — I had hoped.' Though she could not see her face, Marion imagined from her voice that the girl was pouting.

'You'll see him in a few days, don't worry.'

'So you are the people who will be giving me a job?'

'Yes.'

'You have child?'

'No. No we don't,' answered Marion. 'We aren't married, we are brother and sister.'

Anxious that she should have kept her mouth shut, she glanced at John, but his face revealed nothing. As they left the car park, the old Mercedes tottered forward, then stopped. John revved the engine. A car behind them sounded its horn. Marion felt the girl's small strong hands grip her headrest, trapping a few strands of hair so they pulled on her scalp. Then the girl let go and began chattering away, filling the car with her loud, bright energy.

'Is the weather always so horrible in England? You know I like the sunshine. I think I will die of cold fever if is always like this. This is Mercedes car, right? It is very old though, why do you have such an old car? Can you not afford to be in newer car?'

Neither John nor Marion answered these questions, but that didn't stop her from asking more.

'It is very big the house you live in? I will have good room and bathroom all to myself, correct? You will be very pleased with me at house-keeping, I am excellent at vacuum, remove dust, polish glass and metalworks. I learn skills in top five-star international hotel. I am very thorough.

I can also cook many foods.'

Then she recited a long list of foreign-sounding dishes that Marion had never heard of.

'But I only do this job until I can save money to go to fashion clinic and become designer. You understand this? Adrian has told you, I think? I make clear to him in emails. Is not my ambitions to become housekeeper. Just to save money.'

Marion wondered what 'fashion clinic' was. Did she perhaps mean fashion college, or something else altogether? Still, there didn't seem any point in asking her to explain. Listening to the girl prattle on, Marion could not believe that this was the sort of person John was likely to get along with. She seemed too pushy and money minded, interested only in shopping for designer clothes and luxuries; what could they even have found in common to talk about in their correspondence? Of course she was pretty, yet there was a glossy hardness about her, a sweetness you could break your teeth on, like a candied apple.

When they got back onto the motorway, iron-grey nails of rain began battering the car. John drove fast, swerving from lane to lane, while the wipers barely managed to clear the windscreen for more than a split second at a time. Violetta declared she wanted to go to the toilet.

'You should have gone in McDonald's,' said John gruffly.

'I would be embarrassed,' the girl whined in a baby voice. 'You shouldn't go toilet in restaurant if you don't eat something. They don't like it. Maybe the manager shouts at me in front of many peoples.'

'Well, we can't just stop on the motorway — you understand English, 'motorway'? No stopping. Do you have motorways in your country?'

The girl made a high-pitched huff to show that she was offended. Did they even have proper toilets, wondered Marion, or just holes in the ground that you squatted over? But the girl had noticed the little man and woman shapes on the sign for a service station and even she knew that meant there were toilets.

'It is no good, you must stop, or do you want me to go toilet in your fucking car?' said Violetta, instantly switching from spoilt baby to angry vixen.

'Hey,' said John, the stern schoolmaster. 'Mind your mouth, young lady.'

Red signs burning through the rain indicated a speed limit of twenty miles an hour. The traffic had slowed almost to a stop.

'John, we might not be home for a long time,' said Marion. 'We could stop at that place just ahead, where we got coffee on the way up? I wouldn't mind using the loo.'

John kept his eyes fixed on the Tesco lorry in front.

'No. I'm not stopping. You'll both have to wait.'

'But why?' said the girl. 'This is not human,' she cried. 'You can't treat even animal this way.' Then with her voice filled with fake tears: 'Please, I am desperate.'

The traffic crawled forward for another five minutes until they came to a dead stop. Signs advertising Burger King and Marks and Spencer were visible next to the flat buildings of the service station a few hundred yards ahead. The girl saw her opportunity and opened the door.

'You can't bloody well just get out here,' shouted John. 'Get back in the sodding car!'

But it was too late. Violetta, dragging her conspicuous pink suitcase behind her, was running along the steep grass embankment towards the service station. Then the Tesco van in front suddenly darted forward, and the traffic in their lane began to move. They were holding everyone up, and the other cars started beeping their horns.

'Can you believe that?' He turned to his sister. 'What does she think she is playing at?'

'John, just let her go, please. Just keep driving.'

'What if the police picked her up? She's breaking the law running along the side of the motorway like that.'

'It doesn't matter. Just let her go please,' Marion replied.

John swerved into the lane for the service station. There was a look of terrible purpose in his eyes, and the veins in his neck were fat and twisted like earthworms.

'No, I won't let her go. All that bloody planning would be wasted. And she took money. She's not getting away now.'

The service station was very busy, and John got angrier and angrier while trying to find somewhere to park. When they finally found a space, it was as far from the entrance to the building as it was possible to be.

'You'll have to go and find her, Marion.'

'But, John, that girl — I mean, perhaps it

would be better to just let her go — don't you think?'

'We can't just let her wander off like that. The police could pick her up, they'll want to know what she is doing here.'

'But why do I have to find her?'

'Because you're a bloody woman, you can talk to her. And what would it look like me chasing after some young girl?'

She knew John would not leave the car park until she went and got the girl. Frightened and weary, she forced herself out of the car. If only she had put on her raincoat. Her wool coat soaked up the rain as she made her way towards the main building. The car park was nearly full, and impatient drivers looking for spaces kept beeping their horns at her as she got in their way. *I just want to be home again.* She prayed silently, *Please let it be over.*

Marion went through the sliding glass doors of the service station and found a food court, a small supermarket, and gift shop, but no sign of Violetta. She went into the ladies' toilets. The long queue consisted mostly of elderly women who all seemed to be travelling on the same coach trip around England. 'I was very disappointed by Stonehenge,' said one of them. 'Will you hold my handbag and coat, Margaret, I don't like to put anything on the floor, you don't know how often they clean these places,' said another. Catching sight of herself in the mirror. Marion realised she blended in seamlessly with the ladies on the tour. How lovely it would be to slip onto their coach with them and escape!

As she waited, Marion noticed the central cubicle in a row of five remained occupied, and a strip of pink plastic was visible in the gap between the floor and the bottom of the door. Marion took her time using the toilet, and when she came out again, the room was empty except for herself and the occupant of the middle cubicle.

Marion knocked on the door.

'Violetta?'

She heard a sound that might have come from a small trapped animal.

'I'm sorry John wouldn't let you go to the loo, but he was worried that stopping would make us late getting home.'

'I don't like you people,' said the voice from inside the cubicle. 'You English are very mean and have no good manners. You are scaring me. The old man, he scares me the most. I don't want to come work for you.'

'John doesn't mean to shout,' said Marion. 'He's just tired from all the driving. He is a very kind man, really. When you get to know him better, I'm sure you'll like him.' Then she sighed wearily. 'Please come out and get back into the car with us.'

There was a pause, then a sharp: 'No!'

A part of Marion wanted to tell the girl to take her chance and escape. Run away and keep running. Whatever you do, you must not get back in that car. Something dreadful will happen. You will never see your family or the light of day ever again. Please just go. Run. Anything that happens to you will be better than coming with us.

226

Instead, she heard herself say:

'But what about Adrian? You know he is so looking forward to seeing you.'

'But he hasn't met me yet. Only photograph. Maybe when he sees me, he thinks I am ugly.'

'I'm sure he will think you are very pretty. I think you are.'

'Did he talk with you about me?'

'Yes, yes, he said he was excited about meeting you after all this time.'

Marion could hardly believe she was capable of putting on an act like this, but she had to get away from those service station toilets before another coach party came in.

'And is he handsome? Like in the photographs online?'

'Well — of course I'm his aunt, so obviously he looks handsome to me.' She hesitated, then thought of that young man Simon from the estate agents. 'He has a lovely smile and he is very charming.'

'Do you think I will be his girlfriend?'

'Perhaps — he doesn't have a girlfriend at the moment. I think he would like that very much.'

'I — I am scared that he won't like me — that — that he will send me away again.' Her words were punctuated by little sobs and gasps. 'This is my only hope, I just want someone who takes care of me . . . I can't go back home now — Mama, she has this new man and baby — they don't want me — she makes me leave, and I have to sleep on floor of my friend from hotel, but she doesn't want me now either — there is nothing for me except this.'

Marion felt a sudden wave of sympathy for Violetta. She wanted to believe that the girl's dreams would come true, that Adrian was a real person who would rescue her and care for her for the rest of her life.

'Then you'd better come now, hadn't you?'

A woman and her small daughter came into the toilets. The mother gave Marion a suspicious look and then used her hand to guide the child's eyes away, as if to prevent her from witnessing something inappropriate.

'Now, come on, we have to get going.'

The bolt of the cubicle door slid back. Violetta rushed out and wrapped her thin, sharp arms around Marion's waist. Damp curls pressed against Marion's face. The girl was surprisingly strong, and it felt strange to have this tiny, tough little thing pressed against her body. How long since anyone else had hugged her? She couldn't remember. Lydia as a child used to wrap her arms round her just like that, usually when it was time to go back to Judith's house and she didn't want to leave, but that was many years ago. If John embraced her, she would have died of shock. Hugging had not been commonly practised when they were children. Mother, though she might press dry lips against her children's cheeks at birthdays and Christmas, considered overt displays of affection 'classless' and likely to spread infection.

Something about Violetta's fierce embrace made Marion want to cry.

She patted the girl's back, feeling the ridges of small hard bones through her clothes.

'Come on, we have to get back to the car now. John is waiting.'

Violetta slept for most of the journey home. John tuned the radio to a programme that was playing old Broadway hits. They listened to songs from shows like *Oklahoma*, *South Pacific*, and *The Sound of Music*.

★　★　★

They finally pulled up outside the house at 9 p.m. Marion, her head fuzzy from the hours of staring at the road ahead, got out of the car and opened the front door of the house while John woke Violetta. As she walked into the hall, the girl stretched sensuously then looked at John.

'What about suitcase?' she asked sleepily.

'I'll get that later,' said John.

The inside of the house was barely warmer than the street outside, and the air smelled strongly of damp; or perhaps, having been away from it for the day, Marion just noticed it more. As she walked through the hall Violetta looked around at all the piles of newspaper and rubbish with an expression of dreamy confusion on her face.

'Come this way,' said Marion, leading the girl through the dining room into the kitchen.

'Is Adrian here?'

'Not yet, but you'll see him soon. Would you like a cup of tea?'

The girl gave a drowsy nod. Then she looked in her handbag for something and frowned.

'Phone is gone.'

While the girl was sleeping, Marion had noticed John take her phone from her bag and throw it out the window somewhere along the M1.

'Maybe you dropped it in the car,' said John. 'We can go and look for it when we get the suitcase, but let's have tea first.'

The girl seemed too tired to object.

John already had the special mixture ready; he had placed the pills ground up in the blue cup before they went out. He left Marion alone in the kitchen with the girl. She put the kettle on. Her hands were shaking as she poured the tea, but Violetta didn't notice. She made sure to add lots of sugar, just as John had instructed her to do. It was nearly over; she had done all that John asked. Soon she could go and rest. As she tasted the tea, the girl screwed up her sharp little nose, but drank it down anyway. She probably thought all English tea tasted funny. It took ten minutes of anxious waiting until her head began to drop towards the table.

When John came back, his hair was neatly combed over to hide the bald pate. His face looked shiny from recent shaving; he had put on a new white shirt and a fresh pair of trousers. Marion could smell his aftershave. When he looked at the unconscious girl, it was as if he was seeing her for the first time, and his face filled with hope and wonder. No one had ever looked at Marion that way. Suddenly she felt as though she was no longer present in the room; it was just John and the girl. He picked her up with reverence, as if she were a princess in a fairy tale, the sleeping beauty perhaps, with all that curly dark hair flowing down her back. Marion knew that when you cared about someone and they were happy, you should be happy for them, but who cared about her happiness? Certainly not John — he hadn't even thanked her after all she had done for him. He carried Violetta down to the cellar, leaving Marion alone in the kitchen.

Teddy Bear

The weeks following Violetta's arrival, John spent almost all of his time down with the visitors. Each evening he put his dinner on a tray and took it to eat in the cellar. When he did come up, he seemed to have too much on his mind to even say a word to Marion. Not even the occasional 'Good morning' or 'Everything all right, Mar?' So rarely did she talk to anyone during this time, she sometimes worried that she might lose the power of speech altogether.

'You have to get out, Mar,' she said out loud to herself one afternoon in early October, after lying on her bed staring at the ceiling for nearly an hour. She had developed the habit of talking to herself just to make sure her tongue didn't wither away. 'Stop just lounging about, feeling sorry for yourself. Get out of the house and do something.'

Bracing herself against the cutting wind that blew in from the sea, Marion walked into Northport Town Centre. On the high street she stopped at an Age Concern shop. Though many people complained about the charity shops in Northport, with their smell of old books, dust, and clothes that have been put away slightly damp, Marion enjoyed exploring them in search of hidden treasure.

The woman behind the counter wore a blonde wig and makeup that, in Marion's opinion, looked too showy for her thin, wrinkled face. Marion went to the back of the shop where they kept paperback books, old records, and other items that weren't clothing. There was a pile of DVDs with lurid pictures of men with guns and explosions, lovers kissing, and comedians grinning foolishly. They were five for a pound, which seemed very good value, though she wasn't sure any of them were her type of thing.

Looking through the box of secondhand toys, she came across a naked Barbie doll on which someone had drawn nipples and pubic hair with black felt-tip pen. She was shocked that such a thing had been put out for sale in the shop; surely whoever sorted through the donated items should have chucked that obscene doll into the bin, or at least tried to remove the black felt-tip and put some clothes on it? Marion glanced over her shoulder and saw the woman at the counter was watching her carefully.

Tossing to one side a robot with an arm missing and a plastic horse, she came across a huge stuffed dog with golden-brown fur, floppy ears, and an enormous drooping snout. Marion felt a rush of pity for the animal. She wanted to wrap her arms around its cushiony body, to bury her face in its threadbare coat. But the dog was far too big for her to buy; she would look ridiculous carrying it down the high street. After giving its nose a guilty pat, she began searching through another box.

She picked up a sweet yellow teddy; what was left of its fur had set into hard little tufts, and it smelled faintly of sick, so she put it back down again. Then she came across another bear with lovely white fur and a big red bow around its neck. It looked almost brand new.

Marion knew that it was wrong to love the new toys better than the old worn ones, but something about the white bear sent a shot of joy through her heart. Then she found a tiny plush ladybird at the bottom of the box that she didn't have the heart to leave behind. She took both toys over to the cash register to pay for them.

'So are these for your grandchildren?' said the woman, picking up the worn little ladybird.

Marion looked down at her hands gripping her leather purse and noticed the backs were creased and covered with brown freckles. It seemed strange to her that people should think she was old enough to be a grandmother when she still felt like a large, ungainly child.

'I don't know if I'd buy secondhand toys,' said the woman, 'you don't know where they've been, do you? If I gave these to my Karen's kids, well, she would probably chuck them straight in the bin.' She sniffed. 'Little Kieran has asthma, and things like this are a magnet for dust and germs, you know. Karen likes everything new and modern. Anyway, I am sure *your* grandkids will enjoy them all the same.'

'I don't have any children or grandchildren as a matter of fact,' said Marion.

'So who are you buying them for?'

Marion bristled with irritation. Why was this awful person asking her so many questions? Really, she should tell her to mind her own business.

'For myself — I collect them.'

The woman raised eyebrows that had been clumsily sketched with a dark brown pencil.

'Hum — well I wouldn't have thought of them as collector's items exactly, I mean they're not like those posh German bears you see on *Antiques Roadshow*, are they?'

Marion wished the woman would just let her pay for the toys so she could leave. Then she began to examine the big white teddy bear, puffing it up as if it were a throw cushion and straightening out its bow.

'This is a nice one, though, almost brand-new.' Her small circle of shrimp-coloured mouth wrinkled, and she gave Marion a suspicious look as though she had been trying to leave the shop without paying for the toy.

'I'm sorry, but I'll have to charge more than a pound for this teddy.'

'Well — all right, will you please just tell me how much?' asked Marion impatiently. It depressed her to realise that this was probably the longest she had spoken to anyone in weeks.

The woman looked at the bear.

'I don't know, maybe five pounds?'

Marion was shocked. 'Really, that seems a lot.'

'Well, it is for charity, isn't it? And just think how much you would have to pay for a nice teddy like this in a proper toy shop. Ten or fifteen quid at least.'

The woman pressed the teddy's nose between her breasts in a manner that Marion did not like at all. Realising that she had no choice but to pay, she handed over the cash quickly.

* * *

On her journey home, the way she had been treated in the shop churned in Marion's mind. She thought that the awful woman with her cheap makeup and wig probably only took the job so she would get the chance to boss people around; she obviously wasn't charitable by nature. She really ought to write and complain. Then she thought: 'I hope she gets some awful disease. I hope she gets cancer.' A rush of horror that she could come up with such an idea overcame Marion, and she quickly scrubbed it from her mind.

When she got home, she took out the big white teddy to admire him. He really was so lovely with his thick silky fur and blue eyes made from real glass rather than plastic. It had been worth dealing with that awful woman just to rescue him. While she was thinking about what to name the bear, she filled the kettle to make herself a cup of tea. It puzzled her to see the blue ottoman from Mother's bedroom standing by the door to the cellar. Then the door opened and John came out. He normally shut it behind him immediately, but this time he walked into the kitchen leaving it ajar. She felt suddenly fearful, as if some unwelcome spirit might escape through the gap, and she wished he would close it.

'More teddies, Marion? What are you like, you daft old bird.'

She bit down hard on her lower lip to punish herself for being so stupid. Why hadn't she hidden the toys away before he'd seen them? John picked up the new white teddy bear to examine it.

'Well, he's a handsome chap, isn't he?'

'Yes, looks almost brand-new. I wonder why someone took him to the charity shop?'

'So what's for dinner, then, love?'

'I was going to do cod with boiled peas.'

'And mashed potatoes?'

'Yes, I could do some instant Smash if you want.'

As he was about to leave, John did a strange thing. He planted a little kiss on the top of her head and then put the big white teddy bear into the ottoman and carried it down the cellar. Marion was so astounded by the kiss that she barely stopped to think what he might be doing with the ottoman and the teddy bear.

★ ★ ★

After a dinner of cod that somehow managed to be dry and watery at the same time, instead of going straight down to the cellar, John came into the living room and sat down on the sofa next to Marion. He was in an odd mood, as though he wanted to tell her something but didn't know how.

They watched a documentary about a volcano that wiped out a whole city in Roman times. It was not Marion's sort of thing, but it made her happy just to have company and for him to find something interesting even if she did not. Usually when they watched something that was her choice, he would make little huffing noises or remarks about how stupid it was; even if he didn't say anything at all, she could somehow *feel* his boredom and annoyance, so she would be unable to relax.

'The volcano erupted without warning,' said the presenter, 'and many people were killed by falling ash while going about their everyday business.'

'Is everything all right, John?' she asked him after the programme had finished.

He hesitated before replying, as if running several answers through his mind. Then he nodded cautiously. 'Yes, Mar, everything is fine. Better than ever.'

★ ★ ★

While Marion was getting ready for bed she heard a strange noise, a low humming followed by a few musical notes. After a few moments, she realised it was her phone that she kept beside her bed. It rang so rarely that she had forgotten what it sounded like, and was surprised that it still even had enough battery left. She picked it up and fumbled with the keys for a while before managing to read the text:

'hi M hope you well am home from uni this week and wondered if I could pop in say hi tomorrow 2pmish :) xxx Lydia'

Marion trembled with happiness. 'At last something good has happened. This is a sign that things are going to change for the better!' She said it out loud, even though she had spoken to both John and the shop woman that day and would be talking to Lydia the next, so she hardly needed to exercise her tongue in private at all.

★ ★ ★

The following morning, when she returned from shopping to buy things for Lydia's visit, Marion found Mr Weinberg waiting by the gate.

'Did you find your little dog, then?' asked Marion, trying to manoeuvre her shopping trolley around him. Of course she knew he hadn't, but she couldn't think of anything else to say. The old man squinted at Marion as if he had no idea who she was. She was about to go into the house when he spoke.

'Who is the gurl?'

Marion felt as if she had been poked in the chest by an icy finger.

'What girl?'

'I saw her going into your house last week.'

'I don't know what you mean.'

'I know I saw it last week late at night. Going into the house with you and your brother. Young with black hair. She is your relative maybe? I don't think because she does not look English, this girl. Maybe some Eastern European. Hungarian, I think, or Romanian, from the look of her. Maybe she comes to verk for you as housekeeper? I haven't seen gurl since.' He leaned towards her as he said 'gurl' in that strange, northern way. 'But I saw your brother with pink suitcase. Putting in rubbish bin.'

Marion could smell his dirty odour of rotten vegetables and stale sweat. Could he tell that she was shaking? She leaned against the gatepost to steady herself. The best thing to do was to just ignore him. He is a very old man, she reminded herself. He must be over ninety; he lives alone; no one will listen to what he says.

She smiled and then said in a cheery tone: 'No, no, Mr. Weinberg, I haven't seen your little dog, but I will check in the garden one more time just to make sure.' Then she turned away and put her key in the lock. While she was struggling to open the door she felt sure that he was still standing there, staring at her with those grey watery eyes, but when she turned around to look, the old man had gone.

Marion unlocked the door and went into the house; she immediately noticed several large white packages stacked up against the wall. There were so many of them, she could hardly get past. John suddenly appeared and loaded several of them into his arms.

'What in heaven's name are all those, love?'

John avoided her eyes.

'Nothing that you need to worry yourself about, Marion.'

Then he carried the packages back through the house towards the cellar.

Marion was too busy getting things ready for Lydia's visit to think about Mr Weinberg or John's mysterious packages. She filled around a dozen soup bowls from Mother's Royal Crown Derby dinner service with crisps and sweets. The bowls, with their regal red-and-gold design, perhaps did look rather too grand for snacks, but they were the only matching ones that Marion could find. Cheese-and-pickle sandwiches, the crusts cut off rather clumsily, had been placed on the huge platter that must have been intended for use at some formal dinner party with a roast suckling pig or large fish in aspic laid out on it. Much of the junk that had previously cluttered the kitchen she had hastily shoved into the dining room. John had gone to the Royal Oak public house and wouldn't, she hoped, be back until early evening.

★ ★ ★

Marion kept checking the text on her phone to make sure she had got the right day, and each time she read it, she felt a little rush of anxious excitement. She made sure to keep her phone in her pocket just in case there was another message. For the visit she had bought all of Lydia's favourite things: Haribo gummy bears, Cheesy Wotsits, Pringles, and a family-size tin of Quality Street. While she was waiting for Lydia to arrive, she was so nervous that she ate a whole bowl of salt-and-vinegar Hula Hoops and had to replace them.

When Marion opened the door, she was surprised at how tall Lydia had grown. And she looked so beautiful, with those big blue eyes, glowing skin, and long red hair tied back in a ponytail. Dressed in a crisp white shirt over jeans, she could have easily been a model in one

241

of those fancy magazines. She had brought a bunch of the most perfect tulips Marion had ever seen, each flower bright and alert without a tinge of brown. The girl hugged her and they went into the kitchen together, just like old friends.

'Oh, Em, you really shouldn't have gone to all this trouble,' said Lydia, looking at all the sandwiches, bowls of crisps, and sweets laid out on the table.

Marion's glow dimmed when she saw Lydia's face. It had been a mistake putting out all that food. These were the kind of things children liked to eat, not sophisticated young women. Lydia would have no doubt preferred sushi or those little plates of Spanish food. Of course Marion mustn't let it show that her feelings were hurt.

'It wasn't any trouble,' said Marion. 'Don't worry if you're not hungry. I just thought you might feel tempted to have a little nibble at something.'

Lydia's tummy was as flat as an unread paperback; she probably watched her weight carefully like her mother. No doubt if Marion had had a daughter, she would have spoiled her rotten, and she'd have ended up fat just like her.

Lydia sat down at the table, one slender white arm sprawled lazily in front of her, the other supporting her head as if that delicate neck couldn't manage the job by itself.

'Would you like some Coca-Cola? Though I suppose now you are all grown up, you might prefer tea or coffee.'

Lydia yawned, waving a hand across the

healthy pink interior of her mouth.

'I'll just have water, Marion, do you have any bottled fizzy?'

'Oh, I'm so stupid, I should have bought mineral water,' said Marion, then slapped the back of her own hand in punishment.

'Tap water is absolutely fine.' The girl yawned again, then gave Marion a gracious smile. 'Don't worry yourself. I don't know why you went to all this trouble just for me, but it was really sweet of you all the same.' She spoke like someone thanking a child for a homemade birthday card.

They sat and chatted for a while, Lydia answering Marion's questions about university with a sleepily polite voice while sipping from a glass of tap water.

Did she have lots of studying to do? Mmm — *puts head to one side* — Yes, quite a lot. Were the subjects interesting? — *shrug, weary smile* — Sometimes, it depended on the lecturer. You must go to lots of fun parties? *sigh* — They could be quite boring, really — I don't go to all of them, of course — *brushes strands of hair from her eyes* — Only if people I know are going. What are you going to do when you leave? — Oh gosh — *giggles as though this is ridiculously funny, puts hands over face* — I have absolutely no idea — travel for a while maybe, work abroad — *laughs* — Yes, work abroad, but I don't know doing what.

While they were talking, Lydia kept fussing with her phone, stroking the glass screen as if it were a beloved pet. Who could she be messaging? wondered Marion, feeling a sour hatred for them. She imagined a group of attractive young people, picnicking in a park or drinking in some trendy pub, begging Lydia to come and join them. 'I just can't,' Lydia would reply, 'I'm stuck with this boring old woman who keeps asking me endless questions.'

Now and then Lydia picked a crisp or sweet from one of the bowls and nibbled on it, but Marion felt she was only doing this out of politeness. After a while Marion began to run out of things to say and began to worry that she might have asked the same question more than once and Lydia would think she had dementia. If only Lydia were a little girl again, how easy it was to make her happy with sweets and stories about fairies and elves.

As they sat across the table from each other, making stilted conversation, the truth, sharp as a thorn, pressed into Marion's heart: the little girl who loved her was gone and this bored young woman was a stranger. Her hopes of remaining part of Lydia's life as she got older, sharing in the excitement of her wedding, becoming an 'auntie' to her children, even visiting at Easter and Christmas, were silly fantasies, just like those about Neil. Of course if Marion had been a blood relative, things might have been different, but without the ties of family, Lydia would drift into the future without her.

Marion heard the front door open, and her chest tightened with anxiety. John normally stayed all afternoon at the pub on Fridays playing chess.

'John, love,' asked Marion, 'did you have a

244

nice game with your friends?'

'Those drunken cheats are no friends of mine. None of them appreciates the finer nuances of the game.' He pinched his thumb and forefinger together to emphasise this point. 'It's as much as they can do to make a move without knocking the bloody board over. And that little slut of a waitress shortchanges you every time you buy a damn round. It's the last time you'll see me near that fucking dump,' he growled.

What was he thinking to use language like that in front of Lydia? From the smell of him and the colour of his cheeks, Marion thought he might have had more than a few whiskies himself.

'That's a shame — it does you good to get out of the house now and then.'

'Oh yes, and I'm sure you're very glad to get me 'out of the house', aren't you, Marion?' He scowled.

'I didn't mean that, John. I just thought it was nice for you to have some intellectual stimulation and male company.'

'But I've got all the company and stimulation I need right here, haven't I, *love*?'

The look he gave her was full of suggestion, and she feared that Lydia might read into it.

Picking up a handful of crisps, John pushed them into his mouth; as he crunched on them his lips were glistening like wet paint. He was standing right behind Lydia's chair, the zip of his trousers close to her head. He placed a thick hand on Lydia's small round shoulder.

'Don't tell me this is the little brat from next door. Who'd have thought she'd grow up into such a lovely young lady! So, how is the big wide world of university?'

'It's okay,' said Lydia, pulling her hair across her face.

'I bet you have to chase the lads off with a sharp stick?'

Lydia lowered her eyes and forced a smile.

'I don't know — not really.'

'No boyfriends, then? Or do you like girls better?' John winked. 'Is that the modern thing?'

A heat rose from Marion's chest to her face.

'I should be going now,' said Lydia.

'Don't let me break up your little tea party,' said John.

'No, I have to work on an essay. It's due in tomorrow.'

'Yes, you go, love, don't let us keep you,' said Marion, suddenly desperate for Lydia to be gone.

Marion got up, and Lydia kissed her on the cheek. They went towards the door, but John was blocking the way. 'What's the matter, don't I get a kiss?' He leered at Lydia.

Then he grabbed the girl by the waist and pulled her towards him. Marion saw him plant a wet salty kiss on Lydia's mouth. There was a flash of hair fanning into a russet tail and then the front door slammed as Lydia left.

John stumbled his way into the living room, and Marion began throwing all the unwanted sweets and crisps into a big plastic bin liner where they formed a crunchy rainbow of trash. How excited she had been buying those things in the hope that Lydia would enjoy them; it had all been a horrible waste and the poor girl would probably never come back again after what had happened.

She threw the rubbish bag on the floor and, steaming with rage, followed John into the next room, where he was sitting reading the newspaper as calmly as if nothing had happened.

'How dare you touch her like that!' she cried, ripping the newspaper from his hands. 'You are nothing but a filthy pervert!'

'You'll mind your mouth, girl, if you know what's good for you!'

John rose to his feet and stood a full head taller than his sister.

'You should be ashamed of yourself, John Zetland. I always believed you were a decent man, but I was wrong.'

'What right do you have to talk to me like that, you ignorant bitch?'

Marion had never stood up to anyone like this before, and her heart felt as though it might burst out from her chest.

'I have every right, and I want you to know I hate you!'

'Hate your own brother, do you? You watch out, or I'll really give you something to hate me for.'

His fingertips sank deep into her flesh as he grabbed her upper arms. He held her for what seemed an age, his face nothing but wild eyes amidst a mass of purple blotches. Then he shook her before pushing her away so violently her neck bones jarred as she fell backwards onto the sofa. Shock left her too stunned to speak or cry as John stormed from the room. Then the sound of the cellar door slamming shut echoed through the house.

★ ★ ★

When she woke the next morning, at first she couldn't remember why her eyes were sore and swollen. Then the picture of John kissing Lydia with his slick red mouth returned. A nasty, grubby feeling clung to Marion like wet mud. She remembered feeling the same way when John had brushed against her in the wax museum and when Mr Bevan had touched her breast, only this was a thousand times worse. How could her brother behave in such a disgusting manner, kissing a pure young woman on the mouth like that?

He was nothing but a dirty old man. Memories of the way he used to look at Lydia when she was a young girl surfaced, and Marion cringed with horror. 'Why didn't I realise it before? I was blind to his gross, perverted nature. I didn't want to see him for what he really was! That poor girl, I should never have let him near her.'

She rubbed the back of her aching neck and then rolled up the sleeves of her nightgown. The puffy white flesh of her upper arms was covered in bruises the colour of thunderclouds from where he had grabbed her. A noise on the stairs made her shiver with fear. Immediately she went to her bedroom door and turned the key in the lock. Was he strong enough to break it down? she wondered. Feeling the pressure of her bladder, she realised she would have to leave her room at some point.

The look of loathing and anger in his eyes before he flung her away like an old rag doll still smouldered deep inside her. How could she share a house with someone like that? If only she could run away, leave him to that cellar — after all, that was the only thing he cared about. Marion went over to the window that looked out into the rear of the house. The sycamore tree stood at the end of the garden. When she was a little girl, Lydia used to play around it. She had a toy tea set and would pile the little plates with 'salad' made from daisies and grass, then leave it for the fairies to eat. Now several branches had fallen from the tree, and all its leaves were dead. Judith had been right. It was quite rotten and probably dangerous.

Forgiving John for this behaviour was unthinkable, but what choice did she have? To walk out the door? Where would she go? Was there some kind of shelter for women like her? Marion imagined herself in some huge, drab dormitory, a kind of Victorian orphanage for distressed middle-aged women, where she would lie huddled on a narrow camp bed next to rows of other lost souls like herself.

★　★　★

The days following the kiss, Marion felt as though she had been infected by some shivery sickness that disturbed her sleep and took away her appetite. Each time she heard his footsteps on the stairs, she would tremble with fear, imagining John storming into her bedroom to attack her once again. Most of the time she hid herself in the attic, but it was impossible to escape his presence completely. Creaking coming from his bedroom on the floor below woke her around six in the morning, then great racking phlegm-rich coughs were followed by the groan of the bathroom pipes as he washed. His breakfast was heralded by the softer, womanish moaning of the kitchen pipes and the noise of the radio made thin and whiny by its journey through the floors of the house. Then the house fell quiet until noon, when there would be more noise from the kitchen while he prepared lunch. After six in the evening, her brother emerged from the cellar for a short while to get his dinner, and then at midnight he went to bed. By learning this routine, she managed to dodge him, only nipping downstairs to retrieve scraps of food when she was sure he wouldn't be there.

It was around midnight, a week after Lydia's visit, when Marion realised she hadn't heard any noise from the house since the previous evening when her brother had gone down to the cellar. She waited an hour before creeping downstairs to the landing below and saw that John's bedroom door was wide open, the bed empty and still made up.

What could be going on? Was he going to stay down there forever?

Instead of going back to bed, Marion went farther down the landing and into her mother's room. On the bedside table was a little bottle of pills. She picked it up, but the small white label was too faded to read. Marion opened the drawer and found a pack of tarot cards.

The box was decorated with a picture of the sun with a lovely face that stared serenely out at her. Perhaps the cards could help her decide what to do. She seemed to remember that you had to first ask a question out loud, so she shook the frayed pack from its box and began to shuffle them in her clumsy hands.

'Please help me,' she said. 'I can't believe it has come to this, but I am afraid of John. I love him, but I feel like I don't know who he is sometimes. Worrying about things all the time is making me tired and ill. I just want to curl up in bed and pull the covers over my head forever. Please, tell me what to do.'

Marion picked out a card. It was a picture of a knight holding a sword, but she had no idea what it meant. She picked another, the hanged man. Did this mean she should hang herself? The idea of dying did not frighten her, but the thought of pain did. She had heard somewhere that death by hanging took a very long time, as one slowly choked to death. If she killed herself, then she wouldn't have to be scared and worried all the time, would she? And also it would serve John right for behaving the way he did. Imagining how he might react to finding her body gave her an odd feeling of satisfaction.

She picked up the bottle of pills from the bedside table and unscrewed the lid. There were only three inside. That wouldn't be nearly enough to do it; she had to look for more. She began searching through the drawers of the bedside table but found only indigestion remedies and some old eye drops.

Then she glanced towards the door of the en-suite bathroom. The pills would probably be in there, but she hadn't gone into that room since the day Mother was found dead, with her grey hair floating in the cold water, a burned-down cigarette butt still trapped between the fingers of her outstretched hand. The thought of going in now gave Marion chills.

You have to do it, she told herself. Just go and look inside the medicine cabinet. Don't be such a mouse — it will only take a minute.

Marion crept forward and then slid through the doorway. In the corner of her eye she caught sight of something dark in the middle of the bathtub. A huge spider? Dust? She did not dare look at it directly. She approached the cabinet and saw a rust stain snaking towards the plug hole of the small washbasin below. Her reflection appeared in the mottled glass mirror, and for a terrifying instant she mistook it for Mother's dead, bloated face. Snapping open the doors of the cabinet, she found no pills, only discoloured eau de toilette and bottles of cough linctus. Her bravery unrewarded, Marion left the en suite, closing the door firmly behind her.

Mother must have hidden her store of pills somewhere else. She got down on her knees and began pulling out boxes from underneath the huge bed. Most of them contained material, thick velvet, lace, and heavy-glazed cloth that made her nostalgic for the warehouse. There was a box containing odds and ends, little broken ornaments, used batteries, a china parrot with its beak missing.

In her search she came across a whole family of egg-shaped Weebles, a toy supermarket cash register, and a tiny pink kitchen with fake tins of food, little cardboard packets, and plastic vegetables that went in the cupboards. Looking at these old toys filled her with sweet sadness; they had provided small islands of joy in an otherwise unhappy childhood. Would she ever feel so good about anything again? When she was dead, a stranger would come into the house and take all these things and throw them on a rubbish dump. She had once hoped that Lydia might take them for her children, but of course, no one would want them now. Even that nasty old woman in the charity shop would think they were scruffy, germ-ridden things, 'not fit for a modern child'.

She found suitcases full of photograph albums. Inside one of those albums, alongside the many stuffy portraits of her parents at formal functions, there was a black-and-white snap of her and John, dough-faced toddlers perched on top of donkeys, both of them dressed in military-style coats looking serious and deter-mined, like tiny generals about to lead a cavalry charge. Then she found a picture of herself and dear Aunt Agnes standing on Northport Pier. Marion remembered her aunt asking a perfect stranger to take the picture. She had just gone right up to him and given him the camera.

Mother would never have done something like that. A warmth surrounded her heart. Yes, I was happy then, she told herself, I can remember. I loved Agnes, and we had many wonderful times together.

Outside there was a rumble of thunder. Mother used to say it was God moving the furniture. Rain began sloshing against the windows, not in individual drops but as if it were pouring from a burst pipe. Lit by flashes of lightning, the trees that lined Grange Road looked like giant green beasts swinging their furry bodies from side to side.

Perhaps she would rest for a while until she could think of another place to look for the pills. It occurred to her they might have expired anyway after such a long time and she would have to think up another method of doing away with herself. Without bothering to replace all the boxes she had dragged out, she went back to her own room and got into bed, then lay for hours listening to the storm.

She pulled all her animals close, but they just felt like bits of fake fur stuffed with rags and offered no comfort. Then, through the wind and rain, she heard something that sent a wave of shock through her whole body. Could it be the sound of a baby crying?

It was so faint, it was hard to tell if she was imagining it or not. Her mother's baby brother had died in this house, was it his ghost? She got out of bed and opened the door to listen. Yes, she could distinctly hear crying coming from downstairs. A baby crying.

Standing in her nightgown, clammy with sweat and the pulse in her neck throbbing, Marion strained to listen.

Her mind began to race. Could it really be possible? A baby born in this old house? It seemed impossible to believe. Was that what John had been doing all that time? Helping the mother to give birth? A new life couldn't survive down in that cold, damp cellar for long. It needed warmth and fresh air. The child would have to be brought up into the house.

She pictured herself holding the baby, smelling its warm soft head. Tiny fingers glowing with pink light. The baby smiling at her, learning to recognise her face. A brand-new person who would know her as Aunty Marion. Someone to play with and tell stories to.

They would put the child in the spare room next to hers. That room had a nice big window overlooking the garden and got lots of sun in the morning. It would have to be decorated, of course. She would be able to read the child all of her Beatrix Potter stories and let her play with all her toys. She felt sure it would be a girl, and she would call her Agnes after her aunt.

Marion would give herself entirely to Little Agnes. She would be the centre of her world. She would cook good food for her, proper healthy food, not junk. She would buy her pretty little dresses. Perhaps they wouldn't send Agnes to school; instead, John could teach her at home. He was an excellent teacher, after all, and then they wouldn't have to worry about her being bullied by other children.

They would play games together in the garden and go for picnics on the beach. It would be like when Lydia was small, only Agnes would never leave her. How happy they would be together. This was what she had been waiting for her whole life, something that would belong entirely to her.

Throughout the night she would creep downstairs and listen at the cellar door, but she didn't hear the baby cry again. She began to worry that Agnes might need a doctor, and that would require an explanation as to where the child came from. Perhaps they could say they had found it left on the doorstep, but then the baby would be taken away by social services and that would be heartbreaking.

If she pretended that she had given birth to it, would anyone know? Would they examine her medically? Didn't women sometimes have children in their fifties? She knew for certain that she would never let anyone take the child away. She would protect it with her own life if she had to. Of course she would have to forgive John for that awful business with Lydia. He would need her to help him with the baby.

A baby, just saying the word in her head made her feel light with happiness. A new life meant hope for the future, a reason for her to go on living, someone to love and care for — someone who would love her in return. It would be hard work, but she was sure she could do it. Marion went back up the stairs and lay down on her bed; she had been awake all night, so she should get some rest. Later there would be so much to do.

While the storm raged outside, Marion, lulled by warm, comforting thoughts, drifted off to sleep.

★ ★ ★

This time it wasn't a child's cries that disturbed Marion's slumber, but a loud crash that sent hoofed animals stampeding through the forest of her dreams. After a brief struggle to free herself from sleep's clutches, she got out of bed and rushed to the window. The uprooted sycamore tree was stretched across the grass, its upper part having smashed a section of the wall that separated their garden from Judith's. John was lying on the ground next to it.

Marion ran from her bedroom. As she hurried down the first-floor landing she glimpsed a devilish face leering at her through the doorway of the guest room. She let out a little scream, before realising it was just that pattern on the wood of the old oak wardrobe lit by a flash of lightning. Almost down the final flight of stairs she felt something catch her foot and stumbled forwards. Managing to cling to the banister and save herself just in time, she remembered with a chill that according to Aunt Agnes, Mother had tripped at this exact same spot, on the fourth stair from the bottom, falling, then crushing her baby brother beneath her as she landed on the hall floor.

When she got to John, she saw his clothes were soaking wet as if he had just been washed ashore by the tide and his hair flopped to one side like a clump of matted seaweed, exposing his naked scalp.

'What is it? What happened?'

He grasped hold of her hand so tightly, she thought the bones might break.

'I was trying to move it, to lift the damn tree away from the wall, and I got a terrible pain — down my arm and my chest! Please, love, help me.'

She tried to help him up, but she could no more lift him than the sycamore trunk itself, and the muscles in her back screamed each time she tried.

'I'll get help, I'll call an ambulance.'

'No, no, you can't do that.'

'But John what else can I do? I can't leave you out here in the garden.'

Marion went to the hallway and phoned for an ambulance with trembling fingers. When the operator asked for the address, her mind went blank and she couldn't remember the number of her own house.

The operator, a man with a very kind voice, told her to walk calmly to the front door and take a look; he said that happened to people sometimes, that they forgot things when there was an emergency. When she gave him the address, he told her they'd send someone very quickly and Marion thanked him.

Marion wrapped her arms tightly around her body as she stood on the doorstep. When she heard the siren, she felt breathless with terrible excitement. Usually that sound made her think there had been an accident somewhere, some poor unknown soul was in dire trouble, but on this occasion she was the one who had called the ambulance. It was coming for her brother.

When the ambulance stopped in the street, she waved to the driver to let him know which house to go to. It irritated her to see Mr. Weinberg standing on his step, watching everything.

As the two young men in medic's uniforms followed her into the house Marion felt her usual shame at the state of everything. As they went through the kitchen Marion noticed the cellar door had been left open, the key still in the keyhole. While the two men were examining John in the garden, she locked it, then placed the key into a biscuit barrel.

Going outside herself, she heard John arguing loudly with the two young men who were trying to move him onto a stretcher. Each time they touched him, he screamed out in pain.

'Who do you think you are? Get your bloody hands off me!'

'Sir, we need to take you into hospital to get you checked out.'

'I'm not going anywhere, you see, I can't!' said John, slapping the men's hands away as they tried to move him.

'You've got to let us do our job — '

'You buggers need to leave me alone.'

The men looked at Marion for support.

'Please, John, you have to let them help you,' Marion said gently.

He looked into her eyes, and she knew he was afraid. Kneeling down in the mud, she took hold of her brother's hand. The fingers felt cold and limp.

'I promise it will be all right, love. You don't need to worry. Mar will take care of everything,' she said.

John squeezed her fingers very weakly, then his eyes rolled back in his head and he passed out.

Hospital

It was impossible for Marion to make sense of all the words and pictures colliding with one another inside her head. The fallen tree, a blocked blood vessel, and a broken hip: so many awful things at once! Why had this all happened now? The nurse had left her sitting on a small sofa in what was called the 'Family Room' (those words made her feel lonelier than she ever had in her entire life), telling her that someone would come and fetch her when John's operation was over. But she hadn't said how long that would be, and according to the clock on the wall, Marion had been waiting nearly five hours. She watched the black hands, sharp as scalpels, steadily move around the clock's cold, white face.

On the other side of the room there was a table with tea-and coffee-making things. A half-used packet of digestive biscuits stood upright, its torn wrapper unspooling across the tray. Despite having had nothing all day, she would sooner have put sand in her mouth than attempted to eat one.

Before the surgery, someone had asked her who was John's next of kin. She had said that would be Mother. And then, when they asked how to get hold of her, she had told them that Mother was dead, and they looked at her like she was a complete fool. The doctor, a young

261

Chinese woman wearing a pink jumper that didn't seem very doctor-like, snapped at Marion as if she were a child who had been caught telling fibs:

'Do you realise there is a high possibility that your brother might not survive this surgery?'

The thought of his glasses left folded on the bedside table next to a half-eaten roll of Trebor mints, his cable-knit cardigan hung over the back of a chair like the pelt of a slain beast, ripped her apart. She might never hear him whistling along to the radio again or iron another of his shirts. For all his faults, John loved her and she loved him. Without him there would be no one. He was there on birthdays and at Christmas. He might only buy her something cheap or forget to buy her a present at all, but at least he was there. Someone to get angry with for not doing the right thing was better than no one at all. He was her brother. She had known him all her life. Without John, she felt, there would be nothing to fasten her to this world and she might just float off into the clouds.

'Please God,' she prayed, 'I am sorry I was so angry with him. I promise if you let my brother live, I will never be cross with him again. I will do everything he tells me and do my very best to be a good sister and make him happy. Just don't let him die. That is the only thing that matters. If he dies, I'll be all alone, so you might as well kill me too.'

Marion sat up rigid all night on the little orange sofa, too frightened to cry or sleep. Every time she heard footsteps from the corridor, she dreaded it was a nurse coming to tell her he was dead. By morning, no one had come and Marion wondered if they had forgotten she was there at all. Her bladder full, she left the Family Room and walked around the hospital looking for toilets. Eventually she followed a sign for the facilities that took her down two flights of stairs and along another corridor. Then, when she had finished using the toilets, she realised she didn't know how to get back to her small sanctuary.

★　★　★

After walking around for a while, she came to a café but had no money to buy a sandwich or drink. Her handbag, along with her mobile phone and purse, had been left at home. Thoughts of the mobile hurt because John had bought it for her. 'You have to have one, Marion. Everyone has one these days. You can't live in the past forever,' he had told her. Even if she had it with her, there was no one to call apart from Judith, and she would probably be too furious about the wall to want to help. She was so tired and cold and hungry. Her back and her feet hurt, her clothes felt grimy and itchy, and she longed for a hot bath. If only Dad were alive and could bring the big, safe Bentley to take her home.

As long as I can't find out where he is, then no one can tell me he has died. So if I stay lost, he will live, Marion thought. Then Mother's voice scolded her for being so silly. *He's your brother, Marion. He needs you. You have to find him. He is depending on you.*

She wandered around, feeling too timid to ask anyone for help; she trudged down long corridors, not knowing if she had been down them before or not. Endless wards, clinics, waiting rooms, one place in the hospital looked exactly like another. At least if she could find her way back to the Family Room, she could make herself a cup of tea and eat some of those biscuits. How precious those biscuits had suddenly become — why had she ignored them earlier? Finally she came across a map, and after squinting at it for a long time (her glasses had been left at home too), she managed to work out directions back to where she came from. She must have walked a long way, because it took her nearly twenty minutes to get there. When she opened the door, she was surprised to see a young couple sitting on the orange sofa. The woman was holding a naked baby doll by one leg and weeping while the man had his arm around her shoulders. Their heads were lowered, and they were too involved in comforting one another to notice Marion.

It was rather a nasty-looking doll, one of those bald, plastic things that Marion had never liked, even as a child, since they weren't soft enough to cuddle. Wasn't it rather unseemly to bring it to the hospital naked? Though of course they had probably left their home in haste and grabbed anything that might be used to comfort a sick child. The man had a shaved head and a tattoo of a skull on his hand. The woman's hair was dragged back in a scruffy ponytail. They both wore tracksuits and trainers, and Marion thought they looked like the sort of people who claimed benefits.

The doll, hanging upside down, glared at Marion with a surly expression on its plastic baby's face as if to say: 'A child is sick. Your problems are nothing compared to that. Go away and leave us alone.'

Of course she ought to feel terribly sorry for them, but under the circumstances, she could not find even a scrap of compassion to spare for anyone else. And at least *they* have each other, she thought with a pinch of resentment.

Having the Family Room occupied by strangers distressed her. She felt having spent most of the night there in a state of extreme anxiety, it belonged to her. Still, it wouldn't be right to go in and start making tea and eating biscuits with those people weeping on the sofa. Instead, she found a little garden where she sat for a while until she got cold, then she went to read the magazines in the shop. The afternoon she spent watching TV in the waiting rooms of 'Fracture Clinic B'.

One of her Heartfelt Productions, *Always Trust a Stranger*, was playing on the small television monitor bracketed to the clinic wall. She had watched the film at least twice before, and it felt like bumping into an old friend. Of course the sound was turned to mute, but that didn't matter because Marion remembered most of the dialogue.

People came along and waited in the seats for a while before getting called for their appointments.

'How long have you been waiting to see Dr. Palladine, then?' an elderly woman in a blue head scarf and shiny green mackintosh asked her.

'Oh, nearly an hour,' answered Marion, too embarrassed to explain her predicament, yet feeling a little guilty for lying to the nice old lady.

The woman shook her head in sympathy. 'It's terrible, isn't it? I had to wait nearly two hours the last time I came. So much for this so-called NHS.'

Then the old woman told her about her husband who had been a fireman and her children who both lived in Australia. 'They begged me to move over with them, but I wouldn't leave my home for the crown jewels. I go to see Eric's grave every Sunday. I haven't missed a week since he passed. You won't get me on that plane unless you dig him up and put him on it too,' she said rather sternly to Marion, as if she were colluding with the daughters to whisk her over to Australia away from Eric's precious grave.

When the clinic closed and all the patients had been seen, she was forced to leave the waiting room. While she was sitting by a vending machine in a corridor looking hungrily at the sandwiches, an African cleaning woman asked her if she was all right. The woman's eyes, deep brown wells of kindness, brought Marion to tears.

'Not really,' said Marion. 'I need to find my brother, John. He's had an operation.'

The young woman left her cart of cleaning things to take Marion to an information booth near the front entrance.

After making a phone call, the woman at the information desk informed her that John Zetland was in the 'Acute Intensive Care Unit' and which could be found by 'following the blue line' running along the corridor wall. Marion followed the mysterious line upstairs and across floors (ignoring orange, green, and yellow lines), as carefully as Hansel and Gretel following bread crumbs through the forest. When she finally reached John's ward, the door was locked shut and she had to press an intercom buzzer to be admitted. While waiting, her chest filled with an awful tingling sensation as she dreaded the news she was about to be told.

A male nurse came to fetch her, and she was taken to another small room to speak to a doctor. The doctor was Indian and very handsome. He sat leaning forward with his forearms resting on his knees and an earnest expression on his flawless brown face. He referred to John by his first name and spoke about him with as much compassion as he might about his own brother. He told her that John had broken his hip while trying to move the tree, and the shock had given him a heart attack. But he was alive and it was a miracle that he had survived the operation. He said that her brother was a fighter, and that he was very lucky, but he wasn't out of the woods yet.

Before she was allowed to see John, she had to scrub her hands very carefully and put on a flimsy plastic apron. When she found him, he was wearing an oxygen mask and his eyes were closed. He looked pale and crumpled like an old shirt in need of pressing. She took hold of his

267

hand and it felt very cold.

'Oh, John, I am so glad to see you, love! You won't believe what it's been like. I've been worried to death about you.'

John opened his eyes and looked at her warily as if he didn't know who she was. The nurse gave him a little drink of water from a paper cup.

'Your husband is doing great, but he needs to rest,' said a thin nurse with spiky blonde hair.

'He's my brother, not my husband,' said Marion.

'Maybe if you come back in an hour or so, he'll be able to chat with you.'

Marion had to scrub her hands and put on a fresh apron each time she went into the intensive care unit, then take it off again when she came out. When she returned to the ward later, John was sitting up in bed drinking tea.

'How are you feeling, love? I've been beside myself with worry.'

'Not so good — but they're looking after me all right.'

'Well, that's something. The nurses seem nice.'

'Marion, how long have I been here?'

'Since yesterday morning.'

He waited for a nurse to take away the tea things before beckoning her towards him.

His lips began to move, but his voice was so weak, she was unable to understand what he was trying to tell her.

'I'm sorry, love, I didn't hear that.'

She leaned right over him. He smelled of disinfectant with a hint of bad breath.

'And the girls, are they all right?' As he spoke,

a small amount of spittle dripped from his lips onto his chin. She felt she ought to wipe it away but could not bring herself to do so.

'What do you mean?'

'In the cellar.'

It shocked Marion to hear him mention *them* in public.

'Have you checked on them? They'll need food and water.'

'But I haven't been home.'

'Where've you been?'

'I've been here all the time, of course. Waiting for news about you.'

'But they can't take care of themselves. They can't move around.'

'Oh my goodness — John.' She leaned away from her brother.

What did he mean, they couldn't move around? There was a clatter of metal trays as food was being served to the patients. The smell of mashed potatoes and boiled meat turned her stomach.

Then it occurred to her, they couldn't do anything because he must keep them tied up. And without him, they couldn't even feed themselves. An awful sick feeling surged through her body as suddenly the idea of those women trapped in the cellar of their home became very real to her. She glanced around the ward; a man and a teenage son were sitting next to the bed of an old woman. The woman's face was so bloated, it hardly appeared human. There were dark shadows under her eyes, and she seemed close to death. Her lifeless gaze fell on Marion.

The man was holding the woman's hand, while the boy lounged back in his chair, checking his mobile phone.

'You have to go home now, Marion.'

'I came in the ambulance with you, and I don't have any money to get back.'

'Call Judith up and ask her to take you home. It's about time she did someone else a favour.'

'But I don't like bothering her. Anyway, I want to stay here with you,' Marion pleaded. The thought of going back to the house alone, to deal with *them*, made her bones cold with dread.

Straining to sit upright, John gripped the steel handles attached to the side of the bed, but he could hardly move more than a few inches. Exhausted by the effort, he slumped back into the pillow and lay there struggling to regain his breath.

'I could be in here for weeks and you can't stay here all the time. You have to go home and make sure they get food and water.'

She turned her head away, unable to look at him.

'What do you mean? I can't go down there — you told me I should never ever — '

'Marion,' he interrupted, 'listen to me, you have to or they'll be done for.'

'Oh God, John, please don't make me. Please.' She put her hands over her face, unable to bear the look in his eyes.

'I need you to do this for me.'

She remembered her promise, that she would do anything to make her brother happy, just so long as he lived.

'A person can only last for three days without water. Three days at the most.' John shook his head. 'It will be your fault, Marion. And there's a little one now.'

'What?'

'One of the girls, Alla — she was expecting, the child arrived just before I came in here.'

Marion gasped. So it was true. She hadn't imagined the cries, after all. At that moment a nurse dressed in a strawberry-coloured uniform came towards them, humming along with a tune on the radio. She looked so bright and happy. How could one be so cheerful surrounded by all this sickness and fear, wondered Marion.

'Haven't you got your mobile?'

'I left it at home.'

'Then go to the nurses' desk,' he whispered. 'Ask them if they can let you use the phone to call Judith. Tell them the situation, Marion. They are used to this sort of thing.'

'I can't phone Judith. She will be terribly angry about the tree. After all, she warned us — '

'Tell her we'll buy her a new wall, and a new bloody house too if she wants it.'

'Could you give us a minute, Marion?' said the nurse. 'I need to check John's dressing.' Then she whisked the curtains around John's bed.

Another nurse found Judith's number in the phone book. She reluctantly agreed to come to the hospital after a lot of tearful begging from Marion. Marion then had to wait outside in the cold for nearly forty-five minutes before Judith's yellow Citroën appeared. Judith must have seen the damaged wall, yet couldn't really get angry because of John being ill. Storing up her fury for a more suitable occasion, she drove Marion home in silence. The only time she opened her mouth was to scream 'fucking arsehole' at another driver who pulled out suddenly in front of her.

★ ★ ★

It was after 9 p.m. by the time Marion got back to the house.

She sat down in the kitchen for a very long time trying to steel herself for what she must do. Even looking at the cellar door made her sick with fear.

'But I don't want to! I can't go down there,' she cried out loud.

You must, said John's voice in her head. *If you don't, they will die.*

'But I didn't bring them here. You did. They are nothing to do with me. If they die, it won't be my fault.'

'You can't let the baby die. If that happens, you will never forgive yourself.'

Marion took a deep breath and got to her feet. With trembling hands, she prepared meat paste sandwiches and a bottle of orange cordial. But what would the baby eat? Would she need to go out and buy formula? The most important thing, she told herself, was to bring the baby up into the house. Then she would work out what to do next.

After removing the key from the biscuit barrel where she had hidden it when the ambulance came for John, she unlocked the cellar. As the

272

heavy oak door swung open, a thousand little pinpricks of fear sank into her flesh. When she tried to move, something solid seemed to be stopping her from taking a single step forwards.

'Just get on with it,' she told herself. 'Don't be such a coward.'

The tray of food rattled loudly with each step she took down the steep stone staircase. At the bottom was another door that had to be unlocked, then behind that, a large room containing a wooden worktable with a vice fixed to it. To one side of the table lay a dismantled radio, abandoned with its innards still exposed, like a patient that has died on the operating table. Next to it an old-fashioned biplane, strange and exquisite as a dragonfly, was mounted on a stand, waiting for John to finish painting its dark blue surface. Fine brushes, their tips hardened beyond use, littered the work surface along with dozens of miniature tins of enamel paint.

The brick walls of the cellar, once painted white, were now a greenish grey streaked with black. Long cobwebs, woolly with dust, dangled from the low ceiling. She felt one catch on her hair and nearly dropped the tray as she tried to shake it loose.

A variety of tools, screwdrivers, several sizes of saw and a couple of hammers hung on one wall. Off this room were three more doorways. The one to the left led to the back cellar; this had always been used for gardening equipment because there was access to a flight of steps and a door that led out into the garden. The middle cellar had been full of Dad's office things, files and such, and the front, the largest area, was where her parents stored disused furniture and the Christmas decorations.

On one side of the room stood the ancient movie projector that she remembered Dad and John bringing back from Frank's yard to repair. Alongside it were several unlabelled, round metal tins, strips of brown celluloid unspooling from them. John and Dad must have come down here to watch films together. Next to the stack of movies was a pile of magazines. Marion turned away in revulsion when she saw they were the same kind Mrs. Morrison had found in John's bedroom all those years ago.

She put down the tray on the table and found the key labelled 'front cellar' hung up on a peg. She hesitated before unlocking the door. It wasn't too late to run back upstairs, to go and have a hot bath, then get into bed and fall asleep. Pretend they didn't exist. 'No, you have to keep going, you have got this far, you can't stop now,' she urged herself. As she opened the door the smell rushed to greet her. It was the stench of things people didn't talk about. Filth and sickness and shame. Shuffling sounds came from the darkness, noises made by creatures disturbed in their cages. She imagined them lying in wait, ready to pounce upon her and rip the flesh from her bones.

When she turned on the light for a moment, everything seemed too grotesque to be real. The room was around fifteen feet by ten, the whitewash on the brick walls was flaking and mottled with black mould. Plaster had fallen away from parts of the ceiling, leaving the wooden joists exposed like the bones of a rotting carcass. Three mattresses lay on the floor. On one side was an upturned orange crate — these served as a kind of bedside table where the girl's personal items, such as a toothbrush and a washcloth were kept. On the other side was a bucket filled with dark slops.

The small amount of available floor space between the mattresses was littered with debris: dirty cotton buds, scraps of grimy tissues, soiled sanitary napkins, food wrappers. By one wall Marion noticed two rattraps, each of which had ensnared a glossy brown victim. In the centre of the room there was a single, unvarnished wooden chair, and a large blue washing-up bowl that contained an inch of scummy water.

It frightened her to look directly at the occupants of this hideous dormitory. Each of them lay on a mattress, their hands and feet joined together by a tangle of chains, yet more chains connected them to the walls. Their mouths were gagged by weird things that looked like rubber balls connected to a dog's muzzle.

How could she have ever believed he was trying to help them? Was it because the truth was so awful? Nothing in her imagination had come close to this.

The smell and sights of the room were so repulsive, Marion worried she might faint. She forced herself to breathe deeply. Soon it will be over, she told herself. You can get through this. Pretend it isn't real. They are just like the wax-works in the museum, not actual human beings.

The eyes of the girl on the mattress near the

door were closed, and she wasn't moving at all. Though she must only be in her twenties, her bloated face reminded Marion of the dying old woman she had seen in the hospital.

This was Alla. How different she looked from the glamorous woman in her fur coat who had looked down her nose at Marion the first time they met. Her blonde tresses had grown out into a dense dark thatch of hair. The lower half of her body was covered with a blood-soaked blanket trimmed with blue satin. In this corner of the room, behind Alla's mattress, were unopened packets of nappies and formula. She remembered the mysterious packages in the hallway. They must have contained supplies for the baby.

Next to Alla was the blue ottoman; sitting inside was the teddy bear with white fur she had got from the charity shop, and lying next to it was a funny little doll wrapped in what looked like a green-patterned pillowcase. The doll's eyes were closed and its face blue-grey in colour. A wave of horror nearly knocked her from her feet when she realised it was the baby.

That poor little thing, its life over before it even began. A white crocheted shawl lay on the floor next to the ottoman. She picked it up and placed it over the child's body, carefully tucking it in around the sides.

'I'm sorry,' she said, 'you and I would have looked for fairies together in the garden. I would have adored you like my own.' Then as tears blurred her eyes she turned away.

Don't look at it. Don't even think about it. If you think about all of this too much, you will go

276

mad, and you have to keep going. You promised John you would do this, and you must.

Sitting on the middle mattress was a small thin figure, barely recognisable as Sonya, the first of the visitors. She was so nervous when she first arrived, clutching that old suitcase decorated with stickers of ponies and horses. Her face, round and soft when Marion first saw her, now had sharp edges and deep hollows like something carved from wood. She wore a ragged blue dress and an old cardigan that had once belonged to Mother. The girl's legs were red raw and covered in bruises. Sonya's eyes, still large and terrified — the one thing about her that seemed unaltered by years in the cellar — followed Marion's slightest movement.

Beside her mattress there was a collection of toiletries: pine-scented shower gel, toothpaste, conditioning shampoo, a dried-out sponge, and a soiled towel. A blonde, snub-nosed Disney Cinderella was printed on the back of a hairbrush, its bristles clogged with clumps of dry, blonde hair.

'I'm here to help you. That is, if you will let me,' Marion said to Sonya, her voice unsteady. 'Please don't be scared.'

As she got closer the girl leaned away as if she thought Marion was going to hit her.

'I'm sorry,' said Marion. 'I didn't know it was like this. Honestly I didn't.'

The girl started crying. Marion reached carefully round the back of her head to undo the gag. As she was struggling with the fastener she saw there were scaly bald patches on Sonya's scalp. The gag was tricky to undo, but when it

277

finally sprung lose, it was as if Marion had triggered an alarm. The girl began to scream.

'Please, you have to be quiet. If you don't keep quiet, I can't help you.'

'Dink dink,' said the girl, looking at the jug of orange cordial. 'Pees dink.'

'Of course, of course, I'm so sorry, you must be very thirsty.' Marion had forgotten to bring any cups, so she poured the drink straight into the girl's mouth. She began to choke and cough; a lot of the orange cordial ended up soaking into her dress.

Since the girl's hands were chained, Marion had to hold the paste sandwich to her mouth. It was like feeding a wild creature. The sharp little teeth tore at the food so ravenously, Marion worried they might nip her fingers. As the girl ate, Marion found herself reaching out to stroke her head, and in return the girl rubbed herself against Marion's hand as if taking comfort from this contact.

Marion imagined letting Sonya go free. The girl would be interviewed on morning TV, ruddy cheeked and healthy, her hair nicely washed, wearing a clean blouse and new jeans, like a bright young university student. Sonya would tell the story of how she had been rescued by Marion from her terrible ordeal in cellar.

But it could never be like that, could it? said Mother. *If you let her go, then things will be very bad for both of you.*

When Sonya finished eating, she looked up at Marion.

'Peeeease help.'

Marion took a deep breath.

'I want to help, of course. But the situation — really, it is very complicated — you see. I have to think things over — to decide what is best — really, I don't know — '

Marion picked up the gag and went to put it back on Sonya. As soon as the girl realised what was happening, she began shaking her head wildly and screaming as hard as she could.

'No gag no please, no gag help us. You help us, lady, please,' the girl wailed, moving around so much that Marion found it impossible to place the gag around her head.

'You have to be good now,' said Marion, trying to reason with her. 'John is in hospital, see. He is very poorly. He had an operation. For a while I wasn't sure if he would pull through. I want to help you, but you are making it very difficult for me. You don't understand how much strain I am under.'

The screaming was tearing her nerves apart. Surely Judith or someone else would be able to hear?

'Look, if you don't behave yourself, I won't bring you any more food. In fact, I will never come down here ever again. *No one will.*' Marion surprised herself by the stern tone of her voice. The girl stopped screaming and just stared at her stupidly with those big eyes.

When finally she managed to replace the gag, Sonya seemed to lose all hope and slumped back onto her mattress, exhausted.

By the far wall Violetta, dressed in a short black dress, sat bolt upright on her mattress. Her skin was still smooth and tanned, her curls glossy. Next to her pillow was a vase of dead roses. She stayed very still, hardly moving her head while the gag was removed, but her eyes were blacker than anything Marion had ever seen before. Marion's back ached from leaning over to feed Sonya, so she sat down on a wooden chair next to the mattress. Violetta drank and ate without crying or screaming. Only after her mouth had been wiped and Marion was fiddling with the gag did she speak. Her voice was rough from thirst, yet calm and reasonable.

'Marion, you have to do something. You must help us.'

Marion was shocked to hear her name spoken by one of *them*.

'The baby died, and Alla is nearly dead too. Why do you let him do this to us? Why don't you go to the police? Did he threaten to kill you?'

'No.' Marion hesitated, remembering the look in his eyes when he had shaken her. 'John would *never* do a thing like that.'

'Then why do you help him?'

She searched for an answer.

'He's my brother.'

'You are a woman too. You are not evil. Don't you see you have to help us? We will say you didn't know anything until now. We won't tell that you came with him to get us.'

As she turned away from Violetta's black eyes the words of Brendan O'Brian echoed in Marion's mind: *You are evil.*

'I'm sorry, but I have to put the gag back on now.'

'No, no, don't do that!' Violetta ordered. 'You cannot. You have to help us.'

'I *am* trying to help you.'

'Do you even know about the things he does?'

'He's teaching you things like English and mathematics, because he wants to you to have an education.'

'You really believe that? You think he is our teacher?' Violetta began to laugh. 'You think that is how Alla got baby? From *mathematica?*'

The baby had been John's child? That girl had been down the cellar for well over a year now, so it must be his. How could she have been so stupid not to realise? She looked over to the small blue doll tucked in one shadowy corner of the ottoman. That baby shared her blood. Her little niece or nephew had died down here.

'You are evil woman,' screeched Violetta. 'You are a bitch from hell. This is your fault, you have done this to us, you are as bad as your fat fucking rapist brother.'

'Don't call him that!'

'You know he doesn't give shit for you. He laughs at you, his fat stupid sister. He says when you were at school, they call you manatee, big fat sea monster with titties!' She began to giggle.

Manatee. The name thundered through her head like a train in a tunnel. Only John could have told her about that. How else would she have known? He must have remembered Juliet teasing her all those years ago in the department store café.

She imagined John describing his fat ugly sister. The Manatee. Everyone made fun of her at school, and now she was a sad old virgin, all alone with no one to love. How that nasty little bitch must have shrieked and cackled with glee!

Violetta's laughter echoed around the cellar and then suddenly stopped. Marion didn't realise she had hit her until she felt her hand strike that sharp little nose. The girl screamed, more in outrage than pain. 'Oh, oh my gosh, sorry!' Marion said automatically, as if she had trodden on someone's foot in a crowd.

Sonya began bouncing her legs and bottom around on her mattress and making a whining noise through her nose. Marion's heart banged against her ribs like someone desperate to escape a locked room. She had to get upstairs before she fainted, but first the gag must be put back on Violetta, otherwise the girl would scream all night long and someone would most certainly hear.

As she stepped onto the mattress to replace the gag, Violetta swung her chained legs sideways, knocking Marion off her feet. She fell forwards, landing across the girl's tough, wriggling body and losing her glasses. The cellar became a muddle of blurry grey shapes. She tried to prop herself up on the mattress, then felt a surge of sharp pain. Violetta was biting into her neck.

'Stop it, stop it,' said Marion, struggling to get away. Violetta was moving around so much, it was impossible to get upright. She struck Violetta across the face with her elbow and then rolled sideways, knocking over the filth bucket and hitting her head against the wall. As she groped around for her glasses she felt the cold vile contents of the bucket soak into her clothes.

She found her glasses by the side of the mattress and got to her feet. There was blood on Violetta's mouth that Marion realised must have come from her own neck.

'Why didn't you run away at the service station? Why did you come back? It isn't my fault. None of this is my fault!'

'It is your fault. It is all your fault. You could have stopped him. You die in prison, you ugly fat witch. Then you go to hell.'

Before she even realised what she was doing, Marion picked up the wooden chair. She swung it at Violetta's head but missed. She then closed her eyes and brought the side of the chair down hard on her chest. It's like crushing a spider beneath a book, she told herself, you have to hold it down long enough just to make sure. Finally she lifted up the chair and slammed it down on the girl's head. A terrible, wet scream could be heard followed by a crunching sound.

For a few seconds after Violetta stopped moving, a sense of relief overcame Marion. Sometimes when you hurt a living thing it could drain away a little of the hurt that was inside you — she had felt this way when she gave Mr Weinberg's dog the ham seasoned with rat poison, only a person was more than an animal, so they took away more of the hurt.

As she stood there gasping for breath, she realised Sonya was staring at her.

'I'm sorry,' Marion pleaded. 'You know it wasn't my fault, don't you? I didn't mean to hurt anyone — I just *reacted* — I mean — those cruel, horrible things that she said — I would never have done it on purpose. You know that, don't you?'

There was terror in the girl's eyes. No one had ever looked at Marion like that before. All her life she had been ignored, treated as a person of no consequence. Her parents took no interest in her; at school she was invisible; John treated her like a servant. Now, for the first time ever, she was important, she had power, she was the giver of life and death.

* * *

The horror of the cellar formed a dark stain that spread through Marion's mind, tainting every thought and memory. She plunged her head beneath the surface of the bathwater, tears mingling with the grey suds. When she came up for air, a raw moan escaped her mouth.

'I can't go back down there, not ever. I would rather go to hell.' Her voice echoed around the dripping bathroom.

'You could still save me.' Sonya's voice, thin and scorching like an electrified wire, had worked deep into her brain.

'No, I can't! You don't understand. I can't do it. I'm too afraid. I did all I was capable of.'

'Please. *Please.*'

'Go away!' she screamed. 'I did my best, I really did, but I can't help you. Don't you see? My nerves just aren't strong enough to deal with all of this. Now, why won't you leave me in peace?'

Every single cell in her body opposed going

back down there to face those sights and smells. She could call the police, of course, couldn't she? Tell them to go and rescue Sonya, but if she did that, they would see everything. They would know what she had done to Violetta, and no one would ever understand why.

★　★　★

The water had been cold for a long time when she got out of the bath. She dried herself with a large orange bath towel that had belonged to the family since she was a child and was, in places, as thin as a bride's veil.

The only thing she could find to dress the wounds on her neck was a box of tiny plasters. After sticking several of them to her neck and ear with tape, she got into bed.

She woke in the night to find her face stuck to the pillow with dried blood. The memory rose up inside her; all of them, the two dead girls and the baby, all fused into one squirming, purplish-black, glistening thing with Violetta's sharp little teeth and nightmare mass of foul-smelling hair.

Brendan O'Brian's words came back to her in full now: 'You are the kind of evil that comes from nothing, from neglect and loneliness. You are like mould that grows in damp dark places, black dirt gathered in corners, a fatal infection that begins with a speck of dirt in an unwashed wound.'

Yes, she said to herself. Somehow he knew.

Cleaning

For the next few days Marion could not bear the thought of going to see John in the hospital. Instead, she began cleaning the house. Starting with the piles of magazines in the hallway, she stuffed them all into big black bags, and then threw the bags out into the back garden. Then she began picking up other pieces of junk at random, tossing things away without even looking to see what they were. Each time she filled a bag she tied it up and dragged it outside. Soon there was a great heap of shiny black plastic. The things that were too heavy for her to lift, she pushed to one side of the dining room. After a while areas of floor began to reappear that she hadn't seen for several years.

Scrubbing, tidying, dusting, staying busy was the only way she could keep the cellar out of her head. When the white-hot wire of Sonya's pleading began to sear, Marion would repeat out loud again and again, 'It couldn't be avoided; what happened simply couldn't be avoided,' until eventually the voice dimmed and faded away altogether. For the first time in her life she slept alone in the house, yet instead of feeling afraid, she was overcome with a sense of relief, as though an abscess, after troubling her for years, had at last been drained.

★   ★   ★

It was over a week after John's admission to hospital that she went back to visit him. She used one of Mother's Hermès scarves to hide the wounds on her neck and took a bus to Northport General. Public transport was a novelty for Marion, and she had to check several times on the timetable to find out which was the right bus, then look carefully at the map so she wouldn't miss her stop and end up lost somewhere miles from home.

The bus driver, a young Polish man, told her when to get off and where to get the bus back. When she asked him what the number of the return bus was, he said it was the same number but on the opposite side of the street. Though she felt stupid for not knowing, the driver was very polite and patient and didn't treat her as though she was an idiot at all.

When she finally arrived at Northport General, she found John sitting up in bed. The tubes were gone from his nose, and he was reading the *Daily Mail*. It felt as though several years had passed since she last saw him. She thought he would be angry that she'd stayed away for so long, but instead his face was filled with relief, as though he had been terrified she would never come back.

'Marion, love, I didn't know what had happened to you — is everything all right?'

As John reached out and grasped her hand, his pyjamas gaped open and she saw bruises in his chest where the nurses had put needles into the mottled skin. A pretty, brown-haired nurse was attending to a young black man with an oxygen mask over his face in the next bed. Had the old woman who occupied it previously died? It seemed unlikely that she had suddenly got better, though perhaps they had moved her to another ward. Marion sat down in the chair by John's bedside.

'How are you feeling?'

He attempted to prop himself up, then winced.

'The stitches hurt like murder every time I move — but apart from that, not too bad. They let me out of bed today. I managed to shower myself.'

An image of John naked with those women entered her head, and she shuddered.

'I brought you some things.'

From her shopping bag Marion took out pyjamas, toiletries, and a bag of strawberry shoelaces.

'Didn't you bring anything for me to read?' He chucked the *Daily Mail* onto the bedside table. 'I'm sick of this rubbish about pop singers and soap actresses, no real news.'

'I didn't think you'd be up to reading.'

'Maybe the next time you come you could bring me a *Times* or a *Telegraph*. And a good novel. I don't fancy anything too heavy, but perhaps if you see a decent thriller in the bookshop. A bottle of cordial wouldn't go amiss, something sharp like lime. I've got this awful taste in my mouth from the drugs. Make sure it's Robinsons; you know I don't like the supermarket's own stuff.'

John opened the bag of sweets she had

brought him, releasing the sickly sweet smell of artificial fruit.

'Well, I didn't know they still made these.'

As he put a red lace into his mouth and sucked, his eyes brightened with pleasure.

'Mm, that takes me back. A Proustian rush, one might say,' he declared, not to his sister, but perhaps for the benefit of some invisible intellectual who might appreciate the remark.

'Oh, for God's sake, John, don't talk such rubbish. They're only bloody sweets,' Marion snapped. Her brother looked shocked.

'What's up with you? Can't be your time of the month. I doubt you've had that for a good ten years.'

And then he gave a nasty little snigger. Though Marion was faintly disgusted by his remark, she felt no sting. Looking at him, lying there in the hospital bed, she realised that his words had no more effect on her than those of a stranger. It was as if Marion's love for her brother was a kind of sickness she had suffered from since birth. It had given her long bouts of pain and discomfort, mixed with short spells of relief that she mistook for joy. It seemed now that some powerful cure had cleansed her system of all feeling for him.

Before she left, he grasped her arm. It took all of her strength not to pull away as he whispered a message:

'Are they asking for me? I expect they'll be worried, especially Sonya. She is such an anxious little thing.'

'Sonya told me to say that she hopes you get

better soon,' Marion replied, surprised at the ease with which the lie flew from her lips.

Smiling with satisfaction, he let go of her arm.

Eventually of course, she would explain what had happened, that she had done her best and really none of it was her fault. What happened *simply couldn't have been avoided*.

★ ★ ★

As Marion was riding the bus home, two young girls, all bouncy and giggling, got on board and took the seats in front of her. One of them was telling the other about a boy called Patrick. Patrick had got fired for pouring a drink over a rude customer in the restaurant where they both worked. The other girl, who kept laughing a lot about the story, reminded Marion of Sonya.

Poor little Sonya. Of course she felt worst of all about her. Just the thought of those scared eyes and her pitiful crying tore at Marion. Unlike Violetta, she felt she was a decent, thoughtful girl, someone whom Marion would have liked if she had met her under different circumstances.

Perhaps we could have been friends, thought Marion. Perhaps she could have told me things about her past, about her tragic childhood, and I could have comforted her. We could have moved into Aunt Agnes's flat, just the two of us, like mother and daughter. She would have taken a job in a shop, maybe a florist's or one of those gift places on the pier. I would cook dinner for her in the evenings, and we would eat together while she told me stories about silly things that had happened in the shop and we would laugh together. Then we would watch TV until she fell asleep with her head on my shoulder. The next morning I would make her a cup of coffee and toast before she went off to work.

But deep down, Marion knew that this would never have happened. Like Lydia, Sonya wouldn't have wanted anything to do with her. Young pretty girls didn't want to waste their time with lonely, middle-aged spinsters. They preferred to go to parties with girls their own age, and text each other about boys and clothes. Becoming like her was what they feared the most. Yes, the truth was that Sonya wouldn't have wanted to be friends with someone like me, she thought. Not one bit. She wouldn't have given me the time of day. I would be invisible to her, just like I am to those two, she thought, watching the girls as they got off the bus together, still laughing.

★   ★   ★

The turmoil she had undergone had brought about an unexpected transformation in Marion. She first noticed the change while standing in front of the mirror in Mother's bedroom one morning. Lifting off her nightgown, she forced herself to stare directly at her body. Previously, when Marion had, by accident, glimpsed her unclothed figure, she felt ashamed. Today there was instead a flicker of pleasure.

The thighs, though still full and rounded, were no longer huge mounds of chalk-white flesh. Her upper arms and calves were almost slim. Of course the bosom was rather slack, but with the right bra and underclothes, it would look fine. Her body felt entirely different, as though she had taken off a grotesque costume that she had been forced to wear for years. Now she felt lighter, cleaner, smoother, more feminine than she had ever felt before, perhaps someone that a man might want to protect, rather than a big sturdy lump that could fend for itself. Of course she wasn't beautiful, or not even what anyone else was likely to find attractive, but there was an improvement.

In the month since John's admission to hospital she had lost a significant amount of weight. She had been so busy cleaning and running to and from the hospital, there was barely time left to eat. And when she did prepare food for herself, she would catch a whiff of that awful sickly smell that now pervaded the house and be unable to swallow more than a mouthful or two.

She went over to Mother's wardrobe, a structure so large, it almost seemed like a separate building, something old and important like a bank or town hall. Opening the doors, she peered into the darkness. Suspended in a dry cleaning bag was a black long-sleeved dress that Mother had worn years ago for a function at Dad's Masonic lodge.

Breathing in the smell of old sweat and talcum powder, she put the dress over her head. The cut emphasised her newly formed waist and the curve of her hips. Then she found a pair of earrings made from a yellowish stone carved into large teardrops and clipped them to her ears. The woman she saw in the mirror looked like a stranger, someone who might attend dinner parties and flirt with other women's husbands while drinking sherry.

The urge to dance overcame her, and she began to move before the mirror, swaying her hips and waving her arms in the air. She felt blissful and free.

'I will never let myself get fat again,' she said out loud. 'Not ever.'

Suddenly she became dizzy. Sitting down on Mother's bed, she pressed her hands against her throbbing temples. It was so hard to cope with the constantly shifting confusion of life. How could she feel a single second's happiness when so many awful things had happened, after what she had done?

★　★　★

The next day she was walking down Northport High Street when she stopped outside a hairdresser's shop called Shears. A huge pair of pink scissors decorated the window. Marion went inside. The walls were painted pale blue, and several potted plants had been placed between the workstations. A smell of flowers and the balmy breeze of hair dryers made her feel as though she had been transported to a tropical island.

The baby-faced receptionist gave Marion a dimpled smile.

'Heelloo there, can I help you?'

'Yes, I want — please — I want you to do something with — this.'

Marion pointed helplessly towards her riotous hair.

After she'd been waiting on one of the leather sofas for just five minutes, a tomboyish young woman called Ruby, with a tattoo down one arm and a pierced nose, came to attend to Marion. Despite her scary appearance, Ruby was softly spoken and treated Marion as though she was a very special and important person. First the terrible hair was washed in warm, fragrant suds. Then Ruby spent what seemed like hours shaping and cutting it. Products were applied that smelled of delicious fruit. Finally, the hair was blow-dried until it transformed into something quite soft and feminine that flattered Marion's skin tone and the shape of her face in mysterious and wonderful ways. When Ruby had finished, Marion felt sad to leave and wished she could come in every day and enjoy the comforting attention of this pleasant young woman.

★ ★ ★

Every evening Marion took the number 86 bus to the hospital. She began to look forward to the journey, identifying landmarks along the route, like the funny-shaped mosque on Newport Road, a wedding-dress shop with the most beautiful gowns in the window, and Axendale Golf Club, where her father once was a member,

294

though she didn't think he had ever played. She was sorry not to see the young Polish man again, but she supposed the drivers changed shifts regularly.

Marion became used to finding her way around the sprawling hospital building. John's ward was close to the canteen, and sometimes she ate her evening meal there. She ignored the large metal containers that were filled with things like lasagne, sausage, chips and meat pies, all glowing temptingly under orange lights, and instead chose something from the 'healthier options' display, like baked potato with tuna or salad.

★ ★ ★

Just before Christmas, John was moved to a general ward. The atmosphere was more relaxed here than the intensive care unit, and he got along well with the nurses. To them he was polite and obedient, a model patient. The ward sister, a plump Asian lady in her forties, called him 'a real old-fashioned gentleman'. There was a male nurse called Wayne with a high-pitched Scottish accent who made everyone laugh. Some of the things he came out with made Marion think he could be a proper comedian on the TV, and even John chuckled at his gags, though he normally couldn't stand 'queers'.

As nurses were pinning up Christmas decorations around the ward one day in mid-December, John pulled Marion close and whispered in her ear:

'Don't forget to get a little present for each of

the girls. Violetta can't resist dark chocolate — get her a box of Terry's All Gold. Alla loves ballet music, perhaps a CD of *Swan Lake*. And Sonya, anything to do with animals will make her happy.'

On Christmas Day he wore a paper crown while eating turkey dinner in his bed. A group of carol singers from the local Rotary Group came to perform for the patients, and when they sang 'Away in a Manger', Marion noticed John's dull, grey eyes glitter with tears.

★　★　★

Day after day she filled black bin bags with clutter and rubbish. When she looked at the teddy bears on her bed, she was reminded of the white bear in the cellar, so she stuffed them all into bags and was surprised not to feel a scrap of emotion as she cast them onto the growing heap in the garden. She cleaned and cleaned, spending hours scrubbing the kitchen, dipping a toothbrush in bleach to remove mould from the bathroom tiles, vacuuming years of fluff from the hall and the bedrooms. Still, no matter what she did, nothing would get rid of that sweet, rotten smell coming from below.

It reminded her of those strawberry shoelaces John liked so much, tinged with something vile.

★　★　★

'I've brought your *Scientific American* and the *Economist* and some elderflower cordial,' Marion announced as she arrived at the hospital one January evening. John was sitting in bed eating tinned peaches and ice cream.

'The doctor came round today. She said I should be home by the weekend,' he said, licking ice cream from his lips.

'Is that right?' Marion felt a sudden chill in her middle.

'Don't sound so ruddy pleased about it.' John's voice wobbled with hurt. 'Anyone would think you were happier without me.' He let his spoon fall into the metal icecream dish with a clatter.

'Don't be daft. Of course I want you to come home, love. The house doesn't seem the same without you,' she said, trying to sound like a caring sister. 'But we want to make sure you're all right first, don't we? I mean, you hear about them sending people home too early just to free up the beds.'

'You look different, Marion,' said John, his eyes squinting at her like the stone-lidded shellfish that clustered under Northport Pier. 'Is that a new coat?'

★   ★   ★

Marion dreamt that night she was running down Grange Road. She passed dozens of large Edwardian houses and hundreds of poplar trees, yet no matter how far she ran, she never seemed to reach her own home. Then suddenly she found herself at the top of the cellar steps. The door was open, and she could hear screams from below. She ran down the steps and found Lydia lying on one of those awful mattresses and chained to the wall. She rushed to help her, but John was standing there holding a hammer. Before she could do anything, he moved towards her, swinging the hammer, then everything went black.

★   ★   ★

The meter ticked up to ten pounds just as they turned onto Grange Road. John, unshaven and wearing his pyjamas beneath his coat, sat next to her on the wide backseat of the taxi. He kept glancing at Marion.

Marion examined the contents of her purse for a suitable amount to pay the driver; she knew she ought to tip, yet was never sure of the right amount. If she gave him too much, she would be left feeling like a fool, yet if she didn't give enough, the driver might get angry. If only John would deal with it, he was the man after all, but he seemed too busy being an invalid to bother himself with matters like that.

As the taxi pulled up outside the house Marion noticed that Mr. Weinberg was standing outside his house watching them. After John and his bags had been placed onto the pavement, Marion thrust an amount just twenty-five pence more than the price on the meter into the driver's hand, then hurried away without waiting to see if he was annoyed or not.

As she helped John down the path, she realised how much weight he had lost. Illness had chewed the meat right off his bones. He kept clinging to her arm, as if he was frightened of falling over, and had to be detached, finger by tightly curled finger, while she went to unlock the front door and carry his bags inside. She supported him down the hallway and then once he reached the lounge, he managed to make his way across the room by gripping bits of furniture. It seemed he didn't even notice that all the junk and clutter had been cleared from the room.

'Always nice to get back home,' he sighed, then sank into his place on the sofa and picked up their copy of the *Radio Times*.

'You know, Marion, I'd love a cup of tea.'

She stood in the doorway staring at her brother, holding her breath and waiting for him to ask about *them*.

He turned to look at her. 'What are you doing standing there like a wax dummy? Put the kettle on. And let the girls know I'm home. I won't be able to get down to see them just yet. Those cellar steps are a devil.'

★ ★ ★

At night, John slept on the living room sofa. During the day he watched TV and read books, eating his meals from a tray on his lap. To begin with, her brother needed Marion's help with everything: washing, dressing, and even using the bedpan. John didn't seem the slightest bit embarrassed by any of this.

'My toenails need doing. And make sure you don't cut them too short,' he ordered as she was pulling off his socks before bedtime.

Disgusted by the thought of touching his swollen yellow feet, Marion went to fetch the nail clippers. As she was clipping his big toenail he screamed out loud. 'Watch what you are doing, you clumsy bitch. You must have cut right to the bone.'

* * *

Twice a day she unlocked the cellar and then stood at the top of the steps for several minutes, shivering with horror. When she came out again, she slammed the door loudly behind her. By doing this she hoped to fool John into thinking that she was still looking after the girls. It surprised her that he never asked about the baby. Did he really think a child could survive down there with his mother in chains? Perhaps he was afraid of knowing the truth.

A district nurse came regularly to check on John. Despite Marion's cleanup, no amount of Mountain Breeze air freshener could disguise the sickly rotten smell that hung in the air. As soon as Sister Pam walked through the front door her lip curled in disgust. A house that produced such a stink was clearly not a suitable habitat for someone recovering from major surgery. 'You know your brother is still very vulnerable to infection. A squalid environment could prove lethal,' she warned Marion, shaking an immaculately scrubbed finger at her.

Andrea, the terrifyingly cheerful physiotherapist in her crisp blue polyester uniform, came three times a week to bully John into exercising.

After he had been home a fortnight she finally forced him into climbing the stairs by himself.

'If you don't get moving now, you will stay in that chair for the rest of your life.' Andrea had a way of making even threats sound jolly.

As John strained up each step, clutching the banister as he went, Marion willed the carpet beneath his feet to wrinkle so he would slip and tumble down the steep stairs. Then he might never have to discover what lay down in the cellar. But John did not fall; instead, he struggled all the way to the top and then stood there panting and grinning at the physio, desperate for teacher's approval.

'I did it, didn't I? Can you believe that?'

★ ★ ★

One morning, nearly a month after John was discharged from hospital, she heard a roar of misery echo through the house. When she found him, he was sitting at the kitchen table weeping.

'Are you all right, John? What's the matter?'

He refused to even look at her. She knew then that he had found them.

'How could you, Marion?' His voice sounded strained, like a rope was tightening around his throat. 'They were all I bloody had. I loved them. They loved me too in their way. You could never understand.'

The tea towel that he used to wipe away his tears had a map of 'Bonnie Scotland' on it, and the head of the Loch Ness monster peeped out from John's clenched fist.

'I'm not like you. I need love and affection; I need human warmth. I'm not dead inside like you. And the child — you let the child die. That was unforgivable. You killed my son — my own sister, a cold-blooded murderess. You were jealous, that was it — you didn't want me to have anything . . . ' He trailed off as if the rope around his neck had gotten so tight, he could no longer speak.

No, Marion was about to say, that wasn't my fault, the child was already dead. I would have done anything to save it. I would have given my own life. But then she realised she didn't care any more what he thought of her.

She carried on cooking his meals, making his toast in the morning, warming his tins of soup and macaroni cheese, and he ate it all without saying a word or even looking at her.

'I could poison you if I wanted to; I am, after all, a cold-blooded killer,' she said to herself from time to time, thinking of the box of rat poison beneath the kitchen sink.

★　★　★

He did the exercises prescribed by the physiotherapist each day lying on the living room sofa, kicking his legs in the air, lifting tins of soup, flexing his ankles. Eventually he was able to drive himself to the hospital for appointments. Every now and then, she would pass John in the hallway or they would meet in the kitchen and he would glare at her with a deathly look. He was getting stronger, and Marion knew he was thinking about revenge. The danger came from not knowing when or how he would attack, so she would have to be on her guard constantly.

John used a chain saw to cut up the sycamore tree. Its grating roar seemed to cut through her. Looking through her bedroom window late one night, she saw her brother pulling two black bin liners across the grass. He took them to the rear of the garden and threw them onto the heap of rubbish she had cleared from the house. Then he tossed on several logs cut from the sycamore tree. He must have soaked the wood in petrol, because when he lit a match and cast it onto the pile, great orange flames cut into the night.

A dark thrill went through Marion, and she remembered her father burning John's magazines in the garden. But would they burn completely, she wondered, even the bones? Marion seemed to remember reading that when people were cremated, the bigger bones would not burn and had to be ground down like flour in a mill.

★ ★ ★

One afternoon when she was lying on her bed, the doorbell rang. She looked out the window and saw the dusty grey disc of Mr Weinberg's hat below.

If I don't go down, she thought wearily, *he'll be out there all day.*

As she went downstairs she saw the familiar shape behind the coloured glass door panel. *Briing-briing.* Each ring made her heart beat a little faster. Then a blister of rage burst inside her. *I'm not going to let some daft old bugger like him frighten me.*

'What do you want?' she announced on opening the door.

Mr. Weinberg just stared at her with his ugly old tortoise mouth hanging open. Under his coat he was wearing pink and orange pyjamas that must have been fifty years old.

'Well? I'm really very busy. What is it you want?'

'I know that smell,' he said.

'For goodness' sake, what smell are you talking about?'

'The burning. That smell, the burning of bodies. I know from the war. You never forget. A smell stays with you always.'

He tapped his nose with a scaly finger.

'That's none of your damn business!' she yelled at him. 'Just go away. Don't ever come back here again, you dirty stinking fool.' Then she slammed the door in the old man's face and rushed back up to her room.

Immediately Marion felt a wave of self-disgust. She shouldn't have called him those wicked names. But really, someone like that ought not to be allowed out alone; he was clearly suffering from dementia. His family, if he had any, should have him put away in a care home.

* * *

The bonfire went on for days. On the fourth night she saw him throw a white shape into the

304

fire. The teddy bear. Marion felt a stab of sorrow. That poor baby had dipped into the world for such a short time. Didn't he at least deserve some fitting memorial, perhaps a stone angel or a dove of innocence to mark his brief life? When the last bonfire died down, John took a spade and began to turn the soil over until the far end of the garden was nothing but a patch of blackened earth.

'The smell was just awful, Marion. I couldn't even leave my windows open at night,' Judith said as she placed a cup of tea on the table before Marion.

Even though there was no sugar to dissolve, Marion picked up a spoon and stirred out of habit. She was visiting Judith in order to pay her for the damage to the wall. Judith had been unable to hide the gleam in her eye when she opened the envelope of cash. Clearly Marion's payment had been far too generous, yet it was a relief to bring the matter to a close.

'I had some people over the other evening,' Judith went on, after putting the envelope safely into a drawer, 'a local artist who works with things that wash up on the beach, and his partner came for dinner, and you could taste it' — Judith screwed up her mouth and looked as though she was about to spit — 'you could actually taste the smoke on your tongue, even with the windows closed.'

'I'm sorry, Judith, I really don't know what to say — '

'But just what was he burning out there?'

'The sycamore tree, of course. I thought you'd

be glad to see it gone.'

'Why not just pay someone to take it away? I mean, shouldn't he be resting after his surgery?'

'The doctors said exercise is good for him, so long as he doesn't overdo it.'

'But surely just burning wood wouldn't make that awful stink? To be honest, you're lucky no one has complained to the council about it.'

'I suppose it smelled like that because it was rotten.'

Only half-convinced, Judith frowned and sipped her coffee. At least Judith would be away in Greece in a few days, but what if someone had complained? Marion wondered. Then Judith's phone rang. She answered it and began pacing around her kitchen while talking. 'I intend to use my full baggage allowance — if you need to bring that much, then you'll have to pay extra yourself,' she said sharply, followed by: 'Greg, I honestly don't know what you can and can't flush down the toilets in the villa — can't you email them about that?'

'How is Lydia getting along?' asked Marion after Judith hung up, eager to prevent the conversation from returning to the subject of John's bonfires.

'Don't ask,' said Judith, shaking her head. 'She's dropping out of her course.'

'Oh, Judith — what a shame.'

'She says it's a waste of time and money — I just wish she'd decided that two years ago. Anyway, she wants to see the world instead, so she's got a job nannying in Spain.'

'Who is she going to work for?'

'Some couple who live in Madrid. I think one of them works in the oil industry. She mentioned they have a dog.'

'Do you know anything about them? What kind of people are they?'

'Vampire rapists, I expect.' Judith scowled as if Marion's stupidity were giving her a headache, then began clearing up the cups and putting them into the sink, in a way that let Marion know it was time for her to leave. Suddenly remembering her dream about Lydia in the cellar, Marion was filled with panic.

'But a young woman travelling abroad like that on her own, don't you think you ought to find out more about them?'

'Oh, for God's sake, if you had kids yourself, you would realise you can't mollycoddle them, or they'll end up too frightened to go out the front door in case they catch a cold. I mean, do you want her to end up like you?'

'What do you mean?'

'Living in the same house you've lived in all your life, never taking risks, never finding a job or getting married?'

A flash of guilt crossed Judith's face as if she realised she had pinched too hard this time.

'Though I'm sure your life has been rich in other ways,' she said apologetically. 'Perhaps ones that aren't immediately obvious to the outsider.'

Her conciliatory smile wasn't enough to push down Marion's rising anger.

'You think I am this sad, plain little woman, but you don't know anything about me, Judith.

You have no idea what I am capable of.'

Then she picked up a little red espresso cup and threw it on the floor. It did not break but went rolling towards the huge fridge as if for protection.

Judith said nothing, but her look of shock could not have been greater if the cup had hurled itself across the kitchen.

Marion went back home, her heart still pounding from the outburst. The ringing of the telephone in the hallway multiplied her feeling of alarm. She picked it up fearfully, a small, silly part of her imagining Judith had called the police.

'Hello, is that Marion?'

She didn't recognise the male voice on the line. Surely shouting at a neighbour wasn't against the law, was it? The cup hadn't even broken.

'Who is this?'

'This is Simon, from Tyler and Co. Have I caught you at a bad time? You came in to visit the flat on North Beach last summer?' Of course, Simon the estate agent, she remembered liking how his sentences bounced up at the end in a way that sounded hopeful and cheery.

'Oh yes, yes — the flat.' She must have given him her telephone number the last time they spoke.

'Are you all right? You sound like you're a bit out of puff,' he said sympathetically. 'Should I call back at another time?'

Marion forced herself to breathe steadily.

'No, it's all right, I just ran downstairs.'

'We did find a buyer for the flat, but unfortunately the purchase fell through, and now the sellers have lowered the price by ten thousand. I know how much you liked it, and I thought you might want to take another look.'

★ ★ ★

As she made her way along the seafront towards Ocean Vista Court, Marion passed dozens of the benches and little brick shelters where rows of old people in grey and beige raincoats perched like pigeons. She felt they must be staring at her and thinking how ridiculous she looked in the pink wool two-piece of Mother's she had put on to meet the estate agent.

'Look at the state of her,' they were probably thinking. 'Who does she think she is, all dressed up like a dog's dinner? And running around with no coat in February.'

The pink skirt rode up her thighs as she walked, and she had to keep stopping to pull it back down again. She had put on a pair of mother's American Tan tights, but her shoes, a pair of badly scuffed brogues, one tied with a blue lace and the other with black, were Marion's own, as Mother's feet had been several sizes smaller. The tights itched like hell. Marion scratched her leg, then cursed herself when she realised she had made a ladder all the way down her right shin. A strong wind came from the sea, blowing sand into her eyes and upsetting her carefully arranged hair.

And to think she had gotten herself ready with

some vague idea of looking pretty for Simon. It embarrassed her to think of the five other outfits that lay on Mother's bed, having been tried on, then rejected. Did she really imagine it was going to matter to him if she wore the powder-blue trouser suit or the tangerine day dress? And why was she going back to that flat? It was unfair to let him think that she would really buy it, when of course this was entirely impossible. But he had sounded so polite and hopeful on the phone that she hadn't had the heart to refuse a second viewing. If only she wasn't such a coward, then she would have told him the truth and this nice young man wouldn't be wasting his time on a fool's errand.

She arrived ten minutes early for her appointment. While she was waiting by the entrance, a silver-haired man wearing a navy blazer and neatly pressed cream trousers came out of the building. Though his face was deeply lined, Marion thought him handsome and intelligent looking, like someone who might read the news on TV.

The man had a small dog with him. It trotted over to Marion and then looked up at her with its head cocked on one side, as if expecting a treat. She wondered if she should pat its head. She was rather nervous of animals — Mother thought dogs were dangerous and filthy things, and, apart from poor Bunty, Marion had had little contact with them, but there was a bright, friendly look in the eyes of this dog that appealed to her.

'I'm sorry. He's very sociable, you see. He always likes to say hello to people.' The man spoke in a nice middle-class voice, no smear of the muddy Northport accent. Though he was smiling at her, Marion felt anxious that he might be wondering what she was doing waiting outside the entrance. Should she offer some explanation as to why she was there?

He wore a gold band on his wedding finger, but then of course at his stage in life it was possible he might be widowed. She suspected that Ocean Vista Court was the sort of place where well-to-do 'senior' persons moved following the death of a spouse.

'It must be pleasant to have him for company,' she said, cringing with shame as the dog nuzzled her laddered American Tan ankle. Those shoes with the mismatched laces were like two oddball relations, and it embarrassed her to be seen out in public wearing them.

'Well yes, he is good company, but I only wish he could laugh at my jokes,' said the man.

Perhaps this meant he was lonely. His wife must be dead or at least someone with no sense of humour.

'Come along, Treacle,' he said to the dog. Making a clucking sound with his tongue, he pulled on the dog's lead and the two of them went off along the path that ran by the beach.

Her heart bounced as Simon's little blue car turned into the car park. He parked precisely between the white lines of an empty space, then, looking in the mirror, smoothed his hair into glossy waves. It was longer on top than before but still short at the back. Marion was briefly thrilled to think that he was tidying it in anticipation of seeing her; then she reminded herself he would probably do the same before meeting any client, male or female.

He swung his slim, athletic body out of the car and then reached in to grab a red folder. His blue suit was a little darker than the car's paintwork, and it went well with a primrose yellow tie that caught the sunlight like a knight's sword. When he saw her, a broad smile filled his tanned face. Marion realised she was trembling, as though she was going on a date with a boy she had been obsessing over for months. They went into the building together, and Simon pressed the button for the lift. As they waited he asked her how she had been and even commented on how nice her hair looked.

As soon as Simon unlocked the front door she felt a warm, familiar feeling. Looking around the flat, first into Aunt Agnes' bedroom with its fitted wardrobes and huge double-glazed windows that faced the sea, and then the small room that had been especially reserved for her when she was a child, she was convinced she could feel her aunt's presence, smell her favourite rose-scented bath oil in the bathroom and hear her singing in the kitchen.

'You probably think I say this to all my clients, Marion, but I get this feeling that you really belong here, don't you agree?' said Simon.

'Yes — you have no idea how true that is.' There was a choke in her voice that he must have noticed.

'If the price is an issue, the seller might have a bit more room. The previous owner, a senior

312

gentleman, passed away, and the family are keen to sell.' Then he added quickly, 'I hope that doesn't sound insensitive? But these flats are popular with older people and — well of course, the inevitable happens.'

'Oh — it doesn't bother me at all — people have to die somewhere.'

Simon frowned.

'Well, I don't know the details, but I believe he died in a hospice rather than the property itself.'

'Oh, of course,' she added, realising she had embarrassed him by suggesting that the old person had actually died there in the flat, as though this fact might have permanently tainted it in some way.

'So you might be interested, then? In putting in an offer?'

Cold air rushed her lungs as though she were about to jump into a river. Why couldn't she buy the flat? Was it really so ridiculous? Might it not be possible to alter her life after all these years of just drifting along? After all, she had been left money and if she didn't spend it, then who else would?

She had once considered leaving it to Lydia, but the thought of her receiving a phone call or letter and thinking wistfully, 'How sad, that lonely old soul dying with no one to leave her money to but me, and I haven't spoken a word to her in years,' rather angered Marion. I'd rather give the lot to charity, she thought with grim satisfaction. Or leave it to someone who is nice to me, like Simon.

'An offer, well, I suppose so — perhaps — I

mean, why not? Of course, I'll need some time to think it over.'

'Yes, yes, of course.'

This time his sentence did not bounce upwards at the end; instead it was weighted down by disappointment, as if he knew she was lying to him but was too polite to say anything.

'No, Simon, I really mean it. I'm going to buy this flat. I want to more than anything.'

'Great, that's great Marion.' His lovely mouth, with the slightly feminine Cupid's bow, curled into a smile. 'Do you have a solicitor in mind?'

'A solicitor?'

Then her flesh began to prickle with anxiety. There would be so many complicated things to deal with, and she couldn't ask John for help. She heard her mother's voice: *You will never manage this by yourself, Marion. You will probably end up getting conned out of every penny you possess, just like that fool Jean Page.* Shut up, Mother, she told the voice sternly. Not everyone is a thief or a con man. I will manage. People will help me, good decent people like Simon.

'Of course, if you don't, I can recommend someone. And you'll need to get the finances in place,' said Simon. 'Perhaps if you book an appointment with someone at your bank? Or I could give you the number of a mortgage broker. How about I call you in a couple of days, Marion? And if there is anything I can do, please give me a ring.'

'Yes, of course.'

'I think I left the balcony doors open,' said Simon as they were about to leave.

'Don't worry, I'll close them,' said Marion, keen to be helpful.

She dashed into the living room as a chilly breeze was blowing in through the open doors. As she was pulling them shut, Marion looked down to the street below and remembered Bunty lying there, her white fur spread out like an old rug someone had discarded on the pavement. Suddenly the warm sea she had been floating in turned ice-cold. She heard her aunt's voice in her head: *You did it, Marion. You are bad through and through just like your brother.*

And then it seemed impossible to even imagine that she could live somewhere like this, somewhere clean and bright. She would only bring the rottenness with her. After what she had done, didn't she belong in Grange Road? Her father had murdered Sally. Her mother had killed their baby uncle. She had killed Violetta and let the others starve to death.

She suddenly exclaimed out loud: 'No I don't deserve this. I am an evil woman.'

'I'm sorry, what was that?' Simon was standing right behind her in the living room. She turned to face him.

'I have done bad things,' she said plainly. 'When I was a child I killed my aunt's dog; I threw the poor thing over this balcony. I was jealous because I didn't want her to love anything but me. And I once killed another girl's pet because she was unkind to me.'

A look of confusion clouded Simon's face.

'I threw a rock at one of my schoolmates while she was cycling home. It cracked her skull. And I have done *much, much* worse things — I have killed someone.'

She stopped and waited for Simon's reaction, not really knowing if she had said those things out loud or just in her own head. For a while he just stared at her, and then he laughed politely as if someone had told a rather inappropriate joke. Of course he didn't believe a word of it. Marion was an ordinary, rather dull middle-aged woman. No one would think her interesting enough to be capable of evil.

'I'm sorry. I don't know what's wrong with me.' She gasped, putting her hands to her face. Her skin felt cold and numb.

'Are you all right? You look a bit pale.'

'I do feel rather dizzy, it's so warm in here — I have low blood pressure. Sometimes it causes me to faint.'

Marion had no idea what the symptoms of low blood pressure were and whether it might involve fainting or not, but she hoped Simon wouldn't either. He sat her down in the kitchen and, after running the tap for a long time to make sure it was cold and fresh, gave her a glass of water.

Simon was so kind, he insisted on driving her all the way home to Grange Road. She told him that she lived at a house several doors down from her own. What would the neighbours think if they saw her getting out of a car driven by a handsome young man?

Money

Eileen, the special accounts manager, took Marion into a private office just off the main part of the bank. Everything in the room was newly furnished with the reassuring brown and orange colours of the bank's logo. The door of the room closed with a gentle click, leaving the two women alone in an atmosphere that was businesslike yet at the same time warm and soft.

All the business of dealing with banks and estate agents made Marion feel as though she was acting out some charade, involving herself in serious, grown-up affairs when she had no right to do so, and it was only a matter of time before she was found out and punished for wasting everyone's time. Yet if she held her nerve, then wasn't it possible the game might carry on, that she might actually fool people into letting her start a new life in her aunt's flat?

Eileen offered Marion a seat and then sat down behind her desk. She must have been about the same age as Marion, little lines surrounded her eyes and neck, but her hair was beautifully coloured, a sort of burnished gold. She wore a suit and blouse that matched the decor in the room. Even though her attitude was professional, there was something kind and caring about her that Marion liked. She imagined how nice it would be to have her as a friend.

The two of them would visit cafés together and drink frothy cappuccinos, then afterwards look around the shops. They would call each other on the phone now and then, not for any particular reason, just to chat about life in general, recounting little stories about things that happened to them, the sort of thing that no one else would find funny but would leave the two friends in fits of laughter. If Eileen found a lump she was worried about, Marion would go with her to the hospital to get it checked out, and not mind a jot if she had to sit in the waiting room for hours and hours, because that was what close friends were for.

No, Marion, stop being silly, she said to herself, suddenly realising how ridiculous it was to imagine that a stranger was her best friend. She had already spent too much of her life daydreaming. If it didn't stop now, then she would never do anything for real.

'Normally my brother John deals with these things. I mean, just thinking about money and all that gives me a headache,' Marion explained. 'But you see, he was ill recently, and I thought I ought to start taking more responsibility for my finances, you know, in case something happens. I mean, we never know what the future might hold, do we?'

Eileen smiled blandly as though as an employee of the bank, it was not within her role to speculate on the future, one way or another.

'Yes, of course. Won't take a minute to get your details up.'

As Eileen tapped on her computer keyboard

Marion noticed pictures of her family on the desk. It appeared that she had two grown-up children, a boy and a girl, in addition to a husband with a receding hairline and a round, kindly face. There was also a picture of the girl holding a newborn baby. This woman had achieved so much in addition to her career at the bank. How were such things possible, wondered Marion, how in roughly the same number of years had she managed to achieve next to nothing at all? In fact, instead of creating life, she had destroyed it.

'Well, Ms Zetland, it seems you have a very considerable investment account with us that provides you with a healthy monthly allowance in addition to the sizable amount in your current account.'

She wrote some numbers down on a piece of paper as if it would be indecent to speak them out loud.

Marion looked at the numbers written on the paper. Instead of scaring her, what she saw made her feel nourished, like drinking something warm and sweet on a cold day. She hadn't until now realised that her inheritance was so generous.

'So if, for example, I wanted to buy a flat for around two hundred and fifty thousand pounds, that would be possible?'

'Certainly. In fact, you wouldn't even have to get a mortgage. There's more than enough in your current account.'

'And would there be enough left over to live on, I mean for one person to pay bills and buy food?'

'Oh yes, you see, your investments are

providing you with an income that would be adequate to provide most people with a decent lifestyle.'

Marion liked that phrase: *a decent lifestyle.* She imagined herself staying in plush hotels and having doors held open for her by men who called her 'Madame' in foreign accents.

'And is it all my money, I mean my brother — he couldn't take it away from me or tell me what to do with it, could he?'

Eileen looked a little shocked.

'Absolutely, all of this money is in your name.'

★ ★ ★

Mr Weinberg's front garden was overgrown with tall purple weeds that swayed from side to side in the breeze like woozy old maids. Empty tin cans overflowed from the recycling box next to the front door. Only a few tatters of lace curtain hung at the windows, but the glass was so filthy, it was impossible to see inside. Marion peeked through the curtains of Mother's bedroom window. The police car was still parked outside the house. It was now half an hour since she had first seen it.

She imagined Mr. Weinberg coughing out his story to the police with thick lumps of phlegm. He had seen a girl arrive late in the evening. Perhaps he had heard sounds in the night while he was walking his dog. And then of course the burning, he knew that smell, the smell of burning bodies. Could a smell be considered as evidence of a crime? Would the police believe him? He was very old, they might suspect he was just losing his mind, but they would have an obligation to investigate all the same.

It didn't matter how seriously they took his accusations, Marion felt sure that the minute the police spoke to her, she would fall to pieces and confess everything. Even if she succeeded in keeping her mouth shut, her body would betray her. The police were trained to detect all sorts of signs. They would see guilt in her shifting eyes and shaking hands.

How long before they knocked on the door? Of course, she should have known all along this would happen. An awful sick feeling twisted her stomach. Perhaps it was just better to accept what was coming. She deserved to be punished, and so did John. She would admit everything and pay for her crimes. And she would make sure that John paid too. That was the right thing to do, to accept her fate. Wouldn't she feel better once everyone knew the truth?

When the doorbell rang, she got up from her bed, taking a last look at her room in case she never saw it again, and then went downstairs. Two tall dark figures loomed behind the glass. She opened the door. A man and a woman in uniform stood on the step; both of them were so well-groomed and attractive, they looked more like actors from a television crime drama than real-life police. She told herself that she must be polite and co-operate with them entirely.

She waited for them to do something, to grab her and put her in handcuffs, or even push past her to search the cellar for evidence, but instead they just stood there, with sympathetic smiles on their young unblemished faces.

'Would you like to come inside?' suggested Marion.

'That's not necessary,' said the female police officer. 'We just wanted to inquire if you had seen the man who lives opposite lately.'

'Mr. Weinberg?'

'Yes,' said the male officer. 'We received a call from his son in Cape Town. He hasn't heard from him in a few days, and he was quite worried, so he asked us to check on him. Wanted to make sure no one had seen him before — entering the property.'

Later she watched from her bedroom as they took Mr. Weinberg's body out on a stretcher. He looked like nothing more than a pile of sticks beneath the blanket. How lonely it must have been for him in that big house. I expect he just gave up after his dog went missing, thought Marion. She forced herself to imagine what it would be like to end up like that, living all alone and getting old and ill, being unable to wash or feed oneself, getting weaker and weaker until it was too late to get help.

★ ★ ★

As she had her supper of poached eggs and cold ham that evening, Marion thought of Mr. Weinberg eating his last meal, forcing it down even though the taste made him sick. Afterwards he would crawl off to bed and then lie huddled beneath the covers, perhaps suffering terrible

322

thirst or pain. Even then afraid of calling his son in Cape Town and causing him any inconvenience. How long had he lain in his own filth, waiting for the end to come?

Before she went to bed that night, she remembered the meeting she had the next day with the solicitor who would oversee the purchase of the flat and felt a flutter of anxiety. Simon had given her his name with the assurance that he would deal with everything. Could it really be happening? Was she really going to move away from this house where she had lived her whole life and away from John? Surely she was bound to make some mistake that would ruin everything. 'No, Marion,' she said to herself firmly. 'You can change things for the better, you really can.'

★ ★ ★

She woke to the sound of the door handle being turned ever so gently. Finding it locked, he went away. Marion lay there, ice crystals slowly forming in her blood as she waited for him to return. Then there was a clicking and tapping as he methodically went about his work. She heard each rattle as the separate parts of the lock fell onto the floor. When she opened her eyes, a shape was standing by the bed.

How foolish I was to think he could be kept out by that pathetic little lock, she said to herself. It seemed the giant figure that loomed over her in the dark could have lifted off the roof of the house, then reached in and grabbed her right out of her bed if it wanted to.

The hands that reached around her throat smelled of coal tar soap. Had he washed them before deciding to choke her? It hurt very badly, worse than anything had ever hurt before. As she wondered if it would take a very long time, memories came back of tooth extractions and having stitches on her foot after treading on broken glass while paddling in the sea. 'It won't hurt for much longer,' they always said. But it always did. And the pain around her neck was hurting for a very long time.

The squirming, purplish-black, glistening thing was biting into her throat with sharp little teeth, trying to chew right through the bone and sinew. The burn of death spread from her neck to the rest of her body. She almost wanted to laugh at herself for being such a fool in thinking she could escape all the horror. Would he put her body in bags, then burn her out in the garden like he had done with others? The smell floating in through Judith's window, causing her to wrinkle her nose in disgust? This will end for me like it did for them. I am getting what I deserve. That thought came with a soothing dose of calm, like a shot of anesthetic given by a kindhearted doctor.

But it would not be over. When she came to, John was sitting on the side of the bed weeping.

'I can't do it,' he wailed, as if her death were an arithmetic problem that couldn't be solved. 'Why can't I do it, Mar?'

'To think once I believed you were capable of anything,' she said, despising him then, not for what he had done to the women in the cellar, but for his weakness. 'But you're nothing but a pathetic old fool, John.'

Dec 18th

Alla, darling daughter, why don't you call, what has happened to you? We have not had phone call or skype message or letter for over three weeks now. Vava is always asking for you. I saw her the other day trying to prise open laptop with her little baby hands. Because she has seen you on the skype she must have thought her mama is trapped inside there and she can help you to escape. And then she cries when I take it away, I cannot allow her to break it, how would we ever buy new one?

All I care about is that you are safe, and I do not mean to complain but at the same time I must inform you times have been difficult because Vava and I depend so much on the money you send us.

Your mama is not complaining of course. If necessary can try to get my job back at the factory — the trouble is they do not like so much when I take the baby with me because she sometimes gets into mischief. We do not want to be any trouble to you but you must remember Vava is growing very fast and needs new clothes and shoes all the time. Your mama does not need anything for herself, apart from one packet of cigarettes per week that she smokes while standing on the small balcony and looking down at the park where the old men go to walk their dogs, plus one small bottle of English gin per

325

week if there is a little bit of money to spare.

Of course I would give up these luxuries just to see your beautiful round apple cheeks and pinch them between our fingers! By the way Mr. Zhenshavic keeps asking about the rent he gets very angry with me sometimes and is threatening to take away television set. I say please wait one week until I see season finale of *Never is not Enough* to find out if Magda is released from jail — she has been wrongly accused of killing Mara's husband.

Please do not concern yourself about money just call soon, I am so worried about you!

Dearest Alla

I spoke to Det. Insp. Constantin Dimtayin yesterday. I had to wait three hours for my appointment and the baby was crying the whole time. There were some very inferior types in the waiting room, a mother with a whole group of boys whose ears stuck out like batwings and a man with no teeth who said his accordion had been stolen. He spat when he talked and it was really quite disgusting.

Finally when I got to speak to the Det. Insp. he was far from helpful. In fact many of the things he said made me angry and very hurt indeed. I do not even want to tell you I have to put my hands over the tender ears of the baby he was so unpleasant. He said your girl Alla has gone abroad to become a whore we see thousands like her every year. Then he said, 'Go home and forget her, old woman.' Which is very rude as he was barely two years above me at school.

Then he said, 'She has left you with baby, and she is now in London wearing fur coat bought by pimp and drinking champagne. She has gone because she does not want the child and she is sick of having to send you money.' Oh please Alla call soon — tell me these things that the Det. Insp. says are untrue. Call soon, I fear that next week the landlord will take away mobile telephone because of rent and then how will you contact me?

I don't care if you are a whore wearing fur coats who no longer cares about her mama and baby, please just let me know that you are alive and safe!

Oh my darling I am practically dying from a breaking heart. Your cousin Oleg made long journey last week to the city and the Kitty Kat Klub where you were working. He would not tell me many details of this place, but I can imagine what it is like. He says the people there have seen no sign of you for over a year. What has happened to you my darling? I do not know if you will ever read this but still it comforts me to write you. The baby is getting so big now; she can walk and talk and likes to watch ballet DVD. Nutcracker is her favourite, she spins around like a little prima ballerina along with the dancers.

We have so little money that I have taken job cleaning at the sulphuric acid factory. It is not so bad, while I am at work I leave the baby with old Natalya who lives in our building. The baby does not seem to mind and she is getting fat on all the cakes Natalya feeds her.

Every Sunday I go to church and pray for you

and for the baby and for me. I hope if you did run away from us you have happy life.

Dearest, darling daughter
I am so desperate to hear any news of you after all this time that I agreed with old Natalya to arrange a session with a psychic woman she knows.

I know you are saying, Mama you are an old fool and this woman is just trying to take your money. But Natalya swears by her 'special powers'. And I feel a desperate need for what the Americans call closure.

I went to old Natalya's apartment last night. It was all very strange, she had turned off the lights and lit many candles, Mrs. Livchenka was there, a big fat lady wearing a strange fur hat that looked like a black rat sitting on her head! At first I was a little afraid of her. I gave her the money, nearly a whole week's wages, I know this is a lot but I am so desperate to hear news of you my darling what else can I do? The politzia are no help of course and I have no money to hire a detective.

Then we sat around the table, old Natalya's cats were staring at us from the shadows, I gave her your picture and a medal that you were given as a child when you won the ballet competition and one of the leather gloves that I gave you for Christmas when you were sixteen (remember you lost the other when you went skiing in the mountains with Oleg). Mrs. Livchenka touched all of the things and looked at them very carefully. Then she closed her eyes and begins to make these strange noises. I was worried she had become unwell, but old Natalya informed me

328

that this was perfectly normal and part of the process.

Then she took hold of a pencil and piece of paper and wrote down a single word. It said MANATEE. What can this mean?

Afterwards when I asked her about you she just shook her head and this made me very afraid. She said that you and the baby are both with God. At this I panic and rush back home to check on Varvara but she is safe, fast asleep in her bed, thank God, so I know none of it can be true. I am a silly old woman to listen to these mystics!

I pray I will hear from you soon.

Mama

'I'm not ready yet,' said Marion, then added proudly. 'I'm waiting for a friend.' The waitress's smile showed no trace of irritation, and she went away to serve another table.

She was sitting by the window in Stowe's Tea Rooms. A year ago she would have rather bitten off her own tongue than send the girl away without giving her order. She hated even the idea of inconveniencing people in any way at all. And occupying a table that could have been used by another customer, or even group of customers, perhaps some of them elderly or infirm, would make her feel awful with anxiety. In fact, she wouldn't have had the courage to come into Stowe's by herself at all.

But the Marion that sat at the table by the window no longer cared so much about making people wait for her. She had other things on her mind. Edward, the man with the little dog she had first met outside Ocean Vista Court, was joining her for tea.

Since the move to Ocean Vista Court, nearly a year ago, Edward had been such a good friend, helping with all sorts of paperwork and bills, advising her on insurance policies and how to get her phone line and cable television connected. She did not know what she would have done without him.

Sometimes she joined him on his walks along the front with Treacle, and they often went for tea afterwards. Edward said Stowe's coffee was the finest in Northport and couldn't resist their homemade vanilla slices. He hated those nasty modern places like Starbucks and Costa Coffee. Also the waitresses didn't mind Edward bringing Treacle into the café; they even gave him pieces of broken shortbread to eat.

Since becoming friends with Edward, Marion learned that his wife, Celia, had passed away from leukaemia several years earlier. He had moved to Ocean Vista Court because his previous home was too filled with difficult memories. At seventy-one, Edward was quite a lot older than Marion, but he was very physically fit for his age, and in some ways he seemed much younger: he liked to listen to modern music, he still went skiing twice a year, and he even talked of her accompanying him.

Marion took a compact out of her handbag to check her lipstick. The colour was called 'Sunberry' and was supposed to 'intensely moisturise' the skin of the lips. She thought the pinkish-gold shade looked attractive with the highlights in her hair. The beige suit she was wearing had been purchased from Pennington's department store a few days earlier. She had also stopped at the makeup counter and acquired the lipstick along with mascara and a powder compact. She hadn't yet used the mascara — it was the first bottle she'd owned in her life — and wanted to practise more before wearing it in public.

Buying clothes had become something of a pleasure for Marion since she had slimmed down. In the weeks and months preceding her move to Ocean Vista Court the pounds had simply dropped away, but she had to be careful not to put the weight back on again. When Edward arrived, she would order only one small chocolate éclair, and they would have a very long walk afterwards.

Marion saw a haggard-looking woman pass the window. It shocked her to realise it was Judith. Her former neighbour had changed so much, Marion hardly recognised her. A shabby brown cardigan was wrapped around her stooped form, the grey roots of her hair were showing, and she wore no makeup. Poor Judith.

Her art gallery had now closed and there was a big Under New Management sign in the window. There was a For Sale sign up outside her house too. Marion wondered if she would move in with Greg or even if they were still together. She had not spoken to Judith for a long time. Perhaps she never would again. And she doubted she would ever know how Lydia's life turned out either.

Of course since moving to Ocean Vista Court,

Marion had lost all contact with her brother. She doubted if he even knew or cared where she was living now. At times she did miss the old John, but not that scruffy, bearded tramp she sometimes glimpsed walking around town with stains on his trousers and dirty white trainers on his feet.

The day she left Grange Road she didn't even tell her brother she was going; instead, she waited until he was down in the cellar and then walked out the front door, taking almost nothing with her, except her coat and handbag. The first night in her flat she had slept on the bare mattress in Aunt Agnes' bedroom.

Like a bride she had started from scratch, buying everything: underwear, clothes, bedding, furniture, pots and pans. How strange to have lived so much of her life without appreciating the pleasure of money. Before it frightened her. Now she had learned that having money was like wearing well-made shoes or lying on a soft bed. It was simply something that made life easier.

Of course *they* were always with her. Sometimes she felt them, like a lump beneath the skin that your fingers accidentally brush against in the shower. Yet Marion endured this as she had endured many unpleasant things over the years. Grief for the baby settled in her bones, and she still felt a twinge, from time to time, but if the poor thing had lived, then who would have looked after it? She now realised that the demands of a small child would have been far beyond her own capabilities. Certainly they wouldn't allow a baby at Ocean Vista Court. And imagine having to change all those nappies and prepare special food, all those sleepless nights. Why, I can hardly look after myself, she would remind herself, never mind an infant.

'I just couldn't live with myself.' Wasn't that what people said when they had done something dreadful and found themselves forced to confess all to the world? Marion had come to believe this was a lie and that it was, in fact, perfectly possible to carry on with the knowledge of one's horrible deeds and never tell a soul. Perhaps others had discovered this too and went about their lives filled with unseen rottenness, like jars of half-used jam that have been sitting at the back of the cupboard for so long, you are afraid to unscrew the lid.

At that moment, Edward came into the café with Treacle. The little dog saw Marion even before his master and began pulling his lead urgently towards her table. He always seemed pleased to see her. Didn't that mean perhaps that she wasn't entirely bad? Weren't animals supposed to sense things about people? Or was she just fooling herself; did the dog just run towards anyone he recognised?

'Marion, you look well. Is that a new suit?' said Edward. He was such a gentleman, always knowing exactly the right thing to say. When she looked at him, Marion felt a fierce happiness that was tinged with terror, as if she were crossing some deep chasm on a high wire, and a single breath of wind might send her tumbling thousands of feet to her death. And then she allowed herself to be kissed on the cheek.

July 1st
To @kdubrovna
From @ametcalf2
Hi Kristina

Thanks for adding me! Love your profile and great pictures.

You say that you want to improve your English so perhaps we can chat from time to time. A few things about me . . . I am twenty-one and grew up in a pretty seaside town in the UK. I like skiing, playing the guitar and sailing. When I finish uni I hope to become a teacher. I'm quite shy around girls and sometimes feel awkward when I meet them at parties. That's why I prefer getting to know people online first. I hope we can be good friends!

Adrian :)

Acknowledgements

Thanks to Nicholas Thompson for his encouragement right from the beginning, willingness to read drafts, and unswervingly honest criticism; to Jen Barclay, my wonderful agent, who made everything happen; to the amazing Alison Callahan, Nina Cordes, and all the team at Scout Press; to the excellent Lauren Parsons and everyone at Legend Press, Hachette Australia, and of course David Forrer at Inkwell Management. Also thanks to my friends Louise Curtis, Sue Chaplin, Chris and Peter Padley, Mark Frith, Ken and Anne Morrison, and Fiona Bleloch for their love and support.

We do hope that you have enjoyed reading this large print book.

Did you know that all of our titles are available for purchase?

We publish a wide range of high quality large print books including:
Romances, Mysteries, Classics
General Fiction
Non Fiction and Westerns

Special interest titles available in large print are:
The Little Oxford Dictionary
Music Book
Song Book
Hymn Book
Service Book

Also available from us courtesy of Oxford University Press:
Young Readers' Dictionary
(large print edition)
Young Readers' Thesaurus
(large print edition)

For further information or a free brochure, please contact us at:
Ulverscroft Large Print Books Ltd.,
The Green, Bradgate Road, Anstey,
Leicester, LE7 7FU, England.
Tel: (00 44) 0116 236 4325
Fax: (00 44) 0116 234 0205